YOUR WINDING DAYBREAK WAYS

Upcoming titles in the
Your Winding Daybreak Ways series

Happy Hollow

Hurricane Creek

Hollow Rock

McGill

Cabedelo

Thunderwood

Babylon, A Human Requiem

YOUR WINDING DAYBREAK WAYS

GARY BARGATZE

RIGOR HILL PRESS

For Dianne, who always believed

Elegance among misted roses I harbor
Knowing a woman.
Sea-diary, I embrace
Your winding daybreak ways.
White curves to azure;
Diamonds on my lady's hands.

She dances before sweeping walls,
Dreaming.
Daring to love again and again,
As wind rocks haunted wicker.
Spiraling facets catch the light,
Lilac drives the soaring horses.

PROLOGUE:

SUNSET

Measures pulse,
Swirl, fuse.
Prologue and Myth are one.

WARFIELD

1

BEFORE THE WAR I never thought in shades of blue and gray. North had never meant occupation, and South was never synonymous with insurgency. My axis had always been east-west. My only north-south was an abandoned Chickasaw trail bubbling up miles below Shiloh, snaking over the Duck River, and blurring in a thicket of blackberry vine long before reaching the Dark and Bloody Hunting Ground.

The main road running along the front boundary of our farm served Mama and the schoolmaster well. They used this east-west highway to teach us mathematics, religion, geography, and color. I recall Master Hudson mounting his one-room stage and speaking to us in pictures: "All right, boys and girls, stand up; put your arms out straight from your sides—straight like the highway out front. Turn your hands palms up and cup 'em. You're now a balance scale.

"Your body is the fulcrum, your outstretched arms make the beam, and your palms are the weighing pans. Now, let's pretend to put two apples in your left weighing pan. What happens to your arms representing the beam? Yes, the left side of the beam falls and the right side rises. Now, let's pretend to put a small, two-ounce rock in your right weighing pan; then a second; and then a third. The right side of the beam begins to slowly drop, but not to the point where your two weighing pans are at the same level. You add one more two-ounce stone, and the weighing pans are now equal. So, Thomas, how much do the apples weigh?"

I responded confidently, "Eight ounces total, Master Hudson."

"That's right, Thomas, eight ounces or half a pound. Four two-ounce rocks equal the weight of the two apples."

Reflecting now on that schoolhouse scene and knowing all that has happened since, innocents stand there with their arms outstretched echoing the biblical Peter, Andrew, and even Christ himself at the Place of the Skull. Young martyrs living a human arc from oblivion to innocence, from joy to anxiety, from fear to horror and then back again to nothingness.

I don't know whether it was providence or Mama and Master Hudson discussing lesson plans after church, but there were many intersections between what we learned in school and what Mama taught us at home. Not long after learning about the balance scale, Mama taught us the meaning of Belshazzar's Feast. She told us how the king hadn't shown respect for the gold and silver goblets taken from the temple in Jerusalem; how the king ordered all the guests at his feast to drink wine from the sacred vessels; and how the king praised the gods of silver, brass, and stone.

Mama raised her hand above her head, acted as if she were writing, and quoted the scriptures: "In the same hour came forth fingers of a man's hand, and wrote over against the candlestick upon the plaster of the wall of the king's palace." Mama said the king called out for his astrologers and soothsayers, but none could read what the mysterious hand had written on the palace wall. So the king called out for the prophet Daniel, whom the king's father had made the master of the magicians and astrologers. Mama began reading from her Bible how Daniel had interpreted the words on the wall: "And this is the writing that was written, MENE, TEKEL, UPHARSIN. This is the interpretation of the thing: MENE: God hath numbered thy kingdom and finished it; TEKEL: Thou art weighed in the balances and art found wanting; and UPHARSIN: Thy kingdom is divided. In that night was Belshazzar, the king of the Chaldeans, slain. And Darius the Median took the kingdom." Knowing all that we've endured, Mama's prophetic reading haunts me now: "Our country will be divided; we will be tried in the balances; and our land will be lost."

On comfortable autumn afternoons, Master Hudson would lead us outside Sugar Grove School and march us down a curving path to Trace Creek, where he allowed us to ask spontaneous questions. Since he had been to so many places, we always liked asking about his travels. I remember one day in particular several weeks following our discussion of the balance scale. After settling into our customary places along the rocky bank, Master Hudson gave James the honor of the first question. Our classmate leapt to his feet and eagerly asked, "What's Nashville like, sir?"

Instead of responding directly to the simple query, Master Hudson expanded his answer into a geography lesson. "Before we talk about our state capital," he said, "we have to get there first. So, class, can anyone point us in the right direction?"

Paul raised his hand excitedly and pointed to his left. Master Hudson smiled and asked, "Now tell us, Paul, in what direction are you pointing?"

He paused and then replied, "To the east, sir."

"Nashville to the east? Well, not exactly; but you're close. Nashville's actually to the northeast. Now raise your arm a bit farther to point toward the northeast. And our road out front runs from Nashville to where?"

John, who at age thirteen was several years behind me, waved his hand and stood up. Master Hudson nodded, and the little fellow answered, "Memphis, sir."

"Yes, that's right. Memphis. . . . Now, John, can you point us in the direction of Memphis?"

He pointed to his right and responded, "That way, sir."

"And what is the direction of Memphis, John?"

"West, Master Hudson."

"Like Paul, you're almost right, but it's actually southwest. Lower your arm a bit where you stand to show southwest. . . . So, using our balance scale as an example and saying Trace Creek here is the fulcrum and our Nashville-Memphis road is the beam, which weighing pan is up and which is down?"

Mary, one of the prettiest girls in our class, raised her hand and pointed to her left. "The Nashville pan is up," she said, and then pointing to her right, "and the Memphis pan is down."

"Very good, Mary. Since the Nashville weighing pan is up and the Memphis pan down, is Nashville lighter than Memphis?"

The entire class nodded and exclaimed in unison, "Yes, sir."

"So if that's true, why would Nashville be lighter than Memphis?"

We looked at each other quizzically and then shrugged our collective "we-have-no-idea" response to our teacher.

Master Hudson smiled again and finally launched into his reply to James's initial question. "Well, when I arrived in Nashville, I was struck by how light, how bright everything was—the buildings, the ladies' silk dresses, the flowers, the smiles. The folks there had plenty of money from their trade in corn, cotton, and cattle, from their mills, their shops, and yes, even their racehorses. The forests and cabins were quickly giving way to plantations, mansions, carriage houses, and thousands of acres of the richest farmland.

"Everyone and everything appeared to be floating in a heaven on earth. There were warm conversations, cigars, highfalutin dances, music, whirling debutantes, sweeping staircases, grand hotels, the finest china and silverware, imported sculptures, brilliant portraits, and decorative landscape paintings.

"I was really lucky. I got to stay in the city for a time. I got to ride General Harding's horses at Belle Meade Plantation, dine with the Acklens at their Belle Monte villa surrounded by its galleries, gardens, lakes, and even a zoo; and I got to dance away several perfect summer evenings at Carnton Plantation in rooms of dazzling color and bold French wallpapers where the McGavocks had earlier entertained governors and presidents of the United States.

"Besides the mansions and the plantations, there was the Maxwell House Hotel, which was first known as Overton's

Folly. Any of you ever hear your parents talking about the colonel or his folly?"

We all shook our heads in unison.

"So why such a funny name? Well, as the story goes, Colonel Overton was hard of hearing, and one day he stumbled on an auction and bid fifteen dollars for a cow and won. But when he told the auctioneer to deliver the animal to his plantation, the colonel was stunned to learn he'd actually bid on a plot of land rather than on a cow. . . . Making a long story short, Colonel Overton used his folly to build what many believed was a second and even bigger folly, a luxurious two-hundred-and-forty-room, five-story brick hotel in tiny downtown Nashville. He named his new establishment the Maxwell House after his second wife, Harriet Maxwell Overton.

"Oh, for four dollars a day you can live high on the hog there. . . . You get steam heat, gas lighting, a bath on your floor, meals included—and I'm telling you, oh, what meals! Wild boar, buffalo tongue, black bear leg, opossum, Kentucky mutton, asparagus, succotash, oyster plant, and, oh my, the desserts—mince pie, lady and Italian marble cakes, oranges in sherry wine, and pineapples in champagne."

Master Hudson paused and sighed before he continued. "And Memphis . . . Any of you ever been there? Ever hear your parents talking about having gone there? Any idea why Memphis is heavier than Nashville?"

We all shook our heads again and replied, "No, sir."

"Well, when I visited there, it was much more difficult to live. You see, Memphis is forty years younger than Nashville and much less developed. Most folks struggle to make a living, so there are no concerts, picture galleries, or highfalutin dances. I remember hearing about only one estate; I hear it was on East Beale Street near the downtown. Friends, who had visited the mansion, spoke of four massive columns decorating a two-story brick front. They said there were brilliant chandeliers, canopied beds, and three-tiered marble fountains.

"But I believe things will soon be changing in Memphis. . . . Since the navy yard has now opened on the Mississippi and the Memphis & Charleston Railroad has been completed to the East Coast, I suspect the city's commerce will begin to grow. . . . Life will get easier, silk dresses and smiles will appear, the city will become brighter and lighter, and the Memphis weighing pan will start to rise."

But life has a way of tearing up track and bending the rails. As Master Hudson reminisced, teaching us in the steep slant of that autumnal light, neither he nor any of us knew a surprising force would place its thumb on the balance scale beam and accelerate the shift in the cities' positions. After Forts Henry and Donelson surrendered in February '62, Union General Buell forced Confederate General Johnston to evacuate Nashville. With the fall of the city, the high life of mansions and plantations ended. The Union army arrested General Harding at Belle Meade, convicted him of aiding the enemy, and sentenced him to Mackinaw Island, Michigan. Joseph Acklens, who owned Belle Monte, died in Louisiana during the war, and his widow, Adelicia, experienced firsthand the terror of battle, when Union General Stanley established his headquarters in her villa during his defense of Nashville in December '64.

One month earlier the McGavocks had suffered a similar fate at their Carnton Plantation in nearby Franklin. They witnessed the bloodiest five hours of fighting in the war. During that short period, nine thousand five hundred soldiers were killed, wounded, captured, or reported missing. The McGavock home served as a large field hospital for hundreds of dying and wounded, who were taken there for surgeries and medical care. So the blood of dying generals mixed with that of their soldiers and permanently stained the mansion floors.

What about the Maxwell House and Nashville itself? What indignities did the citizenry endure as the thumb slid along the balance scale beam? Shortly after Nashville fell, the bluecoats requisitioned the grand hotel and used it as a prison housing six hundred rebels. The prisoners were confined to the unfinished fifth floor of Zollicoffer's Barracks. One morning in '63, the detainees heard the signal for breakfast and rushed to the head of the stairs. Their weight was so great that the staircase collapsed. Hundreds of bodies crashed through two sets of flooring and landed on the third level. I understand thirty-seven rebels died during their fall. And Nashville? The city also suffered. While their men were off fighting the Federals, the women wandered gloomily among the shuttered shops. And because there had been droughts, the semiliquid sewage, "lollypop," stagnated in the gutters near the Maxwell House at the city's center.

But how did Memphis fare as the thumb slid along the balance beam? Early in the war, the situation didn't look promising. In June '62 thousands of folks lined the hills above the Mississippi to watch the naval battle for Memphis. It didn't last long;

the fight was over before the lunch hour. The Union ironclads quickly smashed the Confederate gunboats; and three weeks later, Ulysses Grant set up headquarters in that one and only mansion on East Beale Street. But the city's luck was changing. After the Union naval victory, Memphis was no longer subject to siege or destruction. Business folk prospered; they sold cotton openly to the Union occupiers and secretly supplied shoes, nails, and gunpowder to southern agents. But the good times didn't last for long. The thumb began to slide again along the beam, and Memphis returned to suffering, ravaged by a number of yellow fever epidemics that killed thousands and forced many to flee the city for good. Not long after the epidemics, Memphis lay abandoned and bankrupt.

While Master Hudson used the east-west highway to explain direction, mathematics, and high society, Mama used the main road to teach us color. She would lead us out to the wide space between our split-rail fence and the road, look from side to side, and pluck a wildflower. She'd use the various plants as props to teach my older brother, Robert, and me their names while teaching my younger sister her colors. "Look, children, daisies. And what's their color, Rachel?"

"Yellow, Mama!" she blurted.

"No, not yellow. Try again."

Rachel paused and then answered haltingly, "Orange?"

"That's much better. . . . Now here are some flowers we don't see too often. You boys have any idea?"

We shrugged.

"They're crow flowers, similar to buttercups. And what's the color, Rachel?"

Our little sister responded correctly this time. "Pink, my favorite color, Mama."

"Very good. They're pink like the morning sky. . . . And here's some fennel. It's the secret flavor in my ham and potato soup. And the color, Rachel? This one's harder so here's a hint: think of your father's coins."

Rachel replied tentatively, "Gold, Mama?"

"That's right, gold. . . . And over there's another herb I use for cooking Rachel's favorite meal, baked chicken and stuffing. You boys know what this is?"

Robert ventured a guess. "Rosemary?"

"Now, boy, how in the world did you know that?"

Robert smiled proudly and answered, "I heard you call it 'stuffed rosemary chicken' a few times when church folk dropped by for Sunday dinner."

"Your turn, Rachel, what color do we have here? Think of Grandma's hair."

"Silver, Mama?"

Mama laughed. "Okay, I'll have to give you that one. You're close enough, but I'd call it gray. Now, Thomas, you see the flowers over there next to the fence post? Any ideas?"

I shook my head, embarrassed, and replied, "No, Mama."

"Well, they're among my favorites. Columbine. And the color, Rachel? This is a tough one."

"Blue?"

"You're on the right track, but I would say lavender. . . . I know it's a strange word, but remember, you should call this lavender. And, boys, here's one you don't see too often, goat's rue or the devil's shoestring. Some folk around here use it for cheese making. . . . And the color, Rachel? It's one of the primaries."

This time there was no hesitation on our sister's part. She quickly asserted, "Yellow, Mama."

"That's right, yellow . . . just like the sun. And I won't tease you with this hard one, but it's easy to remember after you hear it because the flower has the color in its name. This is 'long purple.' . . . And see over there against the rocks? Those are pansies. And Rachel, they're another of your primaries, so what's the color?"

Rachel announced confidently, "The pansies are red, Mama."

"Very good. And here are violets. And the color here? It's the last of your primaries. . . ."

Our sister responded quickly, "They're blue, Mama."

"That's right, blue."

After walking the fence line for almost an hour, Mama would turn and lead us back toward the house. I remember once we stopped along the way to pet a young bull between the horns; and when we got back to the kitchen, Mama gathered the wildflowers into a colorful bouquet. She placed them in a large milk glass pitcher and then proudly centered her arrangement on the breakfast table. Over the next few days when we walked through the kitchen, Mama questioned Robert and me about the names of the flowers and then asked Rachel for their colors. But come to think of it now, I don't remember Mama ever speaking in terms of black and white during or after any of our wildflower walks while growing up.

Decades later I now know the gods were trying to forewarn us. The strong sunlight streaming through the window onto her bouquet meant the wildflowers were about something far more important than beauty, memory, or color. As the king's wall served centuries before, the milk glass centerpiece with crepe around its neck became an oracle, both ominous and arcing: daisies spoke to our innocence, our simple way of life; crow flowers warned of our lack of appreciation for what we had; fennel emphasized our strength and enthusiasm as the conflict approached; rosemary stressed our loyalty to family, friends, and the land; columbine was all about our betrayal; rue was for our sense of loss, regret, and bitter lessons learned; long purple, or dead men's fingers, screamed the chill of death; pansies were for recollection in the aftermath; and, as they were for the wives of ancient warriors, violets meant mourning and affection for the dead. But we only saw the sunlit splendor; we never heard the milk glass murmurs: "Grave's Bend . . . Robert . . . Burnt Bridge . . . Mama . . . Fort Pillow . . . Rachel . . . Israel . . . ."

2

IN OUR AGE of crow flowers and daisies, the summer sun would gently unravel the night, pastel the listless clouds in pinks, aquas, and creams, and signal the bantams to announce a new day. Lying under muslin sheets pulled up to my head, I would first become aware of the morning sounds: crows cawing in the cedars ... Grandma drawing water from the well ... our mule kicking the stable door ... Dr. Simmons's carriage or perhaps the undertaker's wagon passing our front gate on the way to make a delivery.

After a time, my summer mind would move from sounds to morning smells: freshly cut field grasses and pine sap gradually giving way to a hickory fire in our cast-iron stove, yeast biscuits rising and baking, smoked shoulder frying in a heavy, well-seasoned pan. And then I would open my eyes. The first sight was always black Cleary, curled on the pillow and kneading the sheets near my head. Next, a prized possession hanging over the mantel, one of Grandpa's double-barrel shotguns with black walnut stock. And finally Grandpa's wooden leg made of whittled barrel staves standing in the corner, boot and all. As a junior officer, he had carried that gun from the battles of Monterrey and Buena Vista, to the siege of Vera Cruz, and finally to Chapultepec Castle, where

Pickett handed Grandpa wounded Longstreet's colors and where Grandpa later lost a leg topping the castle wall.

I would stretch, swing my legs around to the floor, pull on my mule ear trousers and bark-tanned boots, and slowly descend the narrow elliptical staircase toward the kitchen. I would greet Mama with a "good mornin'" and a kiss, make two shoulder biscuits (one to eat now and one for my pocket), grab my slouch beehive hat from the wall, and head back toward the front room and out onto our wraparound porch. I would sit in one of the three slat-back rockers, finish my first biscuit, and survey our four-hundred-acre farm. Looking to the northeast toward Nashville I could see our log schoolhouse surrounded by pines and ashes. Between Sugar Grove School and our farmhouse were first a hayfield etched by a road winding toward the Andersons' farm, and next to that field stood our family garden with sweet corn, okra, pole beans, peanuts, and a boyhood favorite, early sweet melons.

Turning to my left toward Memphis, I could see the far pasture where the cattle grazed and the near field where we grew feed corn for the horses, hogs, chickens, and cows. Behind the house up the hill to the south was a large stand of timber, which we harvested for buildings, fences, and firewood. And to the north across our east-west highway was a second forage field, bounded on two sides by Trace Creek and on a third by our peach and apple orchards. An old Indian trail ran north through this quiet, distant field, which had once served as a lively encampment for millennia of hunters. Every summer after completing our chores Robert and I would spend hours in this special place discovering their ancient flint histories written in arrowheads, spear points, scrapers, and square-back knives.

Entering the farm through the wooden five-bar gate, you would first see our white, two-story farmhouse with black shutters sitting on a rise at the end of our entry road. At the bottom of the hill to the left were Bella and Israel's cabin, the well house, and the buckeye tree that Grandpa planted before heading off to war. Grandpa's tree was about forty feet tall with a short, gray trunk, scaly bark, and low-hanging branches, many of which he had pruned back over the years. In the summer months the blossom clusters faded away as prickly husks appeared, protecting the budding buckeyes. In the autumn we would collect the fallen nuts and stuff some in our pockets because Grandpa said buckeyes would bring us good luck. But when we crushed the buckeye leaves in our hands, they stank; it must have been nature's way of warning us that all the parts of our tree were poisonous. But on clear, winter nights during full, low-arcing moons, our tree of good and evil would cast the long shadow of a gentle spirit embracing the silver headstones standing, waiting on the nearby frosted hill.

Directly behind the farmhouse, there were two small log buildings with tin roofs, dirt floors, and no windows—our washhouse and smokehouse. Just outside the washhouse, Grandpa had hung a large black kettle on a tripod of long, metal rods hovering over a ring of rocks. Grandma and Mama used this cast-iron kettle to heat water and make soap for the laundry and our baths. They would make the soap using only lard and lye. At the first hard frost in late October, we would have our annual hog killing; render the pork fat; and save the lard for frying, baking, and soap making the following spring.

Grandma and Mama would make the lye out of wood ashes from our stoves and fireplaces. Every day we would take the cool ashes outside to the wooden bin with a spigot on its side. When it was time to make soap, Grandma and Mama poured water through the ashes in the bin and siphoned off the liquid lye through the drain. They would then heat water in the big kettle over a fire and add the lard and the lye. Grandma and Mama would stir the mixture for hours until it thickened enough for the long wooden mixing paddle to stand up straight in the center on its own. They would then pour the soap into metal pans and wait for weeks until it had fully hardened. Finally, they used their sharpened knives to cut the soap into small bars, which they stacked in our washhouse for the laundry and our infrequent baths.

Grandma and Mama would always do laundry on Wednesdays. They would first fetch buckets of water from the well house and trudge back up the rise to the washhouse kettle. They heated the water and carried it into the washhouse, where they kept the large tubs, rub boards, and soap. After separating and soaking the laundry, each would take a tub and begin working the clothes on a worn metal washboard. When they had finished the washing, they would still have hours of rinsing, starching, wringing, drying, and ironing to do.

Next to the washhouse and across the walkway from our kitchen, Grandpa had built the smokehouse, where we smoked the shoulders, hams, and bacon; rubbed them with rock salt; and allowed them to cure for months and sometimes years. Mama would say, "The longer the aging and the more the mold, the better the flavor." Extending off the back of the smokehouse was a narrow porch with a long, waist-high table, where we would dress the chickens. Grandma and Mama would twist off the chickens' heads and hang the carcasses up on the wall to drain. They would then drop the chickens into large tubs of hot water to soak, which made it much easier to pluck the feathers. Grandma and Mama would always get us children involved with the plucking, which I could never do without gagging—not because of seeing my hands in blood up to my elbows, but because of the awful stench rising from the feathers swirling in the dark crimson tub. After surviving the plucking, I would then take a few deep breaths and recover enough to finish the job of cutting open the bodies and clawing the entrails out.

The barnyard was at the bottom of the rise to the right of our house. This large rectangular area had a mucky space in the middle surrounded by a split-rail fence and farm structures on all sides—in the southeast corner, a toolshed; in the northeast, a covered lean-to for the hogs; in the northwest, a shed protecting our wagons, harnesses, chaff cutter, and plows; and in the southwest corner, our towering barn where we handled many of the daily chores.

As a young boy I would spend hours exploring the tools in the southeast shed. There were scythes, hay rakes, hammers, shovels, hoes, dung forks, hayforks, wood splitters, axes, and two-handed saws. At the pigsty in the northeast corner, I would slop the hogs with table scraps, ask them for advice, and then treat them to ears of dried, husked corn. After Father died, I would only visit the northwest corner when I had to harness the horses, use the plows, or drive one of our wagons around the farm, to the church, or into town.

We began and ended our days in the southwest corner in the antique barn. This massive wooden structure had a rock foundation. It was open on both ends and split in the middle by a wide pathway. On the left-hand side on the lower level, there were stalls for our horses and mules and a hen house, where we would collect the fresh eggs every afternoon. On the right-hand side, there were stalls for milking the cows and for occasionally neutering young bulls with sharp wire and medicinal turpentine. The upper space on both sides was used primarily to store forage, but there was a slatted corncrib on the left, into which we enthusiastically climbed as children and then as adults but understandably for different reasons.

So much had changed since Great-grandpa first built his log cabin on the property. The newer six-room, two-story, white clapboard farmhouse stood as a small jewel, elevated at the center of our enterprise. There were ten, black-shuttered windows, five doors including the funeral door, three chimneys, and a bright tinplate roof with only slight streaks of early rust. The first floor held four rooms—the "front" room facing west; Grandpa's room (ironically, at the front of the house facing north, which he no longer used); the dining room, with its long table and woodstove where we would eat on Sundays when company called; and Mama's kitchen, where everyone liked to linger, drinking strong coffee and chewing the fat. Up the elliptical staircase in the hallway, two attic bedrooms boasted windows looking out toward the woodpile to the north and toward our small burial ground to the south.

Before the War of the Rebellion, nine of us lived and worked on the farm: Father, Mama, Robert, Rachel, Bella, Israel, Grandma, Grandpa, and me. Dr. Simmons delivered Father in Grandpa's room the night a storm ripped the roof off old Anderson's barn. Father was Grandma and Grandpa's youngest of four, and from the beginning, he had trouble breathing, especially during planting season. As Father matured, it became clear that although he wanted to take on more responsibilities, he could only do so much without stopping to rest. Grandpa recognized Father's shortcomings; so before leaving for Mexico with Haskell's Second Regiment, Grandpa arranged for his younger brother, Uncle Billy, to spend time on the farm helping Grandma, Mama, Father, and all of us children. By many accounts, Grandma was the strongest, taking on much of the work and comforting everyone else when times got bad. When Grandpa returned from the war with a missing leg, neighbors were more than willing to help their hero and his family, especially during planting and harvest seasons.

Mama was Pastor Reed's eldest daughter. She came to live on the farm permanently six months before Robert was born. Since Father's three older sisters had already married and left home, Grandma and Grandpa thought of Mama's arrival as their daughters' replacement or the birth of their latest child. And their positive view of Robert's birth, the arrival of their first male grandchild, transformed the situation from what might have appeared awkward or tawdry into frequent scenes of joyous celebration. Over the next three years, Mama and Father produced two additional workers for the farm—my younger sister, Rachel, and me. While Grandpa was away fighting the war, Mama did as much as she could to help Father and Grandma with the chores, but she spent most of her time caring for my siblings and me.

There were two other members of our family, Bella and Israel. They came to live on the farm after Father turned six. When they arrived, Bella was a strong, young woman, and Israel was her three-month-old infant son. Along with two hundred acres of real estate, Grandma had inherited Bella and Israel from her brother, who had died prematurely of the fever. His will had valued his land at two thousand dollars and Bella and Israel at seven hundred each. The family whispered for some years that Grandma's brother had earlier sold off Israel's father and two other healthy males to help pay off his growing gambling debts.

Shortly after their arrival, Grandpa moved Bella and Israel out of the main house into their own log home at the bottom of the hill. While their one-room cabin had only one window, a door, and a dirt floor, it contained much more furniture than you would find on other farms in the region. Grandpa had given them two cots, a pine table with two chairs, and an old chest of drawers he had bought from Mr. Anderson for a dollar. Bella and Israel ate what we ate; and whenever either of them became ill, Grandma or the doctor would care for them until they healed.

While Bella performed all of her expected duties over the years, her young son had limitations; he could only work as a field hand. When Israel was going on twelve, he rode with Grandpa to the Warfield market. Along the way, one of the horses threw a shoe; and before returning to the farm, Grandpa and Israel stopped at the blacksmith's shop for repairs. While Mr. Hatcher had the horse in hand with one of its hind feet held between his legs, a bolt of lightning struck near the shop, followed by an enormous crash of thunder. The frightened horse pushed backward and then lurched to the side, knocking Israel off his feet. The boy struck the left side of his head against the anvil, fell to the floor, and lay unconscious for some time. After regaining his senses, Grandpa and Mr. Hatcher loaded Israel into the back of the wagon with the supplies, and Grandpa hurried home.

Two days later Grandpa sent for Dr. Simmons because Israel was going in and out of consciousness and speaking nonsense. Dr. Simmons examined Israel and told Bella and Grandpa that if Israel survived, he might have serious permanent problems. On the third day, Israel began to improve; he was no longer losing consciousness. Bella and Grandpa tried to help him up off his cot, but his right leg wouldn't support him. They also noticed he couldn't raise his right arm from his side and his words were hard to understand. Over time, Israel improved. His limp lessened, his arm strengthened, and his speech became clearer. He continued growing, reaching six feet two inches; but his mind never advanced beyond that awful day in the blacksmith's barn. From then on he was blessed and cursed with a child's innocence.

While he could never work as a craftsman or tend the livestock, Israel would help Grandpa plow the fields and plant the crops and then help keep the fields clear of weeds until lay-by time in July, when crops didn't need as much attention. With his fieldwork finished for a time, Israel would help Grandpa cut timber, build and repair fences, and clear the land. In early September they would return to the fields to begin harvesting the crops.

Perhaps because of the accident and Israel's physical problems, Grandpa would take Israel with him almost everywhere he went. Family and neighbors alike noticed that the two of them enjoyed a certain bond and that Grandpa treated Israel more as a son than as property. In fact, when Grandpa was leaving for the war, he took Israel aside, spoke to this twenty-year-old child as a man, and told him how important it was to help take care of the farm and the family while he was gone. When Grandpa returned as the wounded hero, their relationship strengthened further. Grandpa truly appreciated Israel's attempts to take on more of the work because of Grandpa's amputation.

The next decade was a sweet spot in time. There were great harvests, marriages, births, Christmases, reunions, revivals, and first-longing loves. But the balance beam never remained steady; it began to move almost imperceptibly. It was mid-August and very hot. Master Hudson had come visiting, and many of us had crossed the main road with him to swim in Trace Creek. Late in the afternoon we returned home to find a ladder angled against the front of the house. Since we didn't see anyone, we turned the corner to the west, where we found Grandpa and Israel sitting in their sock feet, up near the chimney on the hot, slick tin. Robert asked Grandpa what they were doing up there. Grandpa explained that the night before he had heard birds building nests in the chimney. We laughed uncomfortably; we all knew it was the wrong time of the year. We glanced knowingly at each other and then turned away. None of us wanted to accept the possibility that anything was wrong. We pushed the unacceptable into the far corners of our memories, encouraged Grandpa and Israel to come down off the roof, and then steadied the ladder for them as they climbed down.

But inevitably, other actions yanked the unacceptable back into our sensibilities, forcing us to confront the reality. Several months later, after we had locked the doors and gone to bed for the night, two shotgun blasts shattered the winter silence. The volleys had come from the front of the house. Everyone jumped out of bed and spontaneously congregated in the hallway outside the front room. No one wanted to be the first through the door. Father turned the knob and slowly allowed a shaft of light to flash across the floor. Father called out to Grandpa; there was no answer. He called again; still no response. Father then opened the door completely and raised his kerosene lamp to light up the room. Grandpa wasn't there.

After we had all scrambled into the parlor, Mama noticed the front door was slightly ajar. We opened it and walked hesitatingly out onto the front porch. Still no Grandpa. We turned the corner to the east, and there he was, illuminated in the full December moon, standing in his silver nightgown with his shotgun raised and smoking. We all began shouting questions simultaneously, asking Grandpa what had happened and why he was shooting into the night. He had heard some- one outside at the woodpile, he explained, so he got his gun and fired at the shadow stealing his wood. Father then gently took the gun from Grandpa, and Mama led him slowly back into the house.

The unacceptable now appeared with increasing frequency. The time between incidents was compressed from months to weeks to days and now to hours. The shopkeepers and our closest neighbors had begun noticing the confusion and the loss of train of thought. When Grandpa began spontaneously talking nonsense, we had to stop his cherished rides to market with Israel and his Sunday visits to Pastor Reed's church, where he loved singing old hymns about peace and redemption. Some months later, Grandpa began wandering off the farm; acquaintances would find him miles away from home in all kinds of weather, partially clothed, confused, alone, and speaking truths to the unknown.

From then on we had no choice but to keep him locked in the front room strapped to his favorite rocker. Grandpa would sit there day in and day out, pushing off with his good leg, rocking to the beat of the pendulum and speaking to the man in the moon on the face of our antique clock. In all his chaos there would be moments of calm and lucidity, especially when Israel entered the room or when Grandpa sang his favorite hymn:

> Stand up my soul; shake off thy fears,
> And gird the gospel armor on,
> March to the gates of endless joy,
> Where our great captain's gone.

3

THE DAY BEAUREGARD signaled at Sumter was the day the gods declared war on us. Father had reluctantly honored a new law requiring Israel to ride up river with the Hatcher boys to ditch. The county had voted to draft Negroes to help build fortifications on the Tennessee River. The call had been for one hundred twenty Negroes; but after Mr. Cooke's tally showed only one hundred forty total in the county, the politicians and slave owners negotiated one Negro per household to stay home. After one particularly difficult negotiation, Dr. Simmons took Father aside, offered to give Israel a physic to loosen his bowels, and then write a certificate dismissing him as too ill to travel. Father thanked the good doctor for his generosity but refused to accept, explaining that if Grandpa were healthy, he wouldn't approve of any plan helping our family while harming the soldiers.

Just before Israel's departure, Robert had left home to join the militia. After the vote on secession in February '61, Robert became increasingly convinced he should use his skills to strengthen a newly formed West Tennessee cavalry unit. The grand sweep of fighting to preserve slavery, states' rights, or tariff-free markets didn't motivate Robert. It was the years of listening to Grandpa's dramatic war stories about honor, courage, camaraderie, duty, and sacrifice.

I clearly remember Robert's send-off just days after his twenty-first birthday. Everyone was there to wish him well, including Grandpa, who shouted repeatedly from his rocker on the porch, "Death to Saint Patrick's Battalion! Hang Saint Patrick's Battalion!" Following family tradition the rest of us gathered under our buckeye tree and watched as Father and Robert led our best chestnut mare out of the barnyard. Robert cast the perfect image of a daring cavalier—tall, lithe, finely cut features, piercing eyes, and long, bright red hair. He wore a uniform designed by the militia commanders and hand sewn by Mama, who prayed as she stitched, "God, please don't let this be Robert's shroud."

His shell jacket was made of coarse, cadet-gray wool, trimmed in yellow with two rows of shiny brass muffin buttons evenly spaced and grouped into pairs. Robert's trousers were also made of gray wool, had vertical yellow stripes down the outside, and covered the shaft of his cavalry boots down to his spurs. He wore a black stag hat with yellow rope and acorn trim and a brass eagle emblem pinning the raised brim on the right side to the crown. Robert had jammed his Navy revolver under his belt and was carrying a double-barrel shotgun in his left hand. And after long hugs, tears, and firm handshakes, Robert swung into his saddle, glanced back for a final time, and turned onto the main road headed west toward Memphis.

With Grandpa, Robert, and Israel no longer available to help us, Father arranged for Uncle Billy and Master Hudson to come for the spring plantings. Father also began depending more on me to help with the daily chores. On that memorable morning when Beauregard attacked Sumter, Father asked me to go with him in the wagon out to the far field to check on the herd. On the way out, Father began singing softly, almost under his breath:

> Among the beautiful pictures
> That hang on memory's wall,
> Is one of a dim old forest,
> That seems the best of all . . .

When we got close to the grazing cattle, we noticed one of the cows standing over its stillborn calf. The questioning mother backed away as we stopped the wagon next to the perfectly formed carcass. Father said, "Hop down, Thomas, and toss the calf up in the back. We need to take it back to the barnyard and burn it." I jumped down, grabbed the lifeless calf by the hind legs, and swung it up into the empty wagon bed.

After surveying the remaining cattle, we started back along the rocky path toward the near cornfield. Father suddenly sat up straight and mumbled, "Boy, I don't feel so good. . . . My arm here's killin' me. . . . Can't catch my breath. . . ." Father gasped, then snapped the reins. "Giddy-up, Nell! Faster! Faster!"

As we neared the barnyard, I spotted Uncle Billy mucking out one of the stables. Father leapt from his seat, yanked the reins toward his chest, and called out, "I see the gate's open." Sensing the tug on the reins, the mare lurched forward toward the open gate. We almost made it cleanly through the gate, but the left rear wheel crashed into the gatepost. I flew off into the soft muck; Father was pinned between the side of the tilted wagon and the edge of the barn. The horse was lying on its side, flailing, with a shattered front leg.

Uncle Billy and I got to Father almost at the same time. I shouted, "Father! Father! Oh my God! Oh my God!"

"Don't just stand there, boy! Help me right the wagon!" Uncle Billy screamed. "Push! Push harder, Thomas! We almost had it! Again! As hard as you can! Damn it!" After each push, the wagon returned to its original position. "Let's try rocking it," Uncle Billy coached me. "Almost! Again now . . . . Harder! Harder!" I gave that wagon everything I had. "There! Got it!"

We could now see Father lying facedown, motionless, with the stillborn calf curled up next to him. Father's right shin was broken and turned up toward his knee. The jagged bone was sticking out, and his foot pointed in the wrong direction. I immediately turned away and vomited.

Uncle Billy knelt close to Father's face and said, "He's breathing." He then quickly scanned the barnyard and pointed toward the pig trough. "Get that handcart over there, Thomas!"

When I returned, Uncle Billy shouted, "After I get down there and support his leg, I want you to roll him over on his back. . . . Easy . . . easy. There! Now hook your arms under his. I'll get his legs." I struggled to get a firm hold on Father. When finally I could grip him, Uncle Billy said, "On three we'll lift him and then swing him over easy into the cart. Ready?"

"Ready," I replied.

"Okay, now . . . one, two, three, lift! . . . Steady. . . . That's it. . . . Steady . . . higher . . . now, easy . . . easy. . . . Now over into the cart. Gentle . . . gentle there. . . . Now let's get him up to the house. You grab the side there and steady us. I'll push."

Uncle Billy grabbed the handles and pushed Father past the helpless mare and up the rise toward the house. Mama and Rachel gasped as we carried Father into Grandpa's old room and gently placed him across the bed.

"Rachel, go find Bella," Uncle Billy said calmly. "Send her over to the Andersons' so they can fetch Dr. Simmons for us."

"I think she's out in the garden, Uncle. I'll find her."

Father's breathing was shallow, quick, almost keeping pace with the mantel clock. Uncle Billy and I moved a small desk over to the edge of the bed and carefully raised Father's shattered leg up onto the writing surface. Grandma entered without saying a word. She slowly approached Father, stroked his scraped cheek, and offered a private appeal to God. When Mama left to get cold water and clean cloths, Uncle Billy went out to tend to the fallen horse. All we could do now was gently stroke Father's hand, hope he could hear our reassuring messages, and wait for Dr. Simmons. A rifle shot pierced the prayerful silence; the mare was now out of her misery.

Bella returned and confirmed one of the Anderson boys had raced off to Warfield for the doctor. We waited almost two hours in silence, closely monitoring Father's every labored breath. When Dr. Simmons arrived, we described the accident and explained Father's symptoms. The doctor then politely asked us to step out of the room for a few minutes while he assessed Father's condition. When he allowed Mama, Grandma, and me back into the room, we asked if Father would be okay and if the leg could be set. Dr. Simmons looked to the side, avoiding our eyes, and said quietly that Father no longer needed his services and we should send for Pastor Reed.

I walked Dr. Simmons out to his carriage where we met Uncle Billy. After hearing the prognosis, Uncle Billy asked the doctor if he would have the hardware owner and undertaker, Mr. Patrick, bring a casket to the farm. Dr. Simmons gently reminded us that once Father was gone, we would have to conduct the wake as soon as possible, since there was not enough ice left in town to construct a cooling board under the coffin.

Day imperceptibly merged into night as we all focused on Father's struggle. Pastor Reed offered hopeful, comforting prayers. Mama clasped Father's left hand, and I held his right. Sometimes when we spoke to him, he would squeeze our hands and then release them. His left eye had swollen, and his lips had become light blue. His breathing became less regular and increasingly shallow. His lungs would fill; and then there would be a long silence. Finally, a rush of air would blow Father's lips outward and then immediately they would be sucked back in by his next gasp for life.

As the morning painted the bedroom window gray, we sensed Father was losing his battle. The sighs of earlier hours were now replaced by long, mournful groans. He no longer responded to our words with his hands. Accepting the end was near, Mama leaned over to the side of Father's face and whispered, "Everything will be fine with us and the farm; you've fought hard; it's all right to let go now." Father kept trying to breathe but managed only to pull his cheeks in while his lips remained closed.

At a little after seven in the morning, Father's chest heaved upward. His body tensed. He squeezed our hands harder than ever, and then everything relaxed. Grandma and Mama began crying softly. I ran out to fetch Uncle Billy; and when we returned, he placed large coins on Father's eyes. Pastor Reed gathered everyone close to the bed and offered thanks for Father's worthy life and his certain acceptance into heaven.

About four hours later, Mr. Patrick arrived with Father's casket, which Uncle Billy and I carried into the bedroom. After explaining he would wash Father's body and dress him, Mr. Patrick suggested we leave so he could get on with his responsibilities. As we left the room, Uncle Billy asked me to go out with him to the barnyard to help dispose of the dead mare and the stillborn calf.

Following Father's plan, we dragged the calf away from the barn and over to a space bordering the cornfield. We collected firewood and two bales of hay, placed the calf on the flammable mound, and started a fire. Uncle Billy and I then returned to the barnyard and harnessed our strongest horse to help drag the dead mare out to a good burial spot. We removed the bit from the dead horse's mouth, worked two large leather straps under and around her belly, and rigged the straps to the stallion's harness. We then led the large horse out of the barnyard to an open area not far from the burning calf. Following the usual custom, Uncle Billy and I began digging a pit to bury the mare. While shoveling, I looked up the hill to my left and saw the neighbors in our family cemetery already working on Father's grave. I then looked to my right and watched the thick white redemptive smoke rising from the smoldering calf.

Since Grandpa lived in the front parlor, Mama decided to hold the wake and the funeral ceremony in the dining room, adorned appropriately with old willow-patterned paper on two of the walls. To prepare the room, we first removed the firewood, ash can, and poker from around the potbelly stove and then pushed the long table and dining room chairs flush against the back wall. After Mr. Patrick had finished his work, we carried Father's coffin into the dining room, opened all the windows as far as they would go, and positioned the casket in front of them, allowing for a maximum April breeze. Word spread quickly about Father's passing and the expedited wake. Neighbors, relatives, and church members began arriving at dusk. They brought every local delicacy; in fact, there was enough food to feed five thousand.

Everyone paid his or her respects. And as the hours passed, some left; but surprisingly, many stayed through the night. Except for his swollen eye and some bruises, Father looked as if he were resting after Sunday lunch. As morning approached, conversation subsided to prayerful reflection. Why Father? Why now? Who will be next?

The morning broke clear; the air was warm. The gods were smiling. It was a good spring day for planting. Pastor Reed and his wife arrived a little after eight o'clock and viewed Father's body once more with Mama and Uncle Billy. The pastor again expressed his condolences and assured us the church would help us any way it could. Around nine o'clock, neighbors and church members began driving up our entry road. Uncle Billy and I hitched their wagons and escorted the mourners into the dining room, where we had arranged some seats for the older folks. The crowd gradually spilled out on one side into the kitchen and the other side into the hallway leading to Grandpa's front parlor.

At the appointed hour of ten o'clock, Pastor Reed asked Mr. Anderson to give the invocation. After the short prayer, Master Hudson led us in two familiar hymns, "Light Shining Out of Darkness" and "The Pillar of Cloud." As Pastor Reed positioned himself in front of the casket, we could hear Grandpa's muffled shouts escaping the parlor. The pastor quietly cleared his throat and began.

"Our text today is from Leviticus:

> And the Lord spoke unto Moses, saying, speak unto the children of Israel, saying, if a soul shall sin against any of the commandments of the Lord, then let him bring for his sin, which he hath sinned, a young bullock without blemish unto the Lord for a sin offering. And he shall bring the bullock unto the door of the tabernacle of the congregation before the Lord; and shall lay his hand upon the bullock's head, and kill the bullock before the Lord. And the priest that is anointed shall take of the bullock's blood, and bring it to the tabernacle of the congregation. And the priest shall dip his finger in the blood, and sprinkle of the blood seven times

before the Lord, before the veil of the sanctu-
ary. . . . And he shall take off from it all the fat of
the bullock for the sin offering. And the priest
shall burn it upon the altar of the burnt offering. And the skin of the bullock, and all its flesh,
with its head, and with its legs, and its inwards,
even the whole bullock shall he carry forth outside the camp unto a clean place, where the ashes from the fat are poured out, and then burn
the bullock on the wood with fire: where the
ashes are poured out shall it be burnt.

After reading the scripture, Pastor Reed paused and then
described the many good things Father had done over
his lifetime. The pastor asked: "Can we be sure this good
husband, father, and neighbor is now in heaven waiting
for us? Our faith says he is; but I believe God has given us
even stronger evidence this time. Let's reflect on his final
moments for clues. I strongly believe it was Providence that
encouraged him to want to burn the stillborn calf. We all
know we usually bury our dead animals; we don't burn them.
So why would our dear brother insist on burning the calf?
I believe it was Divine Will speaking through him. Burning
the perfect, stillborn bull was God's way of ensuring our
brother's sins were forgiven. And there is also evidence he
is now waiting for us in heaven. What were our brother's
last words? 'I see the gate is open.' This was the Lord's way
of assuring us our brother had reached heaven's gate. Yes, I
truly believe he is now sitting at the right hand of God. And

as we sang a few minutes ago, 'God moves in a mysterious way, His wonders to perform. . . .'"

Following some final words of comfort, the pastor asked us to stand and sing the doxology:

> Praise God, from Whom all blessings flow;
> Praise Him, all creatures here below;
> Praise Him above, ye heavenly host;
> Praise Father, Son, and Holy Ghost.

As the room fell silent, Pastor Reed requested all but close family members wait outside the funeral door to escort Father's casket to the family plot.

After the mourners had left the house, Pastor Reed motioned for Mama, Grandma, Uncle Billy, Rachel, Bella, and me to come forward to say a final good-bye. With tears streaming off her face into the coffin, Mama stroked Father's hair and whispered words none of us could ever understand. Grandma then kissed Father's cheek and said she would see him soon in heaven. Uncle Billy stepped up and firmly promised Father he would do all in his power to look out for the farm and the family.

And as Uncle Billy led Mama and Grandma away from the casket, the rest of us moved forward to say farewell, each in our own way as Father would have expected and heartily approved. Rachel gently rubbed Father's folded hands and sobbed. Bella wrapped her loving arms around Rachel and me and swayed to the rhythm of a silent, prayerful song. And I stood there as a southern gentleman with my chin held high, stoically peering into my beloved father's coffin while fighting back the inner tears of a grateful but fearful son.

When we turned away, Pastor Reed motioned for Uncle Billy to come forward with the lid and nails. With Bible in hand, the pastor raised his right arm over Father's body and gave a benediction: "May the Lord bless you and keep you, and may His grace shine upon you. In the name of our Lord and Savior, Jesus Christ, Amen." He then handed me his Bible and stationed himself at Father's head to help Uncle Billy position the lid on the coffin. As Uncle Billy drove the nails into the edges, Mama and Grandma began sobbing, and Grandpa shouted again from his chair in the locked front room. Calvary streaked across my mind.

When Uncle Billy had finished securing the lid, Pastor Reed summoned Father's pallbearers, who were waiting outside in the warm, spring air. The six men lifted the casket onto their shoulders and carried Father out through the funeral door. Pastor Reed led the silent procession along the path running between the large kettle and the washhouse, curving to the right past the blossoming lilacs, and then rising up the slight ivied incline to the cemetery gate. Once everyone had entered the grounds, Pastor Reed gave a final prayer offering Father up to the Lord. The pallbearers then placed two thick leather straps around the casket and lowered Father into his grave. After pulling the straps away, two of the men began slowly dropping shovels of dirt onto the lid, which made distinctive thuds that lodge deep in the memory. We then left the cemetery and walked the short distance back to the house.

While many were reminiscing in the kitchen and dining

room, I escaped outside and sat alone on the large, worn boulder serving as the back step to our porch. Many poor souls had sat here over the years eating a free meal, after walking up the entry road and telling Mama or Grandma they hadn't eaten in days.

I rubbed the back of my swollen hand and studied the expanding blue marks from Father's last grasp at life. I never thought I'd see the day. . . . Despite his weak lungs, he always seemed so indestructible—and so good to me. Took me with him everywhere, proudly introduced me as his "bodyguard" to everyone in Warfield. I didn't understand. How could this happen? Why? Why did it have to happen to Father who never saw a stranger, who'd give you the shirt off his back?

I thought of the funeral service. What did the hymn imply: "Behind a frowning providence, God hides a smiling face"? If everything happening is bad and if it is God's will, why is he smiling? Did he cause Father to die? Did he make Grandpa lose his senses? Did he allow Israel's accident? Did he smile at these things? Newman's hymn speaks of "the encircling gloom" and implies "a pillar of fire." The telegraph in Warfield says we are now at war. Did he cause this stifling gloom and columns of fire? Is he smiling now? Did Pastor Reed get it right? Was the burning calf really about Father's salvation, or was it about God's redemption for what he was about to let happen? As crimson faded to starlit black, I rubbed my hand again and headed for the lighted dining room. I wouldn't ask the gods to reveal the distant scene. I'd just take a stand with humanity and let come what may.

4

BETWEEN THE SPRING and summer of '61 the number of churches in Warfield doubled. Ironically, with every political and military move, religious tensions mounted and the rifts widened in Pastor Reed's church. The theological screws began tightening with the first state votes for secession in December 1860. Pressures mounted as Lincoln assumed office in March '61 and Beauregard attacked Sumter the following month. And after our own state voted for secession in May '61, the pro-slavery and abolitionist factions within the congregation became irreconcilable.

Throughout the six-month ordeal, Pastor Reed tried acting as a voice of reason, continuously negotiating between the opposing forces. He tried to enlighten the factions, contrasting our looming war with other great wars that he said had been fought over religion. He told stories of Israel's religious battles with the Hittites, Assyrians, and Babylonians and explained how Pope Urban unintentionally transformed local, bloody disputes among medieval barons into the crusades, a series of holy wars that entailed two hundred years of massacring infidels, slaughtering Jews, and leaving one man in Europe to comfort every seven widows.

When Pastor Reed finally concluded that his sermons and negotiations wouldn't heal the church's wounds, he proposed a secret ballot on what he called a "schism." After the members voted overwhelmingly to dissolve their religious union, the factions negotiated who would get the church building and who would receive payments and hold their meetings elsewhere. Since there were fifty-four voting members who were pro-slavery and only seventeen who were abolitionist, the negotiators decided the pro-slavery majority would continue their services in the existing building, while the abolitionists, including Pastor Reed and his wife, would erect a revival tent for the summer months and find a suitable building for winter worship. The pro-slavery members said they would replace Pastor Reed with a new minister from the seminary in Danville.

Because Mama and Grandma were women, Uncle Billy wasn't a member, and I was too young, none in our family voted on the proposed separation; but given Mama's blood relationship with Pastor Reed, we decided that despite having Bella and Israel, we had no choice but to worship in the tent even though there might be some tension and disapproving looks. We felt blood was thicker than water.

During this religious strife, Mama and Uncle Billy were also trying to keep the farm alive. They had drafted a letter to the county fathers asking that Israel be released from his ditching duties and sent home because of Grandpa's sickness and Father's death. The officials agreed to approve our hardship case and sent a message to the commander of the Tenth Tennessee Infantry at Fort Henry asking that Israel be released to an escort and returned to our farm near Warfield. One of our neighbors, Mr. Crews, from the congregation of the fifty-four, graciously offered to fetch Israel at the fort and try explaining to him what had happened to Father.

Israel arrived home at the end of August, just in time for harvest. After hugging all of us tightly in the shade of the buckeye tree, he stepped back, smiled broadly, and said he was happy to be back home in the Promised Land. He then asked to see Grandpa. I put my arm around his shoulder and led him up the rise to the house. I took the front parlor key down from the wall, unlocked the door, and slowly opened it. The late-afternoon light burnished the room; Grandpa was a shadow in the corner. I entered quietly with Israel following close behind. Grandpa was sleeping with his head on his chest and tilted slightly to the right. I gently touched his left arm, which was tied to the rocker. He jumped, whipped his head around, and immediately started cursing me.

As I backed away, Grandpa stopped shouting. Israel then stepped forward, whispering, "Grandpa, Grandpa, it's Israel." He studied Israel's face and began smiling faintly. Just seeing Israel had mysteriously jolted him back to his senses. Grandpa began asking calmly, "What is happening to me? Why am I always locked in my room? Why am I tied to my chair? Why am I alone? Did I do something to deserve this? Where is Grandma? Is Robert well? Where have you been, boy? Why don't we go to Warfield Market anymore?"

But as quickly as he had begun confronting his condition, Grandpa retreated to a safe place, where the demons couldn't harm him. "Did you get the birds out of the chimney? Did you catch that fellow stealing the firewood? Did they hang Saint Patrick's Battalion?" As Grandpa slipped away, Israel and I quietly stepped out into the hallway, locked the door, and deposited the key on the wall again.

Our mediocre harvest that year turned to a cold winter. We had had two unusually heavy snows in January. So far, five townspeople had died of pneumonia. We were all healthy; and with Uncle Billy staying on, Israel coming back, and Master Hudson helping out when he could, we were surviving but not prospering. The hard winter had driven Pastor Reed and the seventeen out of the tent and into Mrs. Booker's parlor. It seemed strange holding services in a member's house, but Pastor Reed quoted Jesus: "For where two or three are gathered together in my name, there am I in the midst of them."

In late February '62 the telegraph wires relayed the first big news of the war—Johnston had evacuated Nashville, and the Feds were now in control. Several days later, as I was walking down the front hill to feed the horses and slop the pigs, I noticed a small band of four to five riders galloping toward the farm, moving east to west. The horsemen slowed and came to a dusty stop at our front gate. After speaking for several minutes, one rider turned into our entry road, while the others sped off toward Memphis. As the lone rider approached, he slowed his horse to a trot and waved. It was Robert back from the war! He must have been riding hard for some time; his horse was white with sweat-foam. He shouted, "Hurry! Open the barnyard gate! I don't want to be seen from the highway!"

After drying Robert's mare and feeding the animals, we

walked arm-in-arm toward the house under a limitless, yellow-gray sky. Robert asked, "How's Grandpa faring, Thomas?"

"About the same," I replied. "But the strangest thing . . . he'll be talking crazy and all of a sudden his mind will clear and you'd think he's just as sane as any of the rest of us around here. And then five minutes later he's back in his own world again."

As we passed the buckeye tree, I stopped Robert to tell him about Father. He listened; and when I had finished, he remained silent with his jaw clenched as if swallowing whatever emotion he felt might escape. I didn't know whether his lack of response was because he never was close to Father or because his time in the militia had already hardened his sensibilities. My guess was the former; Robert had seen little military action so far, and his respect for Grandpa's war exploits was so much higher than it was for his frail father's routine farmwork.

I did notice, however, militia life had caused some superficial changes, including perhaps even an air of false confidence. Robert now walked with a swagger and chewed on the stub of a dark cigar. He had also added an impressive saber to his shotgun and pistol arsenal. While his shell jacket and trousers remained the same, he now stuffed his pants legs into his long leather boots. He still wore a stag hat with yellow rope and acorn trim and a brass eagle emblem pinning the raised brim on the right side to the crown. But there were two differences now: the hat color had changed from black to cadet gray, and three red hawk feathers had been replaced by a sweeping ostrich plume. My first impression of the new Robert was a strong, complex brew of jealousy, rivalry, admiration, and resentment about his cool response to Father's death. But Robert was my older brother; so I concluded he looked stronger, more heroic, and even more the part of a daring cavalier.

I motioned toward the house, and we continued our walk up the rise to the porch. Given the time of day, I suggested we not go in through the front door, but go around back to the kitchen and surprise Mama while she was preparing dinner. As we entered the warm kitchen, Mama was stooped over with her back to us; she was adding more wood to the fire. Robert said, "Hello, Mama."

Since there was no reason to believe the voice was any other than mine, she replied, "Hello, son," and continued stoking the fire.

Robert repeated, "Hello, Mama."

Sensing something was different, Mama stood up and turned around. She gasped and began crying. It really didn't matter to Mama; she always cried whether she was extremely happy or very sad. She then nervously blurted out, "The prodigal son's returned just as I've prayed all this time." She extended her arms. "Come over here, boy, and give your mama a big hug."

While Mama referenced the prodigal son, I was reminded so much more of another of my favorite Bible stories from Pastor Reed's canon. As I watched Mama's gradual recognition of the voice standing behind her in the narrow doorway, I repeated Pastor Reed's narrative in my head almost word for word:

Mary was standing outside the tomb crying, and as she wept, she stooped and looked in. She saw two white-robed angels sitting at the head and foot of the place where the body of Jesus had been lying. "Why are you crying?" the angels asked her. "Because they have taken away my Lord," she replied, "and I don't know where they have put him." She glanced over her shoulder and saw someone standing behind her. It was Jesus, but she didn't recognize him. "Why are you crying?" Jesus asked her. "Who are you looking for?" She thought he was the gardener. "Sir," she said, "if you have taken him away, tell me where you have put him, and I will go and get him." "Mary!" Jesus said. She turned toward him and exclaimed, "Teacher!"

Mama turned to me excitedly and exclaimed, "Thomas, go let folks know that by God's graces Robert has come home safe and sound! And fetch Bella and Israel from their cabin too!"

Since it was almost time to eat, I went out to the smoke-house and rang the dinner bell. With it being a harsh winter, I knew everyone would come running to eat Mama's warm, filling meal. I was right; they began flying into the kitchen like moths to the flame just as I returned from inviting Bella and Israel to the homecoming. First Rachel, then Israel, followed by Uncle Billy, Bella, and finally, Grandma, who had to come all the way up the hill from the hen house. After all the greetings and hallelujahs, we sat down to a dinner befitting the real prodigal son. In fact, I began smiling as Uncle Billy included the parable in his dinner prayer: "And bring hither the fatted calf, and kill it; and let us eat, and be merry. For this my son was dead, and is alive again; he was lost, and now is found."

After our memorable meal, Bella and I helped Mama clean the dishes. Grandma, Robert, and Israel tended to Grandpa. And when Uncle Billy had finished stoking the stove, he sat down and rewarded himself with a large wad of twist tobacco.

It was now seven o'clock and time for the rest of us to sit down again at the dinner table to hear Robert's story of the past year. He took the chewed, unlit cigar out of his mouth, removed a small diary from his left vest pocket, leaned back on the rear legs of his chair, and began telling us where he had been and what he had done since he last rode out onto the main road and headed west toward Memphis.

5

"Now, Grandma and Mama, I need to apologize before beginning. When soldiers are away from home, they sometimes do things they learn to regret later on. Since we have the young folk here at the table with us, I won't go into a lot of detail; but don't let your imaginations run too wild. Honestly, it wasn't as bad as you may think. I am sure Grandpa told you worse tales, when he came home from his war."

After making these preemptive opening remarks, Robert paused for a moment, referred to his small leather-bound notebook, and then began his tale.

"Well, after leaving here, I stopped in Warfield to say good-bye to some friends, do some informal recruiting, and meet up with three other fellows who had joined our militia unit. The four of us then rode southwest through Camden to Huntingdon, where we spent the night and did some further recruiting the next morning. We then rendezvoused in Humboldt with a larger contingent of horsemen and rode on to Jackson, where we finally joined our commanding officer. While in Jackson, we learned we were headed for Camp Yellow Jacket, a training center for raw recruits, some seventy miles north of Memphis. When we arrived there, we quickly realized the encampment had been named appropriately; we spent a lot of time swatting wasps that had infested much of the camp. And from reveille to lights out, we suffered the daily routine of roll calls, drills, meals, and inspections.

"Our west Tennessee militia was only one of many units passing through for training. While stationed at the camp, we conducted exercises with horsemen attached to Josiah White's Mounted Rifles, Thomas Logwood's Tennessee Company, and Hardeman's Avengers. And I remember clearly watching one of Captain White's cavalrymen day in and day out racing a magnificent black horse along the country road bordering our mock battlefield; but more of this a little later on.

"After finishing our training at Yellow Jacket, we received orders to travel south to Memphis to help protect the levees, the navy yard, and the Memphis & Charleston Railroad. The war was really heating up. While we had won the battle of Manassas in Virginia, the Feds were making moves on us in Missouri and Kentucky. And a personal note here before moving on: Just before breaking camp for Memphis, most of our Warfield contingent, Will Mashburne, Charlie Rice, and I, all received promotions to second lieutenant.

"While in Memphis we were stationed on the northeastern outskirts of the city with orders to guard the main road and railroad tracks near the Wolf River. Patrolling was exciting; we were always engaged and alert. We knew we could come under fire at any time from the Feds probing our lines. But when we were off duty, our enemy became boredom and loneliness. Each of us had his own way of passing the time— some played checkers, dominoes, or chess; and sad to say, Mama, others loved to play poker for high stakes. While a few of us wrote letters or diaries, others whittled bone necklaces, bracelets, and rings. In fact, one fellow even showed me a ring he said he had carved from a dead man's shin.

"We also had our share of musicians playing concertinas, Jew's harps, fifes, and clappers. The good news, Mama? Many went to hear the preaching, privately read their scriptures, or offered up prayers. The bad news was that there was a lot of tobacco, beer, wine, and gin. Sometimes we would see these mysterious men walking around the camp with canteens by their sides and thimbles in their hands selling what you would call 'pestilence' at two dollars a jigger.

"These strange fellows were not our only visitors. Almost every Sunday after church from spring to fall, the young women would drive out from Memphis and stop their coaches along the road across from our encampment. They would step down and saunter to and fro, waving, laughing, and calling to us. They wore long, rainbow dresses and slowly twirled their open parasols behind their heads as the parasols rested on soft shoulders. Our 'debutantes' gave us both pleasure and pain. After coyly exciting us for a time, they would step back into their buggies, instruct the drivers, and disappear over the arced bridge leading back into the city.

"But I had some good fortune. Having become a second lieutenant, my senior officers would invite me to join them on what they called 'forays' into the city, where we actually spoke to the debutantes. We would stroll along the cobblestoned docks among the piles of raw lumber, the sacks of sugar and coffee, pyramids of whiskey barrels, and towering stacks of cotton bales—all waiting to be hauled up to the large brick warehouses on Front Street. We would lean against the firm bales, smoke a handsome cigar, and watch the pilots patiently nuzzling their steamers up against the shore. Fashionable ladies, wealthy plantation owners, and preying gamblers would follow the first mates down the gangplanks onto the levee lined with twenty or more steamers like the *Dubuque*, the *Bell-Lee*, the *Highland Chief*, and the *Amulet*.

"As the whistles shrieked, the bells clanged, and the calliopes serenaded the stevedores, the disembarking passengers and charlatans would race off to the seedy saloons on nearby Beale Street or to the daunting, five-story Gayoso Hotel, which we called home when we were on one of our forays. The hotel's two-tiered portico and its wrought-iron balconies were easily recognizable from the levee. The Gayoso was a paradise with its own gasworks, waterworks, wine cellar, and bakeries. Our guest rooms had vaulted ceilings, tiled floors, and large windows with great views of the vast, bending river; and the baths down the hall had large marble tubs, silver faucets, and best of all, flushing toilets!

"Now you probably wonder how we lowly soldiers could afford staying in a swanky place like that. Well, we were lucky. You see, our commanding officer was the best friend of Major General Pillow, whom Governor Harris had just appointed commander of the Provisional Army of Tennessee. Both men were from Williamson County, roomed together at the University of Nashville, and fought together at the battles of Cerro Gordo and Chapultepec in the Mexican War. And where did Major General Pillow choose to establish his headquarters? That's right, in the Gayoso Hotel. So as officers in the unit led by the major general's best friend, we were allowed to stay rent-free. So you see, it's true; rank does indeed have its privileges.

"Well, as you enter the Gayoso lobby through the oak-paneled vestibule, you are struck by the massive carved front desk and the rich burgundy wallpaper with highlights of gold floral stenciling circling the top of the room. . . . But there was gold everywhere: gold bracelets, gold fobs, gold coins, gold rings, and gold teeth, all moving elegantly among the many mirrors, murals, pillars, and elaborate stone fountains. Fashionable civilians, officers, gamblers, and hustling girls flowed freely through the long, vaulted corridors connecting the various spaces, from the lobby to the dining rooms, the tea room, the sunroom, the grand ballroom, and the gentleman's bar.

"But the call to move out came in late November; so good-bye to the forays and debutantes. We were to move north quickly to help strengthen new fortifications on the Tennessee and Cumberland Rivers. Our destination was Fort Henry, which was being built to protect the Tennessee River just below the Kentucky border. We rode for several days in a cold, steady rain; and when we finally arrived at the unfinished fortification, we were greeted by a sea of mud and standing water reaching midway up our cavalry boots.

"Fort Henry was a five-sided earthen structure on the eastern bank of the river meant to stop water traffic, not withstand major infantry assaults. The Tenth Tennessee, the Twenty-seventh Alabama, and more than five hundred slaves were working long hours to complete the fortification. We counted eleven cannon protecting the river and six inside the dirt walls defending a possible land assault. . . . I remember now as we rode toward the fort, our commanding officer commented that the place looked hard to defend. The fort was sitting along the riverbank at the bottom of a teacup with a rim of higher terrain all around. Our unit officer said he thought it would be easy for the Feds to occupy the higher ground and bombard us quickly into submission.

"About a month after we arrived, General Tilghman assumed command of the twenty-five hundred men at the fort. Our senior officer, who spoke with him regularly, told us the general was from Baltimore and a graduate of West Point. My impression of him from afar was that he looked the part of a soldier and was determined to hold Fort Henry as long as he could even though many of his men were poorly trained and armed only with shotguns, fowling pieces, and flintlock muskets.

"But, you see, it was the weather that really caused us the most problems in building a strong defense. As we moved into a rainy February, conditions inside the fort deteriorated rapidly. The river rose constantly, flooding large areas of the fort and the surrounding lowlands. We actually saw the fort's flagstaff standing in almost two feet of water, and that's exactly when the Feds finally decided to strike.

"It all began with one of their ironclads gliding up the river and firing off several rounds. General Tilghman didn't respond until the ironclad began retreating toward the rest of the Federal fleet. The general then gave the command to fire the big cannon, and one of our two shots hit the boat and inflicted some real damage. A few more shots were exchanged during the day to feel each other out, but dusk ended these minor probes. After dark, our scouts returned and informed us enemy regiments were moving south toward our position.

"It rained heavily through the night, and at dawn, the general surprisingly gave the order to evacuate everyone except about eighty men assigned to the big guns. Of the original seventeen cannon, only nine remained above water to mount a defense, and the powder magazine was completely submerged. General Tilghman explained that given the circumstances it was better to retreat and live to fight another day. He gave our cavalry unit specific orders to position ourselves in the hills east of the fort to act as skirmishers protecting our infantry's overland retreat toward Fort Donelson some twelve miles away.

"So we rode up onto the ridgeline and watched as General Tilghman quietly prepared his eighty men for the Fed's assault, which finally began around eleven that morning. We could see everything—four ironclads and three wooden gunboats steaming up the Tennessee, while thousands of Federal troops slogged through deep mud headed to the northeastern side of our fort to cut off any attempted escape. About a mile from the fort, the warships opened fire and kept up a steady, accurate barrage, as the ground troops slowly closed on General Tilghman's position. Our small band of men inside the flooded fort gave it right back to them. After about a forty-five-minute exchange, our biggest gun exploded, and only moments later a Federal shell blasted another of our big guns, spraying the artilleryman against the nearby wall. Through my binoculars, I could see the carnage floating in the flooded space between one of the log cabins and the sloping earthen embankment.

"The Union ironclads and gunboats continued their fierce attack until one of General Tilghman's senior officers appeared on the parapet and began waving the white flag. The guns on both sides then fell eerily silent. Because of the widespread flooding in and around the fort, the Feds lowered a small boat from one of their ironclads and sailed it directly through the sally port into the severely flooded fortification. A few minutes later, I saw General Tilghman board the dinghy and travel out to the ironclad to negotiate terms of surrender.

"And it was not long after the signing that we watched the Federal general and his senior officers ride into Fort Henry. It was our signal to leave. So we pulled the reins to the east and raced off to find a good skirmishing position on the way to Fort Donelson. We dismounted and waited behind large boulders and thick brambles for their expected pursuit; and when their cavalry closed on our position, we opened fire from several directions and then quickly pulled back several miles, reloaded, and waited for them again.

"Because of our skirmishes and the sloppiness of the road from the overnight rain, the Feds failed to overtake our re-treating infantry. They made several runs at us without apply-ing any serious pressure, and as dusk approached, they turned back toward Fort Henry. In fact, the miserable field conditions inflicted more damage on our infantry than their cavalry did; we were forced to abandon six field pieces hopelessly mired in deep, muddy ruts. And around seven o'clock on that punishing February night, our infantry finally straggled into their new home, wet, dirty, very cold, and somewhat discouraged.

"Since we arrived at Fort Donelson long after dark, we couldn't really get the lay of the land until the following morning. Compared to Fort Henry, our new bastion looked considerably stronger. Fort Donelson rose almost a hundred feet above the Cumberland River, which would allow us to rain shells down on advancing warships from our fourteen large guns. As was the case at Fort Henry, the troops and slaves here had dug lengthy trenches in a semicircle around the fortification to protect it from an infantry attack. But unlike the trenches at Fort Henry, these were located along a ridgeline, protected by sharpened tree limbs pointing toward the line of attack, and further backed by several large artillery pieces. Within the earthen walls the soldiers and slaves had constructed some four hundred log cabins to house over seventeen thousand men.

"Our new fort was under the overall command of the infamous John Floyd, President Buchanan's former secretary of war. General Floyd had been indicted up north for conspiracy and fraud in connection with 'irregularities' while in office . . . something to do with contractors and suspicious arms deals. Our old friend from the Gayoso Hotel in Memphis, General Pillow, arrived and began shoring up the fort's defenses and working hard to raise troop morale before the bluecoats attacked.

"I also recognized one other fellow from the past. I knew I had seen this cavalryman before, but I was having trouble placing him. Finally, it dawned on me; he was the striking private in Josiah White's Mounted Rifles at Camp Yellow Jacket, the man who repeatedly raced his black stallion alongside our war games. In the short time between our basic training together at Camp Yellow Jacket and our chance meeting at Fort Donelson, this Private Forrest had risen in rank to colonel and now commanded our entire cavalry.

"One week to the day after we left Fort Henry, a Federal ironclad steamed up the Cumberland and opened fire on us. A senior officer estimated we received over a hundred thirty incoming rounds in the early hours, but our gunners fired back and landed the first serious blow that afternoon, ripping a hole through the attacking ironclad and causing its retreat. After that long exchange, everything remained quiet the rest of the day and overnight. The weather had turned bitterly cold, and sleet pelted us as we awaited the next assault, which finally came the following afternoon.

"The lookouts spotted seven vessels moving up the river toward our position—four ironclads in the lead and three wooden gunboats following. This time, General Floyd didn't wait for the Feds to attack; he ordered our gunmen to open fire. Several minutes later, the bluecoats returned the favor with pretty good accuracy; but the closer they came, the more damage we inflicted on their ironclads. Our gunners rained shot after shot down on them, damaging three of their ships so badly they had to withdraw from the fight. The one remaining ironclad continued dueling, and we must have hit it at least thirty times. Finally, around five o'clock that evening, this last ironclad retreated. . . . The battle was over for now; and we hadn't suffered a single casualty.

"So after successfully defending the fort against the iron-clads, General Floyd ordered a counterattack the next morning. At six o'clock General Pillow's infantry surged into the Feds' center, while our cavalry charged on Pillow's left. We ripped a hole in the bluecoats' defenses, but Union reinforcements arrived, pushing us back and almost surrounding us. We then received urgent orders to fight our way back into the fortification. The situation didn't look good; and after a high-level assessment Saturday evening, Generals Floyd and Pillow felt it was time for them to hightail it out of town. So very early Sunday morning, the two generals commandeered an arriving steamer and escaped with a brigade of our troops.

"General Floyd had left a junior officer in charge of negotiating our surrender, but Colonel Forrest would have none of that. He said he knew of one possible open road through Dover and was determined to cut his way out. He told us he had promised many of our parents that he would protect us, whenever it was within his power. He would rather have our bones bleaching on the sides of the hills, he shouted, than have us captured and carried north to rot in prison-pens in the dead of winter. He gave the orders to rouse the cavalry, and about five hundred of us quietly moved out into the night, leaving seventeen thousand infantrymen behind to fall into enemy hands.

"As we cautiously advanced along the frozen road between Dover and Cumberland City, a second lieutenant and several subordinates out on reconnaissance raced back toward our column. They reported seeing the enemy moving around and across our road about a half mile up ahead. Colonel Forrest asked for additional volunteer scouts to collect estimates of enemy strength and position. When no one responded, my unit officer and I rode to the front of the column to join the colonel and his brother on the risky mission.

"The four of us moved slowly up the road to the point where the enemy had been spotted. We scanned the area listening carefully for any sign of the Feds. We then resumed our cautious advance in the dim light and mist of the early morning and watched as perceived enemy sentries gradually dissolved into a line of short-rail fencing. After some laughter of relief, we rode a little farther along the ridgeline and came upon some fires around which were gathered a number of wounded bluecoats. Colonel Forrest asked the disheveled troops about Fed movements in the area, and they responded that they had only seen a few scouts from both armies. We then headed back to the colonel's command, where he reported the good news that the way was in fact clear for us to proceed.

"Having taken all proper precautions of advance and rear guards, scouts and flankers, we continued along the Charlotte Road southeast, finally camping Sunday night twenty miles from Fort Donelson and only fifty miles short of our objective, Nashville. As a safeguard against a surprise attack, we bivouacked on the ground in the frigid air with our horses saddled and our icy shotguns close by our sides.

"Well, our scouts returned from Nashville the next morning and reported they had encountered no Federal resistance along the way; so we moved out quickly and arrived just before noon on the eighteenth. Colonel Forrest directed us to set up camp in the suburbs near the penitentiary; he then left for a summit with his top commander, General Johnston, and several other senior officers. When the colonel returned from his meeting, we learned General Johnston was leaving Nashville for Murfreesboro some twenty miles to the southeast; that we were once again under General Floyd's command; and that our primary responsibility would be to patrol the interior of the city, while General Floyd's troops salvaged as much subsistence and other public property as possible.

"But when we reported for duty the following morning at General Floyd's headquarters, we learned the plans had changed overnight—General Floyd and his troops were about to quit the city for Murfreesboro and we were to remain in Nashville an additional day patrolling before pulling out. There was no longer any emphasis placed on saving valuable materials from falling into the enemy's hands. But by the time we returned to our campsite from the meeting, Colonel Forrest had already decided to radically transform our mission from patrolling to completing the important tasks General Floyd's troops were supposed to have performed—salvaging as much subsistence and other public property as possible.

"The colonel sprang to work immediately, splitting us into several units and ordering us to check the status of the various supply depots. Colonel Forrest said his first objective was to secure food, supplies, weapons, and ammunition for all of us. As we began surveying the sites, we found that all the officers of the quartermasters' and commissary departments had abandoned their depots and thousands of well-dressed, respectable men and women were feverishly raiding the military storehouses. The colonel rode among the frenetic mob imploring them to cease and desist and save the food and supplies for the military. When the greedy crowd refused to comply, the colonel ordered us to draw our sabers and charge the mob. The intruders then retreated, and we closed and barred the warehouse doors. Colonel Forrest left a small security detail at each of the depots and ordered the rest of us to ride with him to survey conditions in other parts of Nashville.

"But not long after we left, we got an urgent request to return because the mobs had once more broken into the depots and resumed their pillaging. The colonel again first tried reasoning with the crowd but finally ordered us to forcefully clear the warehouses and secure the doors. As we evicted the mob from one of the depots, a large Irishman grabbed Colonel Forrest by the collar, cursing loudly that the citizenry had as much right to the supplies as the colonel or anyone else in the military. I whipped out my pistol and crowned the fellow from behind, breaking his hold and sending him to the floor howling in pain.

"So after once again securing the depots and posting additional guards, we rode off to resume our reconnoitering. But the mob made an even stronger third attempt to pillage the depots; and when we returned, Colonel Forrest ordered us to use a new tactic this time: spray the crowd with ice-cold water from the city's fire engine. And needless to say, the shock and novelty of this last counterattack quelled the rioting once and for all.

"And now another personal note, Mama. . . . After volunteering to escort Colonel Forrest and his brother on the reconnoitering mission near Dover, my unit commander and I noticed we were spending much more time with the colonel and executing his direct orders. On Thursday afternoon after suppressing the mob, the colonel ordered us to telegraph a request for more trains and then to requisition as many carts, drays, and wagons as we could to haul supplies and ammunition from the warehouses and arsenal down to the railroad depot. So every one of us in the colonel's command worked tirelessly the rest of Thursday and Friday to transfer the materials to the station; and seeing that this objective had mostly been met, except for some remaining loads of ammunition, the colonel ordered Major Kelly to begin a pullout of most of our five hundred troops toward Murfreesboro late Friday afternoon.

"But Colonel Forrest honored our unit as one of three to stay behind with him to try to save the remainder of the ammunition before the city fell to the Feds. We worked all day Saturday and into Sunday morning until Union General Buell's column appeared at the outskirts of the city to negotiate Nashville's surrender. We rode over to the railroad depot and spoke with the troops loading the last of the supplies and ammunition onto the trains. They read us the final tally of what we had saved for the Confederacy: six hundred boxes of clothing, a quarter million pounds of bacon, and forty wagonloads of ammunition. We then turned our horses to the southeast toward Murfreesboro and rode high in our saddles that day. We had rescued large quantities of materials, which had been abandoned by other troops, whose sacred duty had been to try to save them.

"On Sunday night our small detachment arrived in Murfreesboro, where we rejoined the rest of the colonel's command. The following morning we learned we were to proceed to Huntsville, Alabama, to refit for duty with the privilege of a two-week furlough for outstanding service to the cause. Our unit commander asked the colonel for special permission for us to leave the force in Murfreesboro and ride directly to west Tennessee. Permission was granted; and after vigorous hugs and strong slaps on the back, we left our loyal brothers in Murfreesboro and headed northwest to meet up with the Memphis road.

"Our plan worked well; we bypassed Nashville and didn't see any Feds along the way. When we passed the Irish settlement on the Memphis highway, we began riding harder, knowing the Feds would be moving south after taking Forts Henry and Donelson. Once we reached the farm here we said our 'so longs' and agreed to meet at Bell's Furnace in three days to begin recruiting new troopers to swell the ranks and share our reputation, which has been growing by the day."

As a spent actor at the close of a demanding performance, Robert reinserted his chewed, unlit cigar and placed the stained, dog-eared notebook back in his vest pocket. He slowly lowered his head, paused, and then looked up again surveying his spellbound audience in the flickering February light.

6

ON HIS THIRD day home, Robert rose long before dawn, dressed slowly by candlelight, and carefully negotiated the narrow hallway stairs. As he passed through the empty dining room, he draped his saddlebags over Rachel's rocker and stowed his shotgun and saber in the corner. Trying to lift Mama's spirits, he playfully grabbed the door frame with his right arm and swung around the corner into the kitchen, where Mama was already perking coffee, baking biscuits, and frying country ham.

When Robert's ghostly image glided into her sight, she gasped and dropped her cooking fork onto the stovetop. She had been absorbed preparing a perfect breakfast for this special, dreaded day and warding off every mother's unsettling thoughts during wartime—poignant separation from a beloved son's smiles; fear he may never return home again; and a crushing loneliness even while surrounded by legions of caring family and friends.

Sensing he had startled her, Robert immediately rushed over and gave her a big hug. "I'm sorry, Mama. I was just trying to have some fun the way we used to when we were growing up." He caught my eye as I stood next to Mama. "Remember, Thomas, how we would run through the kitchen here playing tag? Mama would scold us over and over again for getting too close to the stove." I nodded while dipping the corner of a towel in a bowl of water and cautiously retrieving the fork from the blistering stove.

Uncle Billy appeared in the doorway and greeted us with a muted growl. "Mornin,' y'all." He then crooked his finger and raised it to his lips, signaling his desperate need for the first of many cups of strong black coffee. It wasn't long until Bella and Israel arrived; we had invited them up to the house to share Robert's last breakfast before going back to war. Mama began pushing her way through the growing crowd. "Here now. Let me get in there to check on the biscuits." She pulled a crocheted potholder from her apron pocket, opened the oven, and proclaimed, "Breakfast will be ready in a minute. Now scoot on out of here into the dining room and let me stir up the redeye gravy and scramble some eggs."

When every dish had been prepared to perfection, our master cook piled her scrumptious delicacies up to the rims of our largest antique bowls. Mama then called out to the dining room, "Thomas, go fetch Grandma and Rachel in Grandpa's room. Tell them breakfast is on the table." When the three of us arrived, Mama poured coffee for everyone and then slowly sank into her cane-bottom chair. As was his custom, Uncle Billy asked Israel to offer up thanksgiving for our meal. Israel bowed his head, folded his hands tightly, rested them on the edge of the table, and began praying, almost racing and mumbling under his breath: "Dear Jesus, thank you for this food. Please bless our Robert 'cause he's goin' back to fight. Please say hello to Father. And please make Grandpa better.

Amen." Everyone around the bountiful table echoed a firm, meaningful, "Amen."

During the breakfast, we alternated between complimenting Mama's cooking and sharing Warfield gossip gleaned from the latest egg and butter run. None of us dared broach Robert's looming departure or the most recent developments in the war. Mama had little to say, mostly staring into the small, barely touched portions on her chipped dinner plate. She would look up occasionally and smile faintly, responding to our repeated praise for her special meal. But for those of us who knew Mama well, we could detect those small, subtle displays of deep, unspoken despair—the rubbing of her left knee in a soft, circular motion, the continuous twirling of a long, graying curl near her right ear, and the unconscious tugging at the worn fringe on her faded, handmade shawl.

After sensing these subtle movements, Robert moved closer to Mama's chair. He leaned down over her stooped shoulders, softly settled his cheek against hers, and whispered, "I love you, Mama; everything will be all right. You'll see." Responding to his assurances, Mama raised her left hand to the side of his face and pressed her cheek more tightly against his.

Uncle Billy broke the sad silence that had descended around us. "Robert, if you're going to leave for Bell's Furnace at daybreak, you better go in and say so long to Grandpa now. Then we'll go down and saddle your mare."

"I'll go along with you, Robert," I said. "I'll get the key down and unlock the door. But all I ask is you go in first. Grandpa's taken to cursing me."

Grandma quickly added, "I'm gonna warn you boys now. Grandpa had a bad night, and it's carried over to this morning."

But as Robert entered the room in full uniform, Grandpa sat up erect and stared silently through the faint light at the military shadow approaching him. Grandpa repeatedly tried to salute, straining to lift his right arm, which was tightly bound to his rocker. He finally relented and then asked, "Is that you, sir? Is that you, General? How is Longstreet, sir? I still have his colors, sir, over there again' the wall. Have you seen my leg, sir? I think I left it up there on the parapet. . . ."

Having heard the story a thousand times, Robert knew he had become General Pickett and responded, "Longstreet lives, sir, and thanks to you and your men, Chapultepec Castle is ours! Congratulations for leading the brave charge over the wall!" Robert paused, and then becoming himself again, the devoted, respectful grandson leaned over the brittle warrior, kissed him lovingly on the cheek, and slowly retreated into the hallway as Grandpa's man in the moon chimed seven o'clock.

After securing the door, we collected Robert's shotgun, saddlebags, and saber and walked out onto the front porch looking for Uncle Billy. When we didn't find him there, Robert said, "He's probably already gone on down to the barn and started saddling my horse. I'll go down and help him out."

"I'll go back in and collect everyone," I replied. "We'll meet y'all under the buckeye tree."

Since the late February wind was biting, Grandma wouldn't allow Israel and me to carry Grandpa out onto the porch this time. She was afraid he would "catch a death of cold." So the rest of us gathered under our good luck tree chattering, shivering, and watching for any movement near the barnyard gate. Mama was shaking much more than the rest of us; I suspected it had more to do with seeing her eldest son riding off again than to the chilling effects of the winter gale.

Thankfully, after several more minutes, Robert and Uncle Billy emerged, leading the large, chestnut mare from the barnyard. In the dim, early light of that brutally cold morning, Robert's charger appeared as a fierce dragon firing long columns of steam out of its flaring nostrils. Because of the weather, Robert wore a thick cadet-gray frock over his usual shell jacket. It had wide flared skirts, a tall stiff collar, and pointed cuffs with a single strand of gold braid denoting his officer's rank. Despite the shiny brass buttons running the length of the coat, Robert chose to leave the frock unbuttoned, allowing him quick access to his saber and the Navy revolvers tucked under his wide belt.

As Robert was about to say his good-byes, Mama interrupted. "Before you go, son, we have some gifts to remind you of home." She motioned for Israel to step forward with his present: a handmade mourning bracelet given to him by a fellow slave while trenching at Fort Henry. Mama then nodded for Bella to share her gift: a carved figure of young Balthazar, one of only two surviving members of an antique nativity scene whittled by an early slave and passed down to her as a child. While the African wise man's torso, moveable arms, and head had been carved from walnut, his lower body was cattle bone and his turban and robe had been woven from fine horsehair.

To this day I still wonder why Bella offered her Balthazar as a gift. Was it because she cherished the wise man and felt he was the only valuable thing she had to give? Or was there some deeper meaning? Did she know Balthazar had offered up frankincense to Jesus and that its smell represents life? Did she know its trees survive in the most unforgiving places and sometimes appear growing out of solid rock? Was Balthazar then a symbol to her of both life and survival? I never asked her and she never said, but I will always remember that talisman.

Next Mama stepped forward and placed a four-inch, darkly veined rosewood cross in Robert's right palm and curled his fingers up around it. Pastor Reed had given his eldest daughter this heavy, polished memento as a keepsake after baptizing her at fourteen. Mama whispered, "Trust in the Lord, son. He will keep you safe."

After offering each of the gift bearers a sincere thank you, Robert slipped Israel's hemp bracelet onto his right wrist, carefully stowed Bella's figurine in a saddlebag, and slid Mama's cross into the vest pocket over his heart next to his tattered diary. Everyone, even Mama, now sensed it was the right moment to leave. So Robert began moving along the devoted arc of well-wishers, embracing each of us without saying a word. But when he finally came to Mama, he gave her a long, firm hug and whispered again as he had in the dining room earlier: "I love you, Mama; everything will be all right." He walked over to his charger, took the reins from Uncle Billy, and swiftly mounted. He saluted us and declared, "On to Bell's Furnace!" At that instant, the giant dome of a rising sun silhouetted him in a blinding crescent of celestial fire.

As Robert turned and rode out to the highway, Mama whispered Bible verses she had learned as a child: "And these three men, Shadrach, Meshach, and Abednego, fell down in the midst of the burning fiery furnace. Nebuchadnezzar, the king, was astonished and said unto his counselors: 'Did we not cast three men bound into the midst of the fire?' They answered: 'True, O king.' And the king answered: 'Lo, I see four men walking in the midst of the fire, and they have no hurt; and the form of the fourth is like the Son of God.'"

Bella, who was standing next to Mama, began swaying and singing softly:

> Climbin' up the mountain, children,
> Didn't come here to stay,
> And if I nevermore see you again,
> Gonna meet you at the judgment day.
>
> Hebrew in the fiery furnace,
> And they begin to pray,
> And the good Lord smote that fire out,
> Oh, wasn't that a mighty day!
> Good Lord, wasn't that a mighty day!

7

LESS THAN A week after Robert left, the freezing weather finally broke, and we began hearing the ice booming on the Anderson pond. The rumbling would begin several hours after sunrise and continue throughout the day into the night. Grandpa had taught us to never go fishing when the ponds were booming; the thundering would scare the fish and keep them from biting. But the booming now was a good sign; it meant we could begin planting and have all our crops in the ground before Easter. The booming also signaled that Master Hudson would be coming to help us with the planting again. I'd always respected him as a teacher; and when he began helping us after Robert joined the militia and Israel left to trench, he and I grew closer. We discussed a wide range of things, from his storied family history to his unconventional views on literature, religion, and the human condition.

Warfield ladies judged this twenty-five-year-old schoolmaster handsome, intelligent and somewhat shy. He was about five feet eight inches tall, well proportioned, compact, thin but rather muscular. He had long, curly auburn hair, lustrous hazel eyes, a square jaw, prominent cheekbones, and a broad, appealing smile. During his earlier visits, I'd learned his parents were born in Stonehaven on the rugged northeast seacoast of Scotland and that his father had attended the university in Glasgow, become an ordained minister, and returned home to marry his childhood sweetheart before serving his old parish church.

Master Hudson was truly proud he could trace his Hudson lineage to the twelfth century, when a medieval Hudson launched a ship from Dartmouth on the Second Crusade under Henry Glanville's command. He was equally proud of a second medieval Hudson, who a hundred fifty years later helped Wallace recapture Dunnottar Castle from the English during the Wars of Scottish Independence and was then immortalized by the Scottish minstrel, Blind Harry.

Besides relating stories of ancient Hudson warriors, he'd also described his own personal history. He told me his father, the Reverend Hudson, had gotten swept up in the immigration fervor around 1840. So his parents and he left the Stonehaven congregation and sailed for America on what his father called "an errand into the wilderness." They landed in Charleston after a rough voyage, made their way up to Chattanooga, and then caravanned to their new parish in Warberg near Nashville.

Master Hudson said he had a great deal of respect for his father and felt compelled to follow in his footsteps by attending a good college and becoming an ordained Presbyterian minister. When he turned eighteen and decided on a divinity school, his father and mother unexpectedly transferred across the state to Somerville not too far from Memphis. In light of their move, Master Hudson and his father once again reviewed the list of possible schools and decided on a seminary seventy miles northeast of Somerville. They believed it would be an excellent choice because of the school's solid reputation and its proximity to Somerville, thus fulfilling Mrs. Hudson's most important requirement, that her son make frequent visits back home.

The following September he began his studies, which would lead to his ordination; but over the next two years, he concluded the ministry was no longer a passion. He now believed formal Christian dogma would inhibit him from expressing his deeply held views and prevent him from maintaining honest and open relationships with relatives and friends. So Master Hudson spent his third year at the seminary asking himself the hardest personal question: what do I want to do with my life? But it was his captivating advanced studies in literature and philosophy that helped provide the answer—he would become an enthusiastic teacher in an academy inspiring students and instilling a lifelong joy of learning.

After he was graduated, he traveled to most of the larger towns and cities in western Tennessee seeking a position in a respected school. But when this exploration proved fruitless, Master Hudson widened his search to smaller communities east of the targeted area. This revised approach led him to Warfield, where he learned there were no current openings but there might be one near a farm five miles east of town near Trace Creek. The local farmers had just finished building a one-room schoolhouse and were seeking a teacher. Swallowing his pride and prior ambition, Master Hudson rode out to our farm, spoke to Grandpa and Father, and gladly accepted their offer to become the first instructor at the new Sugar Grove School.

So several days now into the booming, almost as if by divine intervention, I watched Master Hudson dismount, open the heavy wooden gate, and lead his mare up the entrance road toward the well house. I loved my family, but I viewed Master Hudson's arrival as my salvation from a numbing routine. I could now realistically anticipate many hours of provocative insight into his latest readings, which would understandably be inappropriate for most of the students at the Sugar Grove School. As he waved vigorously and shouted, "Hello," I raced off the front porch and barreled down the hill toward the buckeye tree, where we greeted each other with a big hug. He turned and pointed to his bulging suitcase rigged to his saddle. "See there? I've brought you more books."

"I can't wait to get started!" I exclaimed.

"With the planting?" he asked lightheartedly.

"You know what I mean," I chided teasingly, and whisked away the suitcase of books.

The planting season didn't disappoint. We began working steadily the week after Ash Wednesday and finished the hard labor by Good Friday near the end of April. During this visit, Master Hudson and I spent every free moment either reading aloud or probing the classics, which he felt were important to my growth. He said he wanted to challenge me because he believed I had potential. Sometimes, half-jokingly, he would say, "Study hard, apply yourself, and you'll be a scribe some day."

Up until this year Master Hudson and I had discussed Homer; some of the Greek plays, like *The Oresteia, Antigone,* and *Hippolytus;* and several of the Greek histories. For me, though, Master Hudson was at his best describing the battles and plagues in Herodotus and Thucydides. He'd become animated, and his voice would rise as he described the battle of Thermopylae. "Has anyone ever witnessed a stronger display of courage than Leonidas and the three hundred Greeks? Holding off Xerxes and the quarter million Persians at the pass for a week before yielding to overwhelming odds!" And then he would lower his voice and adopt a more serious tone, balancing his praise of heroic action with the brutality of war. "But to the victor go the spoils. So to make an example of the slain Greek, Xerxes ordered Leonidas's body sacrilegiously beheaded and crucified in the public square."

Master Hudson moved on from Greek war to an epidemic, which began in Ethiopia, passed through Egypt and Libya, and finally hit Athens, which lost a third of its people in 430 BC. He said the plague caused religious strife. Since the disease struck the virtuous and sinful alike, people felt abandoned by the gods and refused to worship them. He read me quotes he'd copied from Thucydides's *History of the Peloponnesian War* describing the horrific conditions:

> Though many lay unburied, most birds and beasts wouldn't touch them; but if they did, they died after tasting them. . . .The bodies of dying men lay one upon another, and half-dead creatures reeled about the streets gathering round fountains in their longing for water. The sacred places were full of corpses; for, as the

> disaster passed all bounds, men, not knowing
> what was to become of them, became equally
> contemptuous of the gods' property and the
> gods' dues. All the customary burial rites were
> entirely upset .... Some threw their own dying
> bodies on the stranger's pyre and ignited it;
> sometimes they tossed a corpse on top of
> another that was burning and then left.

But midway through the current planting season, Master Hudson just couldn't resist any longer. He eagerly turned to his favorite writers, Dante and Shakespeare. The schoolmaster opened the dialogue. "Well, earlier this season we explored the most effective techniques to analyze a masterwork. What questions did we say we should ask to begin an analysis?"

"Who, what, where, when, why, and how," I answered confidently.

"That's right. And the most interesting of these questions for me is 'why?' So applying this approach to Dante's *Divine Comedy*, why does the narrator take a circuitous journey through hell and purgatory to finally reach paradise? You might remember in the first canto, the narrator admits he's become spiritually lost. He says he'd strayed from the 'True Way' into the 'Dark Wood of Error.' It's the Easter season, and he wants to immediately climb the Mount of Joy seeking redemption during a time of hope and resurrection.

"But the three 'Beasts of Worldliness' block his path and drive him back into his former ways. As he despairs, Virgil, a symbol of reason, appears and explains he's been sent to lead Dante from error but warns him there's no direct way past the beasts to paradise. Virgil explains the journey to true redemption requires traveling a much longer and harder way. First, the narrator must descend into hell (the recognition of sin), climb through purgatory (the rejection of sin), and only then can he enter the kingdom of heaven. And Virgil emphasizes he can only guide the narrator so far. The final ascent requires a second guide, Beatrice, a symbol of divine love.

"Once we understand why the narrator is taking the tortuous journey, we can then ask a second 'why?' Why would Dante employ Beatrice to help lead the way to heaven and redemption? Any ideas, Thomas?"

"None I can think of, sir."

"Well, he's using his own life experiences to add another layer of complexity, another layer of meaning to the work. After the real Dante fell into 'evil ways'—as all of us young men do—he accidentally met a real-life Beatrice, who by her example and smile drew him back toward the 'right way.' But sad to say, as all of us young men experience along the way, Beatrice married another man and then died young. And as none of us ever forgets our first love, Dante remembered her and her engaging smile and dedicated his masterwork to her."

Master Hudson paused to savor the poignancy before continuing. "And what would be the third 'why,' Thomas?"

I responded confidently this time. "Why did Dante write *The Divine Comedy*?"

"Yes, so why do you think he wrote it, Thomas?"

"To describe the evil in his world."

"Yes . . . and to let everyone know that those who live morally go to heaven when they die and that evildoers go to their appropriate circle of hell. So he paints a conventional picture of Christian doctrine arguing we have both reward"— he paused and for dramatic effect pointed toward the glowing embers in the stove before completing his thought—"and punishment in the afterlife."

I nodded approvingly at his bent for the theatrical.

"But let's move on now," he said. "What about Shakespeare's tragedies? Why do the main characters act as they do? What motivates them? Let's take the major works one at a time. Macbeth and Lady Macbeth?"

I thought for a moment and then replied, "It's all about seeking power . . . for both of them."

"Very good. . . . And what about Iago and Othello?"

"I believe it's the same motivation here for both men, but with a slight twist. For Iago, power and revenge. For Othello, simply blind revenge."

"Let's keep going. And what about the daughters in *King Lear*?"

"Again, it's about power," I replied. "They're seeking power."

"And finally, what motivates Hamlet and his uncle?"

I paused for a few seconds and responded, "For the uncle, again, it's seeking power, and for Hamlet, we've circled back again to revenge."

"Yes! And now tell me what the second 'why?' would be?"

I responded tentatively, "Why did Shakespeare write the tragedies?"

"Very good." But regrettably, Master Hudson pushed on beyond my limits and challenged me. "So why do you think Shakespeare wrote the tragedies, Thomas?"

Realizing I'd be diving into uncharted waters, I diplomatically deferred to the stronger, more experienced swimmer. "I'm really interested in hearing your thoughts, Master Hudson."

He nodded knowingly and responded, "Well, Thomas, I believe Shakespeare's telling us that not only can we cause others to suffer, but we can also bring great misery on ourselves. In other words, unlike Dante, who described medieval hell as a punishment beyond this life, Shakespeare was saying that our lives here on earth can be our hell. In the tragedies a character commits a crime against another; the offended character seeks revenge; and the acts of both the offender and the offended wreak havoc on the innocent as well as the guilty. Ironically, while our relationships with others may be our only path to salvation, they're also the source of much of our suffering. That's the genius in Shakespeare, Thomas—his ability to explore life's dualities and irresolvable contradictions."

8

THE TIME HAD passed quickly, and now it was the evening of Holy Saturday, the night before Master Hudson would leave for home. Since the next day was Easter, everyone else in the family had already retired. So Master Hudson and I sat alone in the dining room near the glowing stove to have one last dialogue. Master Hudson leaned back in his chair and opened the conversation. "So, here we are, Thomas, Holy Saturday night, five hundred sixty-two years to the day after the narrator began his quest in *The Divine Comedy*."

"In honor of the anniversary, Master Hudson, what would you like to discuss your last night here?"

"I've learned young trees grow best in the shade, Thomas. So I was thinking of sharing some of my darkest thoughts with you. I believe you're old enough now to explore them with me. You agree?"

"Absolutely!" I responded.

"Well, let's begin then. . . . We asked earlier this year, 'Why did Dante write *The Divine Comedy* and Shakespeare his greatest tragedies?' We agreed they wanted to examine evil in this life—why people and governments commit horrific crimes causing immeasurable suffering to the blameless; what motivates the damned to choose deception and brutality over honesty and affection in the first place; and besides stipulating there's evil in the world, they agreed there's a hell. But while Dante thought conventionally that God rendered punishment in the afterlife for evil acts committed on earth, Shakespeare believed your hell was other people and the pain they inflict during your lifetime.

"But my ongoing assessment compels me to ask another, perhaps blasphemous 'why' question: if there's a creator, a higher force out there, why does this supreme being with absolute power allow cruelty, malevolence, hatred, dissembling, and human suffering? I began whispering that question to myself during my first year at the seminary. We'd read the scriptures about Jacob's first two wives. They were sisters, you see, and Jacob had worked seven years to marry the younger, more beautiful of the two. But their father tricked Jacob into marrying the older sister.

"Jacob persisted and labored another seven years to win the younger sister's hand. And when the younger of the two finally came to Jacob's tent, he said, 'Now the sunshine has entered.' Ironically, her entry into his life was only the beginning of his troubles. The older sister had begun to have children, while the younger, Jacob's favorite, remained barren and distraught. God allowed the older sister to smile, and the younger to shed tears.

"Well, after humbling the younger sister for years, God finally permitted her to have a son, whom they named Joseph. But the joy didn't last long. Jacob decided to move his family on to Canaan. The younger sister became pregnant again and dreamed of a new, beautiful life with Jacob, Joseph, and future sons to follow. But before the end of the journey to Canaan, somewhere between Bethel and Ephrata, the younger sister went into labor, delivered a son, Benjamin, and subsequently died.

"So God didn't allow her to enter the Promised Land or to see her sons grow to manhood. Why did he inflict so much pain on the younger sister, while ignoring the elder? Why didn't he allow the younger to survive and see the Promised Land? Why did he take Jacob's favorite from him, after requiring him to work fourteen years to win her hand? . . . You see where I'm headed, Thomas?"

"I've got a pretty good idea, Master Hudson. But go on, lay out your case."

"Next, our seminary class learned the story of a Moses whom none of us had ever known. We'd all heard how Pharaoh's daughter discovered the infant in the bulrushes and took the Hebrew child in as her son. . . . But what we didn't know was what followed after Moses grew up."

"Before receiving the Ten Commandments on Mount Sinai?" I asked.

"Exactly! And long before leading his people out of Egyptian captivity."

"What happened after he grew up?"

"Well, knowing he was born a Hebrew, Moses must've resented the Egyptian's oppression of his people. One day he saw an Egyptian beating one of his Hebrew brothers. After looking both ways to be sure no one was watching, he killed the Egyptian and buried him in the sand.

"The next day when Moses was walking among the Hebrew workers, he discovered two of the men fighting.

Moses separated them and reprimanded the worker whom he thought was in the wrong. The aggressor challenged Moses, asking if he planned on killing him as he had murdered the Egyptian the day before.

"Moses shuddered. He realized his own crime had been discovered. He knew the Pharaoh would try to execute him. So Moses began his career as prophet and founder of Israel in the role of a fugitive from justice. He fled to Arabia to begin a new life, sat down by a well to rest, met the seven daughters of Jethro, and to make a long story short, married one of the daughters.

"And then one day later on, while Moses was tending sheep in the backside of the desert near Mount Sinai, the Lord appeared to him in a burning bush and told him to go to Pharaoh and 'deliver the children of Israel out of Egypt.' And after God unleashed the plagues on the Egyptians, Moses led the Hebrew slaves out of captivity, parted the Red Sea, led them to Mount Sinai, received the Ten Commandments, and lived to be a hundred twenty years old.

"The questions for me here, Thomas, were obvious: Why did God choose a murderer as a leader of the people with whom he'd made a covenant? Why'd he select a fugitive to communicate his sacred tenets, which have become the basis of the law for millennia?

"After studying Moses, our class moved on to a surprising story about King David. God had made a covenant with the king promising him that his 'throne shall be established forever.' God then allowed David to build a mighty empire. While at the peak of his power, he committed adultery with

Bathsheba, the wife of Uriah the Hittite. She became pregnant, and David sent for her husband, a soldier fighting at the siege of Rabbah. Uriah honorably refused to sleep with his wife while his compatriots were on the field of battle. So King David sent Uriah back to his commander with a sealed message instructing the commander to abandon Uriah on the battlefield so that 'he may be struck down and die.' The plot succeeded, and King David married Bathsheba. The questions for me again were quite simple: Why'd God make a solemn covenant with an adulterer? Why'd he allow the Messiah to be a descendant of David, which was confirmed in the Gospels of Matthew and Luke? . . ."

Master Hudson paused to consider God's mysterious ways and then continued, "Near the end of the first year of divinity school, we studied the early life of Christ and learned the shocking story of the Massacre of the Innocents. The biblical account was dreadful . . . vivid . . . and unsettling. After the wise men's visit to the manger, Joseph had a dream ordering him to take Mary and their son to Egypt to escape King Herod, who was seeking to kill the infant Jesus. And when the king discovered the family had managed to escape, he sent his soldiers to Bethlehem with orders to kill every child two years old and younger, thus fulfilling Jeremiah's Old Testament prophecy that there would be 'weeping and great mourning in Rama' for children who'd been lost.

"So at the time of Jeremiah's prophecy, God already knew there'd be a Massacre of the Innocents and that Jesus would return from Egypt only after Herod's death. Why did God allow Herod to commit this hideous act against a multitude of children? Why did he want the parents of these innocents to suffer like that?"

"My God, Master Hudson, I'd never heard any of this before."

"Nor I, Thomas, until I attended divinity school, where I suspect they felt future theologians should know all the facts, both the positive and the ... let's say ... the inconvenient ones."

"What'd you think, Master Hudson, when you heard these things?"

"At the beginning of my second year at the seminary, I relived the accounts of Jacob's wife, Moses, David, and the Innocents. And I asked repeatedly, 'Why would a loving God allow these things to happen?' Needless to say, my enthusiasm for ordination was waning. My thoughts flowed naturally from biblical horrors to calamitous world events. I remembered reading how a Caledonian leader described the cruelty of the Roman Empire—'where they make a desert, they call it peace'—and I knew historians had validated the Caledonian's claim with estimates of five million people killed as the emperors' legions conquered the world. Then there were the crusades with two million casualties, the Black Plague with twenty-five million victims in Europe alone, and the Napoleonic Wars with four million military and civilian fatalities. Why did God allow all this human suffering?

"My suppressed, unspoken doubts penetrated my nights, first as agitated sleep and then as a recurring dream, which has plagued me up until now. I'm walking along a curved path lined with gnarly oaks and stubby olive trees. After passing a steep outcropping with alternating layers of rust and umber,

I enter a blighted landscape where the trees and large brush are cropped and stripped bare of bark. I hear a lone, crusted beak drilling and sending hollow thumps echoing among the shattered trunks. The wind begins to swirl. When I turn the next corner, a full moon rises; the forest ends; and large stacks of soldiers line the silver way. I pass between frozen emerald lakes where motionless bodies stand suspended in glowing layers of jade. Long, irregular cracks radiate from these frozen dead, as if they had been hammered into the ice. . . .

"I now see people walking in the road ahead of me. As I run to catch up, I shout, but they don't respond. When I reach for their shoulders, my warm hands slice through their hazy forms. After I pass this ghostly crew, the narrow road suddenly widens into a vast city square. I observe a unique cross standing near the entrance to an enormous tent. The left side of the crossbeam is much lower to the ground than the right, thus transforming the traditional cross into a balance scale. I discover your father, mother, Israel, and Rachel feasting at a round table to the left of the main entrance; and when I look to my right, I see you, me, your brother, and Pastor Reed seated at a second table playing poker for money. The pastor shuffles the deck, and you say, 'Robert, cut the cards.' I then hear whispers of 'Dismas . . . Gestas . . . Belshazzar' echoing in my head. . . . I wake with a sudden, violent shaking."

When Master Hudson finished this last sentence, he sat up abruptly in his chair, as if he were truly waking from a nightmare. He rubbed his eyes with the heels of his hands and began nervously running his fingers through his hair. He appeared to be reliving the ghostly dream he'd just described.

Throughout the monologue, the atmosphere had become increasingly mystical. The lamplight painted the room with an eerie orange glow and cast chilling shadows on the willow-patterned walls. Repeated lightning flashes behind Master Hudson's head added to the unearthly aura of a séance or an exorcism. While he became the medium helping communicate with the dead and dying, I played the exorcist helping him cast out his demons. . . .

I finally broke the silence with gallows humor. "Well, it looks like you, Robert, Pastor Reed, and I are all in this together on the wrong side of the beam."

He leaned forward and responded seriously, "I'm convinced there's no other way to fight this. . . . We just have each other."

"Yes," I replied. "We're all in this together, Master Hudson . . . and we do have each other." I paused and added, "It's getting late; and tomorrow morning, you know, we have to roll the stone away to see if he's still there. Let's try getting some sleep before the big day dawns." I picked up the lamp, checked the woodstove, and then led our pilgrimage of two up the narrow, elliptical stairs to our separate rooms.

9

HONORING A LONG family tradition, Mama had risen well before dawn on Easter Sunday to prepare a hearty breakfast before we headed out to celebrate the resurrection. Following another family ritual, I was the second person to wake on Easter morning. I had washed up, shaved, dressed in my Sunday best, and hurried down to the kitchen where Mama was frying the sausage and eggs and baking her special yeast biscuits in honor of "the rising." As was also the custom on Easter, I gave Mama a big hug and kiss and said jokingly, "Mama, you are up again even before Jesus."

After giving me her usual admonition that God was going to punish me, she told me to go wake everyone else up and tell them breakfast was on the table. So I first shouted the alarm up the stairs, then knocked on the door to Grandpa's room (where Grandpa never slept anymore), and finally ran down the hill to Bella's cabin to fetch her and Israel. We always invited them to share meals with us on special occasions and to attend services on Sundays at Pastor Reed's church.

Even before we had the dreadful schism, Bella and Israel had always worshipped with us, sitting alongside the other Negroes in either the back rows or the narrow gallery. This custom was somewhat unique because in most of the other churches in the county, the Negroes gathered in the church-yards beneath the open windows to hear the sermons and the gospel singing. And even after we became the "Church of the Seventeen," worshipping in Mrs. Booker's parlor, our aboli-tionist faction enthusiastically welcomed Bella and Israel into our tiny fold as "family and brethren in Christ."

When everyone had finally settled around the dining room table, Israel offered his usual prayer but included thanks this time for Master Hudson and all the help he had given us during the spring planting. After all the brimming bowls had made their way around the table at least once, Grandma sug-gested somewhat disappointedly, "I guess it's my time to stay home and look after Grandpa."

But Uncle Billy quickly insisted otherwise, interjecting, "We'll hear none of that this morning, Grandma!" He smiled broadly and continued teasingly, "You need the church service more than I do. . . . And while y'all are gone, I'll give Grandpa a nice Easter bath and breakfast." Uncle Billy had watched Grandma's health steadily decline over the past few years as the constant caring for her beloved husband exacted a heavy toll, and he was keen on relieving some of her burden.

Uncle Billy, Master Hudson, and I then excused ourselves and stepped out into a glorious sunrise befitting a holy day. We walked down to the barnyard to fetch the two wagons and Master Hudson's mare. When we had finished harnessing and saddling, we led the horses over to the buckeye tree and shout-ed for everyone to come on out and get on board. We all gave Master Hudson a strong hug for helping us out again; and after he had mounted his horse, Mama handed him a sack filled with some of his favorites—smoked ham, bacon, eggs, and butter. After the rest of us had climbed up into the wagons, Master Hudson led us out the entry road to the main highway. When we turned the wagons to the west toward Warfield, I looked back over my shoulder and watched as Master Hudson gently pulled his reins to the east toward his home.

Pastor Reed based his Easter sermon on the Old Testament prophecy of the Messiah's death and resurrection in Isaiah: "He was a man of sorrows, and acquainted with grief. . . . He was oppressed and afflicted, yet he opened not his mouth. . . . He was brought as a lamb to the slaughter." After congratulating the reverend on his fine preaching, we drifted from the parlor into Mrs. Booker's dining room, where we enjoyed a delicious Easter buffet of baked country ham, fried chicken, potatoes, milk gravy, wilted lettuce, and three kinds of pie. Wanting to be polite to everyone, we stayed at Mrs. Booker's until around two o'clock, when Grandma announced we should be leaving; she didn't think it was right to leave Uncle Billy and Grandpa alone all day on Easter Sunday.

Once the thoughtful church ladies had packed an imposing picnic basket for Grandpa and Uncle Billy, we boarded the two wagons and turned them toward home. As we rode along, all we could talk about was what we had just learned during the church luncheon—that the Feds had recently taken over our old church building from the congregation of the fifty-four, and the pro-slavery members were currently meeting in a tent, while looking around for a permanent home. I must admit there was some sinful gloating among the congregation of the seventeen.

As we rounded the last bend before the farm, we noticed something was amiss. There appeared to be a host of soldiers in blue uniforms lined up and down our entryway. When we turned onto the property, we drove our two wagons up the road between the two lines of Feds toward the buckeye tree. We looked straight ahead and said nothing. When we got up near the well house, we could see Uncle Billy was talking to several of the officers near the barnyard gate.

I handed Mama the reins, hopped down from the wagon, and ambled over to the small circle of men. The young lieutenant was nervously holding his soiled gloves in his right hand and repeatedly slapping them against the palm of his left as he explained his situation to Uncle Billy. "You see, sir, our boys here met up with the rebs for a couple days over at Pittsburg Landing east of Memphis. And when all was said and done, you can be damn sure we put it to 'em. We drove Beauregard and the rebs straight out of Tennessee down to Corinth. But you see, sir, victory comes at a price—we lost some boys and animals fightin' over near Shiloh church. So to be straight-up honest with you, sir, I need your mule there."

Uncle Billy tried politely defending his untenable position. He looked the young soldier straight in the eye and replied, "I'd like to be accommodatin' but that mule there's not mine to give. Belongs to our patriarch, sir."

Becoming increasingly agitated, the lieutenant countered, "Then I suppose I've been wastin' my time here with you, sir. Perhaps you want to run along and fetch the owner for me?"

Uncle Billy continued resisting mildly. "I'd love to, sir, but ya see, Grandpa's mind's not right. We have to keep him bound in a chair. He's not in any condition to be out here giving up anything."

Given Uncle Billy's response, the young lieutenant adopted a conciliatory tone. "Perhaps you're misunderstandin' me, sir. I'm not outright taking the mule, I'm offering you a hundred and fifty dollars for it. That's well above the market price."

Uncle Billy smiled, thrust his hand out, and replied, "If that's the case, Lieutenant, I'm sure Grandpa would be willin' to deal. Now all's left is for us to shake on it and then for you to hand over the cash."

"There's . . . ah . . . one fly in the ointment, so to speak, sir," the officer said haltingly. "I'd . . . ah . . . love to pay you right here on the spot. But, you see, I haven't got that kind of money with me. I'm sure you understand."

"Well, sir, how ya expectin' to pay us for the mule?"

"Not a problem, sir. Just ride into the county seat and file a formal claim for reimbursement at the postmaster's office."

Uncle Billy didn't respond for the longest time. He just stood there staring at the lieutenant. We all knew his wheels were spinning. He finally cleared his throat and said, "I guess it's better to live with the expectation of gettin' paid than never gettin' paid at all. I'm sure you'll agree with that notion, sir."

"Absolutely. So we'll fetch the mule right there and move on out. . . . Thank you for your time, sir. It's been a privilege." He tipped his hat, turned away, and swung up into the saddle. He then tipped his hat again, smiled, and repeated, "Yes, sir, it's been a real privilege." He raised his right arm above his head and shouted, "Fall in!" And his company of bluecoats fell in to formation and marched out the entryway.

As the blue tide receded, Uncle Billy pulled a cigar from his vest pocket, bit the end off, and wedged the stogie between his teeth. He didn't say a word until the Feds were safely out of earshot on the main road. He slowly lowered the unlit cigar and said sardonically, "Boy, ya just witnessed the fine art of stealin' in broad daylight."

"Stealing, Uncle Billy? We're going to get the money for the mule."

Uncle Billy laughed and replied, "Sometimes, boy, what is . . . really isn't."

"What do you mean?"

"There's a snowball's chance in hell we'll ever see that money. The Feds will never honor a formal claim filed by a citizen of secessionist Tennessee, and I fear this won't be the last of the stealin' either. Not just by the Feds, but by Johnny Reb, too, when he gets hard up."

"Why didn't you just politely refuse to give up Grandpa's mule?"

"We'd be walkin' a mighty fine line there, Thomas. Sayin' no might've been just enough to set him off. And only really bad things would come of that—like burning down the house and the barn. All that for a mule? Not a fair bargain. Just have to agree to give it up and live to fight another day." He wrapped his arm around my shoulder and said, "Let's head on into the house and let the folks know we're a little lighter now in the hip pocket."

After all the blurred distractions of Easter breakfast, Pastor Reed's sermon, Mrs. Booker's luncheon, and the Feds' mule rustling, I finally had a chance to sit alone on the back step and quietly reflect on what had transpired over the past two months, especially as it related to Master Hudson and our ongoing dialogue about his brave quest. I had sat in this very spot during the late afternoon following Father's funeral; and surprisingly, I was now having thoughts and feelings similar to those I had had then. First, there was a sense of separation from someone I respected, relied upon, and loved. Second, there was a deep sense of loneliness knowing it could be a long time before I would see either of them again. And third, Father's death and Master Hudson's doubts had led me to ask probing questions about God's deliberate hand in death and human suffering.

10

HAVING REGAINED HER strength several months after Easter, Mama decided it was Mrs. Hunter's key lime pie at the Booker luncheon that had made her deathly ill. While the rest of us knew others had partaken of the same Hunter delicacy that Sunday afternoon, we could not argue rationally with Mama. Once she had made up her mind, then that was that; it was the key lime pie.

It all started about ten days after Easter. Mama said she was just not feeling right; she had started having severe headaches and dull aching throughout the body. She next lost her appetite, became very sluggish, and was no longer capable of doing all the cooking and her other usual chores. Finally, she developed a fever, which gradually rose to the point where she had to stay in bed constantly and was beside herself much of the time. We sent for Dr. Simmons, who examined Mama and determined she had contracted typhoid fever.

Grandma, Bella, and Rachel tried caring for Mama and taking on many of her chores, but Uncle Billy could see that many things were beginning to fall through the cracks. Grandma was taking care of Grandpa, and her energy was steadily waning. Rachel was still too young to do much of Mama's work, and Bella could not finish all her chores and then do Mama's too.

So in his usual relaxed way, Uncle Billy announced he would be leaving on Sunday to conduct some business and would be returning the following Tuesday afternoon.

But unbeknownst to any of us, he had privately decided to get us help until Mama could get back on her feet again. He knew if he disclosed what he was really up to, he would get serious resistance from the ladies on the farm, especially from Grandma, who cherished her independence more than anyone else.

Like clockwork, on the following Tuesday afternoon, I spotted Uncle Billy driving the wagon down the highway toward the farm. Someone was seated beside him. Since the front gate was closed, I ran down the entrance road, slipped the rope loop off the post, and swung the gate open. As the wagon passed through, I jumped up into the bed and hitched a ride up to the buckeye tree, where Uncle Billy stopped to discharge his passenger.

He turned around and said, "Jump down, Thomas, and help Beth get her suitcases up to the house."

"Yes, sir!" I replied. I then eagerly leapt out of the bed, ran to Beth's side of the wagon, and motioned for her to place her right foot on the top of the wheel. I reached up and clasped my hands around her thin waist, gently pulled her away from the wagon, and very slowly eased her to the ground. I stepped back and instantaneously made an indelible picture of Beth standing there before me. She was about twenty years old, several years my elder. She was tall, fully formed with an upright figure. Her dark curls cascaded down over her shoulders and shimmered in the slant of the warm afternoon sun. She had large, lively dark brown eyes, high cheekbones, a clear brown complexion, a small nose, small chin, and full, glistening red lips, which curved upward into an adventurous smile.

"Nice to meet you, Thomas. Father here has told me a lot about you."

"Likewise, Beth," I responded distractedly, wondering what Uncle Billy had been saying about me. I collected myself and added, "I'll get your things and we'll head on up to the house."

"Hold on there, Thomas!" Uncle Billy interjected. "A change in plans. I'll help you with the luggage and tend to the mare later. Better I go up and make the introductions." He applied the brake, jumped down from the wagon, and tied the reins to one of the branches on the buckeye tree.

As we entered the house through the side porch, Uncle Billy called out, "Hello! Hello! Everyone come on into the dining room. I've got someone for you to meet!"

After Grandma, Rachel, Bella, and Israel arrived, Uncle Billy introduced our surprise guest. "I want y'all to meet my beautiful daughter from my second marriage. This is Elizabeth; but we call her Beth. She's a good, hardworking girl who's agreed to come over here and help us out until Mama fully recovers."

Everyone responded simultaneously, creating a jumbled murmur of "Nice to make your acquaintance" . . . "Welcome, Beth" . . . "Pleased to meet ya" . . . and "Hello, ma'am."

"Any change in Mama while I was away?" Uncle Billy asked.

"Her fever's about the same," Grandma responded. "And now I'm beginning to hear some rattling when she takes deep breaths. Don't like the sound of it. Remember, Doc Simmons warned us to watch out for any signs of chest congestion. Could be pneumonia. I think we should send for Doc again."

"Better safe than sorry," Uncle Billy replied. "We can send one of the Anderson boys to fetch him." He paused and turned to his daughter. "One thing, Beth, before I forget it. We keep the door across the hall there locked. It's where Grandpa stays. We don't want him wandering off and getting hurt or lost. He's just not the same anymore, ya see." He then turned toward me. "Thomas, you and Israel grab Beth's suitcases and carry them upstairs to Master Hudson's bedroom. And when you're done with that, how about giving Beth the fifty-cent tour of the farm."

Israel and I grabbed the valises, hurried up the narrow back stairs, and deposited the bags in what had come to be known as Master Hudson's room. Not wanting to miss anything, I raced back down the treacherous steps into the hallway. As I reentered the dining room, however, I slowed to a saunter and moved nonchalantly to a corner opposite Grandma, Rachel, Bella, and Beth, who were busy divvying up Mama's usual chores.

When the interminable meeting finally ended, I casually walked over to Beth and asked, "You now ready for that fifty-cent tour?"

"Ready when you are," she replied, smiling.

"Okay then. . . . We'll start with the farmhouse here and sample some of the history linked to the various rooms. . . . So let's go out into the hallway there and climb the 'scary stairs' to the second story. You'll see soon enough why as children we called the steps 'scary.'"

Acting every part the gentleman, I discreetly helped Beth negotiate the notorious, curving staircase leading to the small second-floor rooms. Our first stop at the top of the stairs was the bedroom I shared with Uncle Billy. As we stared in, I pointed to some of my finest treasures. "On the table there's Grandpa's bowie knife, and over there in the corner? That's his double-barrel shotgun. He used both of them during the Mexican War. . . . Saw a lot of fighting, from Monterrey to Vera Cruz. . . ." As I described some of Grandpa's exploits (which he had vividly portrayed for Robert and me a thousand times), Beth would stop me to ask specific questions about the battles, some of which I could proudly answer, while others I embarrassingly had to admit I'd probably known but had forgotten now at my advanced age.

When I began highlighting another unique treasure, Cleary, my large black cat, jumped down off his special pillow, strolled out into the hallway, and began rubbing against Beth's long, pale blue dress. She must have had cats as pets. She bent down, rolled Cleary gently over onto his back, rubbed his stomach, and laughed as he began playfully kicking her on the wrists without baring his claws. The purring became deafening; she had made a friend for life.

When Cleary finally tired of the attention and returned to his bed, I resumed the discussion of my treasures by pointing to the wooden leg standing in the corner still wearing its boot. I then described how Grandpa had lost his leg topping the wall at the decisive battle of Chapultepec Castle, or as some say, the "Halls of Montezuma." Beth said Uncle Billy had often mentioned how proud he was of his older brother's war record but that he had never really discussed the details of any of Grandpa's battles. So it was not very long into the tour that I sensed Beth was intelligent, curious, and respectful. She was truly interested in other people's feelings, their hopes, and perhaps even their fears.

I nudged Beth's elbow and said, "Turn and cross the hall. . . . That's your bedroom there." To enliven the tour with a bit of mystery, I offered a riddle. "Sometimes a soldier and a gentle fellow who dislikes wars stay in the room."

Beth smiled and said jokingly, "For their sake, I hope not at the same time."

"Oh, I don't think it'd ever be a problem; but as it turns out, so far that's never happened."

Remaining engaged, she casually inquired, "If I might ask, who are these fellows?"

"As strange as it sounds, Beth, two of my favorite people in the world—my older brother, Robert, who's in the rebel cavalry, and my teacher, Master Hudson, who helps us out with the planting and harvesting. And by the way, there's even something else special about the room."

"I'm curious," Beth probed.

"Well, unlike the other bedroom up here, yours has a name: the 'Master Hudson Room.'"

"Why the name?" she asked.

"The room always takes the name of the last person who occupied it for any length of time. . . . So in the past few years,

it's been 'Robert's Room' and then 'Master Hudson's Room.'"
And I added smilingly, "If you stay for a spell, who knows, it
might well become 'Beth's Room' in the future."

After carefully negotiating the stairs again, we next stood
outside Grandpa's old room, which had become Mama and
Rachel's bedroom after Father died. I whispered, "The door's
closed. That means Mama's in there resting, so I can't show
you any of the family treasures. But one thing I can tell you
is that without exception, everyone in the family ever born in
the house here was delivered in that room."

Beth shook her head and said, "Delivered in that room
there. Hmm, that's really something. . . ."

"Well, there's even more to the story than that. Everyone
who's died on the farm here passed on in that very room too!"

When we had finished touring the farmhouse, we exited
through the back door, passed the washhouse and Grandma's kettle, and then climbed the stairs onto the wraparound
porch to have a sweeping view of the land and the various
farm structures. I first turned to the east and pointed out
Sugar Grove School at the far end of the property, the hayfield abutting the Anderson farm, and closest to us, the family garden, where the Bibb lettuce and kale were now ready
for harvest.

I then turned to the west and explained that the far field
was for cattle grazing and the near field was for growing feed
for most of our animals. I next pointed out Bella's cabin, the
well house, and our lucky buckeye tree, which had forever
been a focal point for family meetings and farewells. I then
explained there was a special forage field across the highway

bounded by Trace Creek and thriving orchards, which we would surely visit in the coming days.

Since it was getting late and almost time to finish my evening chores, I politely rushed Beth along to the barnyard and pointed out the toolshed, the lean-to for the pigs, the wagon shed, and the big barn, which we briefly visited to see the hen house and the horse and cattle stalls. And there was method to my madness; I had saved just enough time for one last stop before officially calling it a day. I led Beth back up the rise toward the house where we joined a path curving to the right past the ancient lilacs and ending abruptly at our moss-laden cemetery gate.

Concealing my conflicted thoughts, I began this last stop with a quip. "Well, Beth, since we both surely believe in the resurrection, I guess it's appropriate to end our tour here at the family burial ground." I didn't really know why I had saved the cemetery for the end of the tour. Was it because I viewed the tour as a symbol of our "brief walk through life," which for our family always began in the farmhouse and ended no more than fifty yards away here in the graveyard? Or was it a first hesitant attempt to engage her in a more challenging dialogue about the Black Plague, Uriah, or the Massacre of the Innocents? After pointing out Father's headstone and the ivied tombs of others I had never known, I declared the tour over and walked her back down to the house.

Over the next few weeks Mama's fever lessened, and she gradually regained her strength. Dr. Simmons stopped by again to examine her and confirmed she had fought off her slight touch of pneumonia and should in time make a full recovery. But we really didn't need Dr. Simmons's examination to confirm Mama was improving; all the signs were there—her appetite was returning; she was now sitting up in bed and reading; and she was beginning to give everyone orders about what needed to get done around the place.

During those first few weeks Beth was with us, I focused on devising plans to spend increasingly more time with her. Since all the crops were in the ground, I only had minor chores to finish during the day. So I would hurry to complete them and then head up to the house to see how I could help the ladies out. And it was during one of these helpful visits to the house that I experienced feelings I had never really sensed before—intense emotions infused with ambiguity, which I both questioned and treasured.

I knew the following morning Israel and I would be doing the usual egg, milk, and butter run on the east side of Warfield. So when I had finished my chores, I went by the barn and offered to take the brimming pails of warm, raw milk up to the house for Uncle Billy. And after he eagerly accepted my offer, I carefully hauled the heavy buckets up the rise to the back of the house, thus successfully implementing the first phase of my ambitious plan.

As I approached the kitchen, I could hear through the open window as Beth and Grandma planned their day. I deposited the pails on the back porch and strolled inside. I tipped my cap and greeted them with the ancestral lilt, "Top of the morning to you, ladies!" I pointed to the window and continued the performance. "It's a fine morning out there! By the way, I just brought the morning milk up from the barn. I suspect there's some churning to be done, and I'd love to help you ladies, seeing I've finished my morning chores."

Keenly aware of my intentions, Grandma played along. She turned to Beth and said, "Now isn't he just the sweetest boy?"

Beth smiled and deflected the charged question. "I suspect . . . especially when he's asleep," she said.

Grandma turned to me and said, "Okay, Thomas, it's time for you to get to work. Go back out and strain the milk you just brought up. Don't leave any straw in it, you hear? Then take it to the milk closet and exchange it for the old milk and cream, which has surely turned by now. When you're done with that, bring the old milk into the dining room and get started churning. Time's awasting."

Strictly following Grandma's orders, I fetched the aged milk and cream; poured the three gallons of thick clabber into the churn; threaded the wooden dasher through the hole in the lid; and then firmly seated the top. I found a comfortable slat-back chair and then called out, "You ladies drop by occasionally to see how things are progressing. . . ." And as I settled into a comfortable rhythm, I smiled; I had just completed the second phase of my operation.

It seemed I had been churning for a lifetime without any visits from Beth. But just when I was about to declare the third part of my plan a failure, she glided into the room and said, "So let's check your progress."

I nodded and stopped churning. While I thought my right arm was going to fall off after an hour of abuse, I refused to reveal my pain. I carefully lifted the lid away and proudly presented a rich, thick layer of fresh butter floating on gallons of warm buttermilk below.

Beth peered in and congratulated me. "I'm impressed . . . . There's a lot of butter in there." She then hurried off to the kitchen and returned with a wooden bowl, which she positioned on a small table next to me. She turned and started toward the kitchen again. "Don't make a move. I'll be right back. I forgot the salt and the butter mold."

But while she was gone, I couldn't resist an urge to close my eyes and thrust my hands into that warm, thick golden layer floating on top. I gently squeezed, repeatedly forcing the soft, flowing substance out through the spaces between my thumbs and forefingers. With my eyes closed, and locked in reverie, I didn't hear Beth reentering the room. When she cleared her throat, I jumped, opened my eyes, and sheepishly began withdrawing my arms from the scene of the crime.

She wagged her finger teasingly and said, "Shame on you, Thomas!" She paused and began laughing. She gazed into my eyes and slowly lowered her arms into the soothing layer next to mine. As she gently kneaded beneath the surface, our oiled fingers touched, gradually engaged, and interlocked for a brief irreligious, religious moment. She slowly unlocked our fingers, smiled enigmatically, and lifted her hands out of the warm liquid. We both stared at the sensuous rivulets flowing down her raised forearms and dripping off her elbows onto the floor.

And then as if nothing had ever happened, she abruptly suggested we transfer the fresh butter to the wooden bowl and mold it into what Uncle Billy called "tasty one-pound squares of gold." When we had finished the molding, Beth excused herself, explaining she needed to go help Grandma change Mama's sheets.

I didn't know how to interpret what had just happened. During the past two weeks as we walked along, the backs of our hands would inadvertently touch; and, at first, she would draw her hand back immediately. But as the days progressed, those spontaneous touches began lasting an instant longer. I also noticed she had begun gently leaning into me as we strolled along the shaded path behind the house. And now this interlocking—what did it mean? What was she feeling? Was she merely repeating something she had enjoyed as a child, dipping her hands into a churn and squeezing the thickened liquid time after time? Or was there something more to this? Was this Beth's attempt to connect with another human being, to melt into a warm, gentle maelstrom of forgiving affection, and then bravely face together a threatened, uncertain future?

During the next two weeks, Mama's health continued to improve, and her fever completely subsided. She now took all of her meals with us and even insisted on performing some of her less demanding chores. My formal relationship with Beth had remained about the same, but my unspoken feelings for her had ripened into unknown emotions. The world was less bleak now. Everything was brighter. Weights had been lifted off me. Anything was possible. I wanted to spend all my time with her. I didn't need to sleep. Her frequent smiles drove surging warmth through me. Her happiness had become more important than my own.

Since it was an idyllic Saturday afternoon, I decided to keep my earlier promise and invite Beth to tour the special forage field across the highway. The early summer sun shone brilliantly on a dark blue sky, framed by gilded columns of translucent clouds widening from purple, smoky bases. As we passed through the deep shade under the buckeye tree, our entry road appeared parched white in the intense summer light. When I stopped to find Beth a pristine buckeye, she continued walking out into the sunlight. Her luminous muslin dress ballooned in the gentle, westward wind. I caught up to Beth, handed her the lucky buckeye, and explained the dubious folklore.

We then crossed the highway, climbed a low hill, and stood at the top of the slight rise watching a timeless canvas of swaying grasses and flowering meadows dissolving into charcoal shadows near Trace Creek. As we descended the hill and joined the path winding north through the waist-high grasses, I explained we were now walking on an old Indian trail coursing a quiet field, which in the past must have been the site of a thriving camp for ancient tribes. I described how excited Robert and I became when we played here as boys and discovered arrowheads and spear points to add to our extensive flint collections.

But as we continued along the path, I noticed Beth's demeanor had changed. She was no longer smiling and had become quiet and distant. I stopped, turned to her, and asked, "Is there anything wrong?"

She answered with a question of her own. "Do you know anything about my family's past? . . . I mean on my mother's side."

I shook my head. "Afraid I don't, Beth . . . but I'd love to hear about it."

We resumed walking along the trail, but now an unfamiliar, awkward silence followed us. When we reached Trace Creek we sat down on a flat boulder abutting the rippling stream. Beth gazed into my eyes and began narrating her past: "As you know, your great-uncle, Uncle Billy, is my father; and in 1837, he married his second wife, Mahaley, who's my mother. Well, my mother is a full-blooded Chickasaw; and up until the day she married my father, she lived a Chickasaw lifestyle, following the tribe's traditions and practicing its religion.

"But to fully understand who we are as a people and what we value, you have to know something of our history in this country. Our Chickasaw story begins sometime in what you would call the Middle Ages, when our tribe migrated from the west to the east, perhaps from the Oregon territory. According to legend, our priests set a pole vertically in the ground each night, and when they awoke the next morning, they would travel that day in the direction the pole was leaning. The pole always pointed east, until one morning they awoke, and it was no longer leaning, which meant they had finally arrived at their new home on the Tennessee River.

"And almost from the beginning, our people were under attack. Like the Hebrews in the Bible, our enemies surrounded us—the Creeks, the Cherokee, the Illinois, the Miami, Iroquois, Shawnee, and the Choctaw. And after the Europeans arrived, we also had to navigate the political waters between the French, the Spanish, the British, and even the Americans. As Mama says proudly, 'We were known among these Europeans as the "Unconquered and Unconquerable" or the "Spartans of the lower Mississippi Valley."' We defeated all of them, driving the French from the territory, frustrating Spanish ambition, and even defeating the Americans in our only battle during your War of Independence.

"Our real threat, though, didn't come from our enemies; it came from within. After many foolish negotiations with your Congress, nearly all our lands were gone by the 1830s. So about five thousand Chickasaws had to pack up their belongings and migrate westward to southeast Oklahoma."

"But your family stayed here, Beth. . . . Why not move to Oklahoma with the rest of the Chickasaws?" I asked.

Beth nodded and replied, "That's a story in itself. Just months before my mama and the rest of her family were to leave for Oklahoma, my father had gone to a town near our village to sell his vegetables and buy supplies. Before returning home, he made a last stop at the saloon to see old friends. A commotion erupted near the bar; two strangers were forcing one of our warriors against the back wall and demanding money. Father jumped up from his conversation, pulled the strangers off the Indian man, and helped calm things down. He then asked the warrior where he lived. The brave explained his house was nearby in the Chickasaw village of Lower Creek. Father then suggested he escort the warrior home, just to be safe; and, under the circumstances, the unarmed brave agreed to Father's offer.

"As they arrived at the warrior's cabin, they saw an older fellow sitting on the front steps repairing a leather harness. They dismounted, and the brave introduced Father to the older man, who was the warrior's father. After learning how Father had saved his son from a sure beating, the warrior's father invited my father in for a meal with his wife and only daughter, Mahaley. Now, Thomas, you can pick up the story from there. . . ."

I smiled. "So I assume Uncle Billy married Mahaley, your mother, not long before your family was to migrate to the southwest."

"Yes, that's right."

I shook my head. "That's quite a story. I'd never heard any of this before. I mean about you, your family, your tribe. . . . Sad how everyone was forced out to Oklahoma."

"Yes, which raises questions I can't answer: why did our Supreme Being, Ishtohoollo Aba Eloa, the big holy one above who thunders, select the Chickasaw as his chosen people and then surround them with their enemies? Why did he allow your government to cheat us out of our lands and force us into another war zone in southeast Oklahoma? I don't understand how living in a world of evil and suffering prepares us for the joy and perfection of our afterlife."

Beth paused, started to speak again, but silenced her thoughts. She lowered her head for a moment, then turned and looked deeply into my eyes, attempting to assess my reaction to her history and lonely exploration. Not knowing exactly what to say or how to say it and knowing it was getting late in the afternoon with evening chores looming, I didn't respond; I simply nodded my understanding and approval of her questioning. I slowly stood up and extended my hands, signaling it was regrettably time to return to the farm.

As we walked along the ancient path toward the highway, Beth locked her arm around mine and slowly pulled herself up against my side. When the wind would blow her dark hair down across her smile, I would affectionately sweep the curls back again behind her perfect ear. About halfway back to the farm, we stopped, turned, and located our distant, sacred niche on Trace Creek, which had now become a glimmer of late-afternoon light.

I couldn't wait for tomorrow to dawn; I was sure we'd begin openly sharing our most dangerous thoughts. Master Hudson said the real quest lay beyond the question of human action and more in the furtive realm of God's intent. As Beth described her ancestors' history, I kept repeating to myself, "Go on, Beth, probe, probe deeper now, deeper." And when she asked, "Why'd our Supreme Being . . ." I knew then I'd found my Beatrice. I would pour oil on our Trace Creek boulder, consecrate the blessed place, and call it Bethel; for I knew now we had become a pilgrimage of three.

11

WHEN I WAS twelve, I watched a man hang for murder. I've tried imagining what he felt, standing on that makeshift scaffold; listening to the judge's final orders; plunging into burlap darkness; gauging the executioner's random steps; ignoring the perfunctory psalmist passages; and then facing the sure unknown. But now I know.

On Saturday evening we celebrated a milestone. It was the first time Mama had prepared a meal from scratch since coming down with the fever. No one at the table knew it was my favorite meal, but Mama had promised me the dinner the first time she could cook again. There was roast pork, boiled potatoes, mustard greens with hog jowl, fried okra, and Mama's special buttermilk cornbread. There was laughter at the long table again, and Beth was sitting directly across from me.

What more could I ask, until Uncle Billy casually declared, "While you two were out walking this afternoon, I had a chance to chat with Grandma and Mama, and we all agree it's time now for Beth to go home." I didn't hear anything after Uncle Billy announced the verdict. I immediately glanced toward Beth, who sighed and lowered her head. My heart began pounding; I was breathing rapidly. Pinpricks jabbed my forearms; electricity surged into my numbing fingertips.

I pushed back from my unfinished plate and asked to be excused. I left the house through the funeral door and wandered out onto the moonlit cemetery path, hoping Beth would follow; but she never appeared. I lay awake that night on top of my covers, fully dressed, sweating, encased in a thick, suffocating darkness, hoping to wake at any moment from this impossible, wrenching nightmare. I thought briefly about getting up, crossing the hallway, and softly tapping on Beth's door. But what good would that do now? What could she do to prevent this preordained descent into hell?

As the tortured hours passed, I listened reluctantly for the first chiming of the cast iron in the kitchen. I knew Mama would want to rise early to prepare Beth and Uncle Billy a good breakfast before they left. Regrettably then, a faint summer light began tinting the wavy windowpanes. The rooster crowed, Cleary butted my head, and the dreaded clanging began. I didn't move. I didn't want to see anyone that morning. How could I hide the horror of my hopelessness?

Mama summoned everyone to breakfast. I knew I had no choice but to rise and shine. I splashed cold water on my face; changed my shirt; ran my fingers through my hair; took a long, deep breath; and descended the back stair. As I entered the dining room, I assumed my obligatory role and greeted everyone with a half-smiling, "Good morning." Beth was missing; Mama said she was still upstairs packing her last bag.

Everyone in the kitchen and dining room was ebullient this bright summer morning—everyone but me. Mama was joyful, having overcome her months-long fever, weakness, and lethargy. Grandma was looking forward to having what she called her independence again, since everyone would now be back performing his or her regular chores. And I knew Uncle Billy had every right to be happy; he was going home to see his sweetheart, his grandchildren, and his grown sons, who had been tending his farm for months now running on into years.

Bella, Israel, and Beth entered through the hallway door; and the hurly-burly of multiple "good mornin's," "how ye' doin's," and Mama's admonitions to "sit down before everything gets cold" eclipsed the formal, uncomfortable greeting Beth and I shared. Israel offered the prayer and added thanks to the Almighty for Beth, to which I added a rare, hearty "Amen." Throughout the lively breakfast, Beth and I remained silent, exchanging occasional forlorn glances.

When Uncle Billy finished his last piece of slab bacon, he asked me to run upstairs and collect Beth's luggage. I excused myself and dejectedly climbed the hall stairs to Beth's room. Her packed suitcases were lying at the foot of the bed. The morning wind had pushed the long gossamer curtains back across the edge of the colorful quilt. This time, Beth had followed me. She didn't say anything as she entered the room and walked toward me. She leaned in, cupped her right hand behind my head, kissed the side of my face lightly several times, and whispered, "Thank you, Thomas. . . . Thank you for everything."

Beth eased back, reached into her deep left pocket, and withdrew something I could not see. With her eyes on my face, she held her left hand out toward me and gradually released her fingers to reveal a pristine buckeye cradled in the palm of her hand. She motioned for me to take the buck-eye, and I hesitantly complied. Beth read my unspoken concern perfectly—she was sadly returning the special buckeye I had given her yesterday on our walk to Bethel. She smiled, reached into her right dress pocket, and pulled out the twin to the first buckeye. I now understood Beth had just given me a priceless gift.

As I leaned in to embrace my Beatrice, Uncle Billy shouted loudly up the stairs, "Let's get goin', y'all." I moved back instinctively and turned immediately to grasp her suitcases. We walked out into the hallway. Beth paused and then headed over into my room. She sat down on the side of the bed; scratched a lifetime friend under his furry chin; nuzzled his cold, wet nose; and then rejoined me in the hallway to descend the narrow, curving stairs for a final time.

We walked slowly down the rise to the buckeye tree, where Uncle Billy and the others were waiting for us near the wagon. There were hugs and best wishes all around. I helped Beth climb up onto the high wooden bench next to Uncle Billy. And as the wagon began turning away toward the entry road, Beth gazed down into my eyes. I mouthed pensively, "So long, Beth, so long." She responded with a slight nod and faint, knowing smile.

After the wagon eclipsed the rising sun and disappeared beyond our schoolhouse, I told my folks I was going down to the barnyard to finish some chores I had started the day before. But honestly, I simply didn't want to be with anyone; I didn't want to share my pain. I realized I might never see Beth again. I was trapped here. I would never be able to go along with Uncle Billy to visit Beth because I would have to stay here to help out while he was away. And I would never be able to go over to Uncle Billy's alone because of Mama's fear I would be killed or forced into the service of one of the two warring armies. So I had become Jeremiah assigning blame: "Is it nothing to you, all ye that pass by? Behold, and see if there be any sorrow like unto my sorrow, which is done unto me, wherewith the Lord hath afflicted me in the day of His fierce anger."

I walked aimlessly about for some time, reacting in the same manner as the soldier whom Robert had described earlier—mortally wounded, and yet, marching forward for some paces before dropping to his knees and falling facefirst into the thick clay mud. I then found myself retracing the steps we had taken on Beth's first day here; and as with her tour, I finished again at the family cemetery. I draped my arms across the gate, rested my chin on the top board, and stared in at the lichened headstones rising out of the ivy.

My emotions arced from one intense feeling to another—missed opportunity, loneliness, guilt, and fear of the routine. Why didn't I broach God's alleged complicity in human suffering? Why didn't I reveal the strong feelings I harbored for her? Why didn't I try reversing Uncle Billy's verdict? Why didn't I experience my usual loneliness while she was here?

I had always felt isolated and gloomy even when I was happy and enjoying myself; I knew the joy wouldn't last. But for once I didn't feel the solitude and sorrow, and I didn't continually dwell on Beth's inevitable departure. In some ways it was better not knowing until the last moment that she was leaving.

I was like that fellow on the scaffold; I would only suffer for a short time before plunging through the trapdoor to eternal blackness. But unlike that poor soul, I've experienced what Hamlet feared: "To die, to sleep; to sleep: perchance to dream: ay, there's the rub; for in that sleep of death what dreams may come, when we have shuffled off this mortal coil. . . ." With her departure, I'd been thrust into a hopeless, nightmare world.

Besides the lost opportunities and the loneliness, there was the guilt associated with Mama's illness. Why did I ever entertain even the slightest thought that I wanted Mama to remain ill so that Beth could stay longer? I didn't want Mama to die, just to remain sick enough to require Beth's presence. And I only conjured up these fleeting thoughts toward the end of Mama's fever, when I knew she would recover. But even then I knew it was selfish, immoral, and wrong.

Why should I fear returning to our timeless routine once Beth had gone home? Grandma associated her independence with returning to a schedule. Why should I dread facing the status quo? I loved everyone here and respected them for what they had chosen to do with their lives, but Master Hudson and my Beatrice eased my suffering for a time and thrust me into an uncompromising mind-set, where I could fearlessly challenge God's agenda and motives.

Yet, I knew I had to carry on, and I comforted myself with the knowledge that Master Hudson would be returning in the fall to help with the harvest. That joyous reminder would help me bridge my loneliness. I also realized I needed to conceal my anguish just as Dante had done when his Beatrice had left the city and traveled to a distant place:

Now I have lost all my eloquence,
Which flowed so from love's treasure:
And I am grown so poor,
In a way that speech barely comes to me.
So that I desire to be like one,
Who to conceal his poverty through shame,
Shows joy outwardly,
And within my heart am troubled and weep.

12

I<small>T</small> <small>WAS</small> <small>ONLY</small> a week after Beth's departure that my new resolve faced its first real test. As I was corralling calves into the barnyard, I saw a soldier leading a horse down the switchback path behind the smokehouse. Whoever it was didn't want to be seen; he was walking the path farthest from the highway. When I moved over to the side gate to get a better look, the fellow shouted out, "Thomas, open up! . . . Let your tired brother in!"

After a big bear hug and heavy slaps on the back, I held Robert at arm's length and asked, "Why the switchback?"

"The main road's crawling with Feds," he replied. "I left my boys at Grave's Bend south of Warfield and worked my way over here on the back trails skirting Slaughter Hill. . . . Can't stay long—just overnight and then I gotta get back." He smiled and explained, "I'm a captain now, Thomas. I've got to look out for a hundred horsemen."

As he spoke I assessed his physical condition. He didn't look too much the worse for wear, but he had only been gone for about five months. The only physical changes I detected were a new red, closely trimmed beard, some dirt on his right trouser leg near the vertical yellow stripe, and some fraying at the edges of the cuffs on his shell jacket.

Robert pointed toward the stalls and said, "Let's get my mare in, dry her off, and get her some hay."

As we tended the horse, he asked, "How's everything going around here? . . . Taking much grief from the bluebellies?"

"So far so good," I said. "See them ever' now and then watering the horses over at the creek. I just smile, wave, and get on my way."

"That's the best thing to do . . . keeping your nose clean. So tell me, how's everyone doing around here?"

"Doing just fine now."

"Now?"

"Yeah . . . Mama came down with a bad fever. She's going to tell you all about Easter and Mrs. Hunter's key lime pie, but no one else got sick like Mama. And besides, Doc Simmons confided it was the fever. He just played along with her views—didn't want to start a second war. . . . You know how she gets when people cross her."

Robert laughed. "Yes, sir. Like waving a bandana in front of a bull." When we'd finished feeding the mare, he said, "Now that that's done, let's grab my bags and head on up to the house. . . . Really been looking forward to seeing everyone again . . ."

Well, we didn't surprise Mama this time. She was looking out the window in Grandpa's old room and saw us coming up the rise. As soon as she saw us she ran out onto the front porch, where Robert met her and gave her a big hug. "The Lord's answered my prayers!" she said. "You're home safe and sound."

"Only for the night, Mama. Gotta get back to my boys. . . ."

"That'll do just fine. Seeing you here—it'll keep me going

for a spell. Hearing all those horrible stories in town scares me to death. But by his grace, you've returned home safe and sound."

After finishing another of Mama's inspired dinners, we all filed out onto the front porch to sit in the moist, warm August air and receive a full accounting of Robert's exploits over the past five months. Some of us sat in country rockers, while others claimed the front steps or sprawled out on the floor close to Robert's slat-back chair. Since the summer days were so much longer, it was still daylight, but we had come prepared with oil lanterns if his story carried on into the night.

Robert extinguished his stubby cigar on the bottom of his boot, tossed the butt out onto the front lawn, and pulled a worn leather notebook from his left breast pocket. He flipped through the pages, paused, looked up, and then began: "So when we left here at the beginning of March, we headed over to Bell's Furnace, did some local recruiting. We then rode southeast to Columbia and Pulaski, picked up several more recruits, and then rejoined the regiment in Huntsville, Alabama. I believe it was around the ninth or tenth of March." He briefly scanned his diary and then looked up. "Yes, I see here it was actually the ninth.

"Well, several days later we received orders to move westward to Iuka, Mississippi, and after that it was on to Burnsville southeast of Corinth on the Memphis-Charleston Railroad line. While we were mustering in Corinth, Grant moved his troops down from Fort Donelson to Pittsburg Landing some twenty miles to our north."

Uncle Billy interrupted. "Pittsburg Landing, Tennessee?"

"Yeah, Tennessee," Robert replied.

"Been around these parts a long time, never heard of the town. Must be pretty small. A hole in the wall?"

"You got that right, Uncle Billy. It's not really a town, just a warehouse and a couple of cottages along the Tennessee. But it sure got our generals' attention."

"Why's that?" I asked.

"We'd heard through channels Buell was planning on joining forces with Grant at the Landing. Would then be some seventy-five thousand strong! Imagine it: the bluecoats plunging south into Mississippi, driving us out of Corinth and destroying our supply lines. . . ."

Mama interrupted. "So what'd they end up doing?"

"Our generals?"

"No, Grant and the other general, Buell?"

"It's not what they did, it's what we did that counts. Our generals rolled the 'iron dice'—deciding to attack Grant at the Landing before Buell could get his troops there. Sever the head, so to speak, before the bluebellies could wreak havoc on us and Corinth."

"Now that's a plan, I say!" Uncle Billy exclaimed. "I'd heard you boys had strong leaders and that says it's so."

"You heard right, Uncle Billy. Yes, sir, I'd charge into hell with 'em any day!"

"So'd you boys go through with it? I mean, attack the Landing?" Uncle Billy asked.

"Yes, sir, we moved outa Corinth the third of April and reached the vicinity of the Landing the following evening. The next morning's when the fun began. We got orders to patrol along Lick Creek to the south of the Landing, and it wasn't long before my unit was tussling with the web feet. Our back and forth lasted most of the day.

"Late afternoon I received orders to return to camp, where I had the honor of reading General Johnston's address to all our cavalrymen." Robert reached into his coat pocket and pulled out some loose papers. "Here's a copy of the order." He cleared his throat and began reading in a much deeper, stirring voice:

> Soldiers of the Army of the Mississippi: I have put you in motion to offer battle to the invaders of your country. With the resolution, and discipline, and valor becoming men fighting, as you are, for all that is worth living or dying for, you can but march to a decisive victory over the agrarian mercenaries sent to subjugate and despoil you of your liberties, your property, and your honor. Remember the precious stake involved. Remember the dependence of your mothers, your wives, your sisters, and your children on the result. Remember the fair, broad, abounding land, the happy homes that will be desolated by your defeat. The eyes and hopes of eight millions of people rest upon you. You are expected to show yourselves worthy of your lineage, worthy of the women of the South, whose noble devotion in this war has never been exceeded in any time. With such incentives to

brave deeds, and with the trust that God is with us, your generals will lead you confidently to the combat, assured of success.

(Signed) A. S. Johnston, General Commanding.

Robert paused and looked up. "I found the general's message comforting. It echoed the last sermon we heard before leaving Corinth. Our chaplain had appropriately chosen Saint Paul's letter to the Corinthians as the text for his homily. Yes, the same verses we learned as children: 'If I speak in human and angelic tongues, but don't have love, I am a resounding gong or a clashing cymbal. And if I have the gift of prophecy and comprehend all mysteries and all knowledge; if I have all faith so as to move mountains but don't have love, I'm nothing. Love doesn't rejoice over wrongdoing but rejoices with the truth. It bears all things, believes all things, hopes all things, and endures all things. Love never fails. So faith, hope, love remain, these three; but the greatest of these is love . . .' During his sermon the chaplain emphasized we had to love God, our cause, our families, and our fellow soldiers. He said God would be on our side and bring us a great victory, if we held this kind of love in our hearts.

"So at sunrise on Sunday, the sixth, thirty thousand of us advanced on the Feds who were hiding in a thicket draped in a heavy mist. My horsemen and I were under strict orders to hold our position protecting the right flank. The bluebellies had no idea we were about to attack. Many of 'em were sleeping, some washing and dressing, and others eating breakfast. When we slammed into the Feds, our boys began firing—

shooting 'em crawling out of their cots. Many of 'em ran away half-naked—ran like scalded dogs, I wanna tell you—and left their guns right where they'd put 'em the night before.

"We began pushing all of 'em back toward the river and Pittsburg Landing. Over where we were on the right flank, we could hear the roar, the yelling, the explosions coming from the center, which bore the brunt of our attack. . . . Wasn't long until I got orders to move my men up Lick Creek toward the heavy fighting to our left. And when I realized Cheatham's division was stalling, I ordered my men to charge the bluecoats, to ride across an open field and break their will. And then after they broke and scurried away, we spent the rest of the afternoon consolidating our gains and setting a perimeter for the coming night. We knew the bluebellies weren't defeated, but surely on the run, forced to set up defensive lines way up north with their backs to the Tennessee.

"So it was time for us to call it a day. A good day at that. My boys and I had a real sense of pride about what we'd accomplished, and we bivouacked toward evening with broad smiles on our faces because we'd be staying that night in the very spot where their General Sherman had headquartered earlier that day. And after I got my boys settled into camp, I walked up a rise; and from my vantage point, I could make out in the last dim light of day a small, log-cabin Methodist Church called Shiloh, which they tell me in Hebrew means 'place of peace.'"

Mama spoke up excitedly: "I remember my father talking about Shiloh. I believe he said the Israelites set up their first tabernacle there. Believe he said it was capital of Israel for hundreds of years before they moved it to Jerusalem."

Robert reacted kindly to the interruption. He shook his head and responded, "I had no idea about the history behind the name, Mama. Someone said it meant 'place of peace.' That's all I ever knew."

Picking up on the loose end of the narrative, I encouraged Robert to continue. "So what happened next?"

My brother looked over and winked. He knew what I was up to. "Let me see now.... Well, later on that night I was sitting on a tree stump at the edge of our bivouac finishing a tasty Federal meal, when a Lieutenant Sheridan walked up, said he had been looking for me, and asked me to come along with him. I dropped my mess kit over at my blanket and followed him to an officer's tent. When we entered, there were already six other fellas there; one of them mentioned we were supposed to wait in the tent until Colonel Forrest arrived.

"It was only a few minutes later when the colonel and an aid-de-camp entered, a number of Federal cavalry overcoats draped over their arms. After a hearty greeting and congratulations on a great victory, Colonel Forrest drawled, 'I've got two things to discuss with ya this evening. I'll start with the bad news. General Johnston's dead.'

"There was an audible gasp followed by anxious whispers. A stunned Lieutenant Sheridan asked somberly, 'What happened, sir?'

"'As was his wont, the general was leading a final charge against the Feds in a peach orchard over to the left of Sunken Road. They tell me that several bullets had already nicked his uniform, and another'd ripped his boot sole in half. But being so caught up in the battle, he didn't know he'd taken a bullet to the back of his knee, cutting an artery. Well, a few minutes later, the Feds broke and began running back towards the river. Seeing the fighting was winding down, the general rode back to headquarters, and while still on his mount, he thrust an arm in the air and shouted out to the officers on the porch, "The Feds didn't trip us up this time!" He started saying something else but reeled in his saddle. Governor Harris, who was on a horse beside the general, prevented him from falling. And when the general's aides lowered him to the ground, they discovered his boot was filled with blood. Well, wasn't too long afterwards the general died peacefully, died in his brother-in-law's arms.'

"Colonel Forrest paused to respect the solemnity of the moment and then moved on to deal with the battle at hand. 'General Beauregard's now in charge, and for now, you men must hold the news here about the general. Sometime after we whup Grant's boys, y'all get the okay to tell your men.'

"The colonel next handed each of us one of the Fed cavalry overcoats and reminded us, 'Make no mistake about it, men, this battle here's far from over. I want y'all to ride up through their lines now as far as the Landing and then report back. Put the Fed coats on after passing our pickets. And I don't need to remind y'all to keep a keen eye out. Grant's men'll be looking out for any probing on our part seeing their backs are tight up again' the river tonight. Any questions? . . . Well, okay then. Dismissed!' I wheeled around, exited the tent, and began running. You can't imagine how tired I was from the fighting that day; but when I grasped the risk and

125

the importance of our mission, my strength returned immediately. I raced back to our bivouac and quickly saddled my mare; and twenty minutes later, we were passing through our picket lines and pulling on our overcoats.

"When we returned from the Landing an hour later, we hurried over to Colonel Forrest's tent. He looked up from behind his portable desk and asked me, 'What'd y'all find out?'

"'Feds, sir, thousands of 'em coming across the river at the Landing. Coming from the east, sir.'

"The colonel slowly rose to his feet. 'You say thousands? . . . Dammit! Must be Buell. . . . Gotta tell Beauregard right away.' He scanned the room and added, 'Not the news we wanted to hear, but good work, men.' He saluted and said, 'Dismissed.'

"The other officers turned and left, but I stayed behind to speak privately with the colonel. 'With due respect, sir, seeing I went up to the Landing and saw things firsthand, may I express an opinion before you go inform the general?'

"'As long as it's quick. What are you thinking?'

"'We should attack 'em now, sir. Hit 'em during the night.'

"'Why's that?'

"'They're not set, sir. The Feds are scurrying about everywhere, many of 'em still waiting to cross over from the east bank. It'll sure be a tougher fight in the morning once they have all their troops in place.'

"'Thanks, officer. No commitments, ya hear? . . . But I'll take it up with Beauregard. You tell the others to stay within shouting distance just in case.'

"Well, around one o'clock in the morning, Colonel Forrest called us all back in. I got all excited. I was bursting with pride. The general must have agreed to the immediate attack. But when we entered, we quickly learned nothing had changed. Nothing was going to happen before daylight."

I interrupted Robert. "So what'd the colonel want you for in the middle of the night, if it wasn't to plan an attack?"

"Y'all won't believe this, but the general had asked Colonel Forrest to provide him with an up-to-the-minute assessment of what was happening at the Landing. So the colonel ordered us to repeat our prior mission."

"What'd you find out this time?" Uncle Billy asked. "What did you tell the colonel?"

"The news wasn't good, Uncle Billy. We told him we suspected the Feds would have about twenty-five thousand fresh troops facing us in the morning.

"What'd he say to that?" Uncle Billy asked.

"Nothing. He just nodded and motioned for us to stay put there in his tent until he returned."

"What did he have to say when he got back?" Mama asked.

"He relayed the general's latest order to 'keep up a vigilant, strong picket line and report all hostile movements.' And after that, the colonel dismissed us."

Uncle Billy commiserated. "That must have really burned your shinny."

"It sure did, Uncle Billy. When we were all safely outside the tent, we just shook our heads and muttered to one another, 'If only the general had seen what we'd seen.'"

Robert paused, reached into his shirt pocket, and lit up a fresh cigar. He took a deep breath and then jumped backed into his narrative. "So by eight o'clock in the morning, the battle had begun again in earnest, their fifty thousand attacking our thirty thousand weary men. We fell back, counterattacked, and then fell back again with our guns blazing as we retreated. Late in the afternoon General Beauregard issued a directive to start an organized retreat back toward Corinth. But ya see, my boys hadn't finished fightin' yet. . . . Colonel Forrest had ordered us to remain behind and help him cover the infantry's retreat.

"So the following Tuesday morning while out scouting near Fallen Timbers, we saw Federal cavalry and infantry coming down the road toward us. Colonel Forrest ordered us to charge, and we smashed into their cavalry, driving the horsemen back into their infantry, which had already fixed their bayonets! Many of their infantry were knocked down in the melee, and many of their cavalry horses were impaled on the infantry's rifles.

"We fired at 'em from short range, yes, emptied our revolvers, pulled our sabers, and began slashing away. And as these bluebellies fell back behind a second line of Feds, Colonel Forrest and I kept on charging—charging right into their new brigade. In the heat of the battle and feeling our strong push, the colonel and I hadn't noticed that the rest of our men had pulled up about fifty yards behind us. We were surrounded by the enemy. . . . And they started screaming, 'Shoot 'em! Knock 'em off their horses.' As I hacked away with my saber, I pulled my second pistol from my belt and began blazing.

"Well, somehow we managed to escape back to our squadron, and the Feds didn't try pursuing us. My mare had been shot twice, and I had a minor nick in the shoulder. Otherwise, I was still in one piece. But when we got back to camp, the colonel told us a musket ball had entered his left side above the hip, and the bullet was still in his body somewhere.

"After our close call, we continued guarding our infantry's retreat and finally reached Corinth the following Sunday afternoon. Colonel Forrest went to Memphis to recuperate and returned to Corinth at the end of April ready to take up the fight again. We stayed there until a strong Fed siege forced us to retreat at the end of May. And believe me, we didn't leave the Feds anything—not a sick prisoner, a rusty bayonet, no, not even a bite of bacon. Those boys marched into an empty town."

"Where'd you go? What'd ya do then?" Uncle Billy asked.

"No more fighting for a time. So ya see, after pulling out of Corinth, several of us rode with the colonel over to Memphis, where he placed an ad in the paper for new recruits: COME ON, BOYS, IF YOU WANT A HEAP OF FUN AND TO KILL SOME YANKEES. And then in the middle of June, a small detachment of us handpicked men rode with the colonel over to Chattanooga, where he assumed his new command as brigadier general. We trained new recruits for a couple of weeks and then headed north to Altamont, Tennessee, where we joined reinforcements from Georgia and Kentucky, bringing our total up to about fourteen hundred cavalrymen.

"We then moved on to Woodbury, Tennessee, twenty miles east of Murfreesboro. The women in town were happy to see us but were also really upset. They said the Feds camped around Murfreesboro had rounded up their men, jailed 'em there, and threatened to execute 'em as rebel sympathizers. But after General Forrest promised to rescue their men, the Woodbury women cheered up and provided us with some real fine victuals.

"Well, we left the Woodbury ladies around one o'clock in the morning and arrived just outside Murfreesboro an hour before dawn. We formed into columns of fours and advanced at a slow gait until we saw the tops of the Feds' tents. General Forrest gave the command to charge, and fourteen hundred of us spurred our horses and gave the rebel yell. Hearing our curdling screams and the thunder of hoofbeats on the paved road, Fed officers, infantrymen, and cavalrymen stumbled out of their tents and the town offices. We began blasting away and captured a lot of bluecoats before they could get off a single round!"

Uncle Billy jumped up and shouted, "Now you're talking, Robert! Now you're taking it to 'em real good! Did ya ride on into town and spring those Woodbury men?"

"Hold your horses, Uncle Billy. I'm getting there. . . . Let's see. . . . So according to the general's plan, my boys and I helped execute the second-wave attack on the town center itself, especially the jail where some of the Woodbury men were being held, and the courthouse, and the Murfreesboro Hotel, where most of their officers had holed up. But some things didn't go according to plan. As we attacked the town center, the jail burst into flames. We learned one of the guards had set fire to it to keep the Woodbury men from getting out alive."

"The bastards! The cowards! Trying to burn 'em alive!" Uncle Billy roared. "What'd ya do then, Robert?"

"We immediately stormed the lockup before the fire fully caught and got 'em all out alive."

"Praise be to God!" Mama exclaimed. "Go on! Go on!"

"Well, right in the middle of the fighting, the general rode up and shouted, 'Ya get 'em all out of there alive?' 'Sure did!' I yelled. 'And the guard that set it just took cover over there in the courthouse.' 'Let's go get the son of a bitch!' the general ordered.

"So we attacked the building from all sides, and my men used a big pole they'd found to smash the front doors. Up to then everything had been so easy. But when we charged in, the Feds opened up with everything they had, and it was now hand-to-hand combat, real up close, almost dark in the hallway, no windows to speak of."

"Oh, mercy!" Mama shrieked.

"Go on, Robert!" Uncle Billy urged. "So what happened next?"

Knowing he had all of us hanging on his every word, Robert paused, took a long drag off his cigar, and then held it out appreciatively staring at the bright red glow. He then lowered his prop and continued. "So after emptying my pistol, I drew my saber and started slashing anyone wearing blue. And I kept on swinging away until the fighting stopped on the first floor.

"My men and I then began working our way upstairs, but we came under heavy fire, and it didn't take us long to figure out the stairwell was just way too narrow to advance. So we backed off to regroup on the main floor."

"What'd you do then?" I asked.

Robert looked over at Uncle Billy guiltily. "I'm not proud of this, Uncle Billy . . ."

"Well, what'd you do, boy? Tell us. It's okay."

Robert sighed and then confessed, "We decided to give 'em a taste of their own medicine. We set fire to the courthouse to smoke 'em out."

Uncle Billy quickly let Robert off the hook. "You were just giving those bluebellies a taste of their own medicine. Sometimes turnabout's fair play. So what'd they do after you set the place on fire?"

"What any sane man would do, Uncle Billy. In very short order, everyone raced out of the burning building, including their commanding officer and the runaway arsonist from the town jail."

"So what'd y'all do then, Robert?" Mama asked.

"Well, after securing the courthouse, the jail, and the hotel, we rode out to the far west end of town to mop up the rest of the Feds. And after things quieted down, sensitive negotiations ensued and the final bluecoats surrendered. Murfreesboro was now under our control."

Robert paused to take another long drag off his cigar. It was clear he was getting tired, but there was no way we would let him stop his tale now. "After lining up all the captured Feds for a headcount," he went on, "General Forrest rode over to the long line with one of the Woodbury prisoners and said, 'They tell me these fellows here treated you inhumanely while you were over there in the jail. So point 'em out to me. I wanna make things right.' The prisoner responded reluctantly. 'I don't wanna cause any trouble, General,' he said, 'but there's really only one man who roughed us up—the fellow who tried burning us alive.' The general and the prisoner then rode along the line until the prisoner identified the guard who had set the fire."

"What'd the general do with him?" I asked.

Robert's lip arced into a satanic grin. "Well, several hours later when we called the names of the private soldiers we were holding prisoner, the arsonist's name was called and no one answered, 'Present.' General Forrest then said, 'Pass on, it's all right.' No explanation needed. Everyone there understood exactly what the general meant. They'd heard the pistol shot a few minutes earlier. . . .

"Our final assessment of the situation at Murfreesboro indicated we had captured twelve hundred prisoners; burned two hundred thousand dollars' worth of stores; destroyed the railroad and depot; and collected sixty wagons, three hundred mules, two hundred horses, and four field pieces. So for the assault on Murfreesboro, General Forrest had developed a very potent form of warfare. He estimated his guerrilla tactics of hit and run with two thousand men could tack down an army of forty thousand in Tennessee. Yes, sir, tack 'em down for a month, a year, or forever."

Robert puffed on his cigar and then launched into the denouement. "As we were about to depart for McMinnville, the general ordered several of our cavalry units to move westward toward Humboldt, Warfield, and Jackson to continue hitting the Feds and then quickly disappearing again. General Forrest called us his 'guerrillas,' his 'lone wolves,' who'd be cutting the telegraph wires, destroying the railroad tracks, burning bridges, torching warehouses, and spreading fear among the Feds patrolling western Tennessee. And he specifically ordered me to provide weekly updates to his central command.

"And there's one last thing. As I told Thomas earlier today, I can only stay the night 'cause the general's promoted me to captain, and now I have to look out for over a hundred men, who affectionately call our unit 'Robert's Raiders.' So I'll have to get an early start in the morning. And Mama, I hope you're up to making me some of your best bacon, eggs, and coffee, which I've missed so much." He smiled and teased her, "Even the Feds' tasty rations don't compare to your cooking, Mama."

Robert slipped his worn leather notebook into his left breast pocket, signaling the performance had ended. He stood up, took one last puff on his cigar, and then flipped it out into the night. Uncle Billy groaned as he rose from the front steps and said he'd check the house before going to bed. Robert and I went back through Grandpa's old room to the hallway and climbed the stairs to our bedrooms.

Robert grasped my arm as I was turning to enter my room. "Give me a minute, Thomas. There's some things I wanna tell ya I didn't wanna say downstairs. . . . Things are going to get a lot rougher around here now. Most of our officers don't think there's a good way to win battles around here and hold the territory. So the new strategy's gonna be hit 'em and run, which is gonna frustrate the hell out of the Feds. If they find out I am related to y'all—connected to this farm—there'll be serious hell to pay. My God, look what they did over at Woodbury; they were going to hang the men as rebel sympathizers. Now don't tell Mama, but you won't be seeing much of me from now on. It's just too damn risky for y'all.

"And there's another threat, this one from our side. There'll be more demands for recruits. Conscription's gonna become a big deal. Now I've put every officer I know on notice that you and everyone else associated with the farm are off limits." Robert saw the look of astonishment on my face and added, "I told 'em you're far more valuable working the farm here and providing supplies than you would be if you were conscripted into one of their units."

I gave Robert a firm hug and went to my room. I opened all the windows as far as they would go and then climbed into bed next to Cleary. As I lay there in the diffuse light of the August moon, I tried unsuccessfully lulling myself to sleep by wrapping myself in the soothing summer sounds of childhood—crickets chirping, bullfrogs croaking, and the faint, doleful barking of distant hounds.

But disquieting thoughts about Robert, Beth, and me frustrated my attempts to drift into a calm, untroubled, forgiving sleep. I lay there reflecting. The thumb on the balance scale had moved along the beam from Robert toward me, and now again back toward him. Every time he appears at the gate, he's the prodigal son . . . the courageous young cavalier receiving the adulation of family and friends. Luck and good fortune have always blessed him.

But then Beth came along, and everything changed. The balance beam began moving in my favor. But no, the thumb couldn't allow too much pleasure or happiness here. Pain is its realm; suffering its purview. So, it's now sliding away, sliding back toward Robert. And the supplicant here has been reduced to thrusting his arms into the air and assertively asking, "Why?"

13

I **ALWAYS LOOKED** forward to waking early, hearing Mama building a fire in the kitchen stove, inhaling the aromatic blend of coffee and biscuits, and then rushing downstairs at breakneck speed to savor the joys of a new day. But after my Beatrice left, I dreaded the early light on the windowpane, the kitchen smells and sounds, and the waking realization that Beth's departure wasn't a nightmare, but a tortured reality.

A constant weight pressed on me; I longed to stay in bed with my knees pulled up to my chest. A feeling of abject hopelessness drained me of my will to finish even the most routine chores, and I became extremely irritable, responding sharply to everyone's comments and actions. After snapping at them, I felt ashamed; I knew they didn't understand the source of my misery, if they realized I was suffering at all.

And I must admit that more than once I cried privately, when the anguish just seemed too much to bear. As a child, I depended on God when I experienced stinging disappointments; but now, how could I look to the creator of my suffering as the wellspring of my solace? That was a question certainly worthy of Master Hudson.

So again on the morning of the eighth day after Beth left, I sensed I couldn't go on; but then, again, I knew I had to keep fighting to overpower my despair. It pounded me to my knees. I'd get up, and it would slam me down again. But I had to remember Master Hudson was coming again in time for the harvest, and mercifully, harvest was only a month or so away. Besides that, Robert was leaving that day and that meant we had to give him another proper send-off. So I slowly swung my feet to the floor, pulled on my trousers, and repeated, "Keep moving . . . keep moving. . . ."

After finding a clean shirt in the top drawer of my dresser and absentmindedly struggling to fasten the buttons on the cuffs more than once, I marched myself over to Robert's door and knocked lightly. "Robert. . . . Robert. . . . Time to get up."

"I'm already dressed and packing my saddlebags," he replied. "Tell Mama I'll be down in just a minute."

I continued standing outside his door remembering that only yesterday I'd been frustrated when he appeared; but now that he was leaving again, I felt a strange loneliness and regret. The fact that my older brother had been here proudly describing his successful exploits was actually a distraction from my awful pain. So I didn't want him to leave; I'd be alone again with my loneliness, waiting for another night to come.

Robert opened the door in a hurry, jolting me from my reverie. I jumped back and blurted out, "Good morning, brother!"

"Morning, Thomas," he replied, looking at me askance. "Whatcha doing still standing out here?"

"Avoiding the kitchen. . . . Dreading Mama's mood. . . . You know how she gets when you're leaving."

I didn't know whether he was buying what I was selling; but

he came over, put his arm around me, and said, "Everything'll be just fine, you'll see. . . . Let's get down to breakfast."

We descended the back stairs and entered the dining room, where everyone had already gathered to spend a last hour with our young captain heading back to war. But it was strange; all during breakfast I sensed we were dining with a ghost, that the real Robert had already left us. He responded to every question mechanically, with short answers and very few smiles. Perhaps he was thinking about his men over at Grave's Bend or about an imminent attack he'd be leading against the Feds. As Master Hudson had taught us last fall, "Uneasy lies the head that wears a crown."

After Mama's fine meal, Uncle Billy and I walked with Robert down to the barn to saddle his horse; but our return route this time was different than in the past. We wouldn't be saying good-bye under the buckeye tree and watching him ride out onto the main Nashville-Memphis road. Robert said that would be just plain suicide. So we exited the barnyard out the side gate and walked the path running closest to the woods.

Mama, Grandma, Rachel, Bella, and Israel were waiting for us up behind the smokehouse. We all gave Robert a big hug, then watched him lead his mare up the switchback path and disappear into a dense bramble headed southwest toward Slaughter Hill. Everyone sensed the added burden he now carried, but none understood how much I was hurting, how much I wanted the pain to go away. For me, the weeks would drag on until Master Hudson appeared, and I would have to fight hard to get back into the routine of things. It was while lying in bed on the bleakest of those nights that I learned the dark could help illuminate the light.

Harvest season finally arrived; and ironically, on one of the gloomiest autumn Sundays I'd ever experienced, Master Hudson arrived. I watched from the front porch as he rode up the entryway, his right hand covering his face to protect it from the driving rain. He stopped for shelter under the buckeye tree and waited as I raced to greet him. We embraced. He turned and pointed to a soaked but overly stuffed valise, bulging with new books for me to read.

And Master Hudson's stay this time didn't disappoint. Throughout the harvest, we continued our forbidden discussions laced with informative private lectures on humanism, Erasmus, and Cervantes. Master Hudson's genius lay in his ability to link specific authors to our most probing quests.

He began our autumn dialogue with two quotes from the early Greek sophist Protagoras. The first reflected Master Hudson's biting humor and his willingness to tweak the noses of supreme beings: "Concerning the gods, I have no means of knowing whether they exist or not or of what sort they may be, because of the obscurity of the subject, and the brevity of human life." After I pondered that sentiment for a moment, he presented me with the second: "Man is the measure of all things." And with that we launched into a deep and rewarding philosophical discussion of humanism and the Dutch Renaissance scholar Erasmus. It was pure joy to have my old master back.

Master Hudson argued that Protagoras's assertion linked directly to the rise of the humanist movement in Florentine architecture, sculpture, and painting. He quoted the architect Alberti: "To you is given a body more graceful than other animals . . . to you most sharp and delicate senses, to you wit, reason, memory like an immortal god."

He then moved on from Florentine triumphs to Erasmus, who discounted outward displays of religion in favor of deep analyses of one's own soul: "Creep not upon the earth, my brother, like an animal. . . . Rise above the body to the spirit, from the visible to the invisible, from the letter to the mystical meaning, from the sensible to the intelligible, from the involved to the simple. Rise as by rungs until you scale Jacob's ladder."

And after proudly presenting my own insight that darkness can help illuminate the truth, Master Hudson opened a sweeping, weeklong study of Cervantes, which concluded with a quotation linking us back to earlier discussions of God's complicity in human suffering and man's indomitable will: "Bear in mind, Sancho, that one man is no more than another, unless he does more than another. All these tempests that fall upon us are signs that fair weather is coming shortly, and that things will go well with us, for it is impossible for good or evil to last forever. Hence it follows that the evil having lasted long, the good must be now nigh at hand." Master Hudson then reminded me that Don Quixote had made this cutting observation only after his brain had become addled.

Our schoolmaster stayed until almost the end of October; and his deep friendship and the continuous discussions we both loved helped bridge the loneliness and speed my healing. I never told him about Beth. I was reluctant to compare my loss to the human suffering he'd described earlier last spring. So standing now in a golden swirl of buckeye leaves, we all thanked him profusely for his help and then waved "so long," as he rode out onto the main highway and turned into a biting northeast wind.

I thought the time from now until next planting season would be challenging. It would be quiet, cold, and depressing. With fewer chores, shorter days, and no one coming to visit, my only buttress against a relapse would be the small collection of books Master Hudson left for me. I was thankful once again for Master Hudson's friendship. Though he knew it not, he was the one person able to help me through my loss of Beth.

I began my study with a volume of poetry, *Lyrical Ballads*, by Wordsworth. I found the preface intriguing. Wordsworth explained he was experimenting with a new approach to poetry—discarding the formal, learned styles of earlier poets; creating works based on the "real language of men"; and using simple country folk as worthy literary subjects. So why this tack? Was he highlighting the commonality of human emotion from beggar to merchant to king? Should I extend his argument to its logical conclusion that it was nigh impossible for even the innocent to completely escape despair and human suffering?

Since I'd finished my afternoon chores and it was a blustery November day, I climbed the stairs to my attic room, sat at my applewood desk, and began reading Wordsworth's "Lucy Gray." The poem describes the death of a young girl who wanders out into an evening snowstorm and is never seen again. When Lucy's parents discover she is missing, they trace her footsteps to a wooden bridge, where the footprints end on the middle board:

> They followed from the snowy bank
> Those footmarks, one by one,
> Into the middle of the plank;
> And further there were none!

I paused to reflect on the narrative, gazed out the front window, and was alarmed to see a bluecoat running up the entry road with his revolver drawn. I immediately dropped the book on the desk, grabbed my shotgun from the wall, and ran down the back stairs to Grandpa's old room. I slowly opened the front door and eased out onto the north side of the porch.

At first I didn't see the Fed but kept scanning the front property. And finally, there he was, hiding at the back corner of Bella's cabin, staring out toward the highway with his gun still drawn. I positioned myself on the west side of the wraparound porch, where I could see him and still have some protection in case he opened fire.

I yelled, "Raise your hands and drop the weapon!" For an instant I thought he was going to swing around and start firing up the hill at me; but after a split second, he stopped turning and slowly raised his arms above his head. I shouted, "Drop the pistol or suffer the consequences!" And this time he complied, letting the revolver ease out of his hand. "Now turn around slowly and face me!" I ordered.

"Don't shoot!" he shouted.

"I don't mean you any harm, soldier," I responded. "Now start walking up the rise there toward me."

As he neared the porch, I could more clearly make out his features. He appeared to be in his early twenties, about five feet eight inches tall, medium build, long dark, curly hair with thick sideburns, a fair complexion, dark eyes, a small, straight nose, and a bushy mustache with goatee. He was wearing a sky blue junior officer greatcoat and cape with three eagle buttons on each cuff and a double row of gold eagles running up the chest. A half-inch dark blue stripe ran the length of his light blue pants, which were stuffed into his cavalry boots. More notable, however, is that he was bareheaded and covered in mud up to his knees.

When he got to the bottom step, I said, "Okay, that's far enough." Trying to decide what to ask first, I started with the basics. "What's your name, soldier?"

"Ah, ah, the name's Burns."

"Whatcha doing running up our road with your gun pulled?"

"The Feds are lookin' for me."

Considering the uniform, I repeated skeptically, "The Feds?"

"That's right, the Feds. And if they find me here, they'll shoot me on the spot. I implore you, young man, take me in. I need to hide."

"So why are the bluecoats chasing you?"

"It's a tangled story that'll take some time to tell. I swear I'll tell you in due course." With his arms still raised the soldier twisted his torso to check the highway and then slowly turned back toward me. He radiated anxiety. "For God's sake," he cried, "please get me inside! I'm out here in the open for all to see. Please, take me in now!"

As I considered my next move, I spotted Uncle Billy walking up from the barnyard. I shouted out to him, "Hurry over to Bella's cabin, and fetch a gun lying on the ground at the back right corner."

Uncle Billy quickly retrieved the soldier's revolver and rushed up the rise toward the front steps. "What's going on, Thomas? Who's the soldier here?"

"He says his name's Burns, Uncle Billy. . . . Says the Feds are out to kill him."

Noticing the uniform, Uncle Billy reacted suspiciously as I had a few minutes earlier. "The Feds?"

"Yes, sir, the Feds," Burns interjected. "I swear I'll explain everything. But please, just get me in out of the open before they come along and see me here."

Uncle Billy stroked his chin for several seconds and then muttered, "It's against my better judgment taking you in like this. . . . Somethin's just not right here." But then he turned to me and gestured toward the house.

"Okay, soldier, let's get to moving!" I ordered, knowing Uncle Billy had my back. "Turn to your right now and start walking over to the side of the house. . . . That's it. . . . Now make the turn there and head toward the back porch . . . . That's it. . . . Now step up and take a seat in the chair there."

Uncle Billy moved directly in front of the Fed and said, "Okay, soldier, we're all ears. Let's hear what you have to say."

"With all due respect, sir, I'm a southerner through and through. Just like you and the boy there. You know we keep our promises, and I swore I'd tell you everything, but sir, I haven't had a bite to eat for goin' on two days. You have somethin' to tide me over?"

Uncle Billy stroked his chin again and then, adopting a more serious tone this time, answered, "Fair enough, Mr. Burns. I'm a southerner and a Christian. But once you've been fed, then you'll tell us what's been going on."

The soldier smiled nervously, raised his right hand, and replied, "I swear to ya on the Bible, right after I get somethin' to eat."

"We'll do you one better, Mr. Burns. Why don't you wash up first and then have some biscuits, and after that we'll hear your story."

Becoming noticeably less tense, the soldier smiled again and responded lightheartedly, "Y'all are gentlemen and scholars—and there're damn few of us left anymore."

Uncle Billy looked over at me and said, "While I take him out to the washhouse, you find Mama. Tell her we have a guest. Have her fetch some of your father's old clothes for me, too. I think they'll come close to fitting Mr. Burns. And tell her afterwards to rustle up some leftover biscuits. Tell her we'll be bringing Mr. Burns to the dining room to eat."

"Yes, sir," I replied and turned to leave.

"One more thing, Thomas. You better let Grandma and Rachel know what's going on too."

When Uncle Billy and Burns entered the dining room a half hour later, the ladies came in from the kitchen to deliver the biscuits and evaluate our "guest." They stayed just long enough for introductions and then shyly backed away toward the kitchen protesting they had so much to do to finish preparing dinner. It was clear they were enjoying the excitement of having a stranger in the house.

After the ladies retreated, Uncle Billy motioned with the soldier's revolver to one of the chairs. "Why don't you take a seat over there on the other side of the table across from Thomas and me. And without wasting any more time, you can start telling us your story while having your biscuits."

"Willin' to oblige ya, sir," Burns responded agreeably.

And after taking his place and devouring the first of the leftovers, he looked up and began: "My given name's Andrew. I spring from a long line of soldiers. In fact, generations of 'em. Fought in all the wars—Revolutionary, 1812, the Mexican—and my favorite uncle, my uncle Paulie, was really high rankin' durin' the Mexican War. Let's see . . . fought at Monterrey, Buena Vista, Chapultepec Castle . . ."

I interrupted excitedly, "Our grandpa here fought in some of the same battles! Lost a leg scaling the wall at that castle!"

Uncle Billy looked askance. "Thomas, let the man tell his story."

Politely ignoring Uncle Billy's admonition, Burns smiled broadly and responded to my enthusiasm. "Well, imagine that. What are the odds? I'm sure old Uncle Paulie would love meetin' your grandpa and sharin' some stories. You know how it is with old soldiers, reminiscing and the like."

I couldn't resist setting the record straight. "I'm sure Grandpa would've loved sharing some stories, but ya see, that's out of the question now."

Burns could sense something was wrong and asked me to explain.

"Grandpa's no longer right in the head," I said. "We have to keep him locked up in his room, confined to his chair. Don't want him getting out—getting lost or hurting himself, ya know."

"Sorry about your grandpa. It's always sad seein' a warrior lose his way." Burns paused to collect his thoughts and then resumed his narrative. "As I was sayin', I spring from a long line of soldiers. My grandfather, father, and uncle all went to West Point, and in fact, my grandfather was in the first class graduatin'."

"Any of your relatives besides you fighting now?" I asked.

"Sure are," Burns responded proudly. "My father went to medical school after West Point, enlisted with me the same day! His last letter said he was in Virginia with Longstreet. Promoted to major. Been designated surgeon of his rebel regiment."

Trying desperately to get the conversation back on track, Uncle Billy asked, "Well, what about you? How do ya fit into all this? What ya been doing during the war? Let's hear it."

"Hold on there, sir," Burns responded lightheartedly, "It was just comin' there around the bend. If ya don't mind, I'll start from the—"

Just as Burns was launching into his past, Rachel entered. "Hope I'm not disturbing anything, Uncle Billy, but Mama sent me in to tell ya dinner's ready."

Uncle Billy stroked his chin, sighed, and replied, "Well then, ya just tell Mama to come on in and set another place for Mr. Burns here."

Rachel smiled and returned to the kitchen with a spring in her step, anxious to share the good news with Grandma and Mama.

When the ladies arrived with the dinnerware, Uncle Billy, Burns, and I stood up to stretch our legs and give the ladies space to set the table for six.

Uncle Billy rubbed his hands together vigorously and said, "If ya don't mind, Thomas, throw that thick hickory log there on the fire. The November wind's picked up and put a shivering chill in the air."

After Mama, Grandma, and Rachel had ferried in the last of the heaping dishes, we sat down for the mandatory family prayer. With Burns's revolver resting on his lap, Uncle Billy offered up his usual thanksgiving and then, as is our custom, included a special blessing for our guest, about whom we now hoped to learn so much more.

Perhaps it was our mysterious guest's visit that inspired the ladies to prepare a meal worthy of kings; but they had really outdone themselves this time, rivaling the finest Easter and Christmas meals I could ever remember. And Mr. Burns chivalrously returned the favor by complimenting their "tasty haute cuisine," as he called it with charm, wit, and warmth.

Knowing we were all eagerly waiting for him to unlock his secrets, the soldier thrice began speaking about himself and then quickly interrupted his thoughts with another compliment for someone or something in the room. But when Burns sensed Uncle Billy had finally reached his limits, he glanced over toward Grandma and Mama and said with a smile, "Well, I believe it's nigh time I get on in earnest with my story. If ya ladies don't mind, I'd love first firing up a cigar to help settle my memory."

"By all means, Mr. Burns, if it'll help you with your tellin'," Grandma replied. "I must admit I used to enjoy it when my husband indulged before headin' off on one of his wartime stories."

"Much obliged, Ma'am," Burns drawled as he pulled a thick, black cigar from the breast pocket of one of Father's old denim coats. He leaned his chair back against the wall, blew several gray spirals into the air, and began unlocking the mysteries.

"I guess it doesn't hurt to go back near the beginnin' again and pick up where I left off before your ladies' fine dinner," he said. "I've already told the gentlemen here about my father's side of the family. Suffice it to say, ladies, most of the men joined the army and fought in all the wars—from the Revolution on up—so I'll move over now to my mama's side. . . . Let's see now. . . . Well, Mama was born in Kentucky. Her folks had a lot of money and property and doted on her, seein' she was an only child.

"Yes, sir, they gave her the best of everything money could buy. And as was the custom in Lexington among the wealthy, when she finished her private schoolin', she became what you call a debutante. And it was not long after her steppin' out into society, she met my father at a summer dance. Mama's told me they fell in love immediately and would've married on the spot, but her 'Pappy,' as she called him, insisted on my father finishin' medical school before allowin' a weddin' to take place."

"Sounds a bit harsh," Mama observed and then quickly added, "but I can understand your grandfather's thinking here. He was making sure your father followed through on his studies and became a doctor. Yes, sir, your grandfather was making sure your father had the wherewithal to provide handsomely and deservedly for the light of his life."

Burns used the interruption to take several long drags off his cigar before launching into the next chapter, an all-important personal one about his own birth. He chuckled in anticipation of what he was about to say. "Well, let's see. Mama and Papa hadn't been married very long when I made a surprise appearance in this world. . . ."

Having been completely drawn in by Burns's narrative and his relaxed persona, Rachel overcame her shyness and blurted, "I'm always curious, Mr. Burns, what's the first things you remember? For me, it was going to the city—seeing relatives, playing in the big park. What's the first things you remember?"

Burns laughed out loud and replied enthusiastically, "Well, can you imagine that? What are the odds? Hard to believe, but it was almost the same for me, Rachel. Some of my earliest and fondest memories are spendin' time at the estate of one of Mama's cousins by marriage. This cousin and her husband had built this thirteen-room brick mansion, Georgian style, on a brook runnin' through their five hundred acres of farmland.

"And contrary to everyone's strongest superstitions about the number thirteen, it was a happy, blessed house. Ya see, thirteen was everywhere! Besides the mansion's thirteen rooms, there were thirteen large windows in both the front and back of the structure. There were thirteen steps to every staircase ... thirteen-foot ceilings . . . and even thirteen-inch-thick walls.

"And of all things, when I turned thirteen, the master of

the house allowed me to visit the mysterious chamber that had always been locked when I was there goin' back as far as I could remember." As Burns continued his narrative, he lifted his hand in a twisting motion for dramatic effect. "So the master slowly opened the thick oak door and guided me into a stunnin' library, lined on three walls with hundreds of leather-bound volumes, stretchin' from the decorative plaster ceiling all the way down to the yellow poplar floor.

"The fourth wall held a massive brick fireplace with an elaborate marble mantel, which the master explained was the handiwork of a freed Negro tradesman. He then pointed to a couple of large portraits hangin' on either side of the mantel. 'That's my grandma and grandpa there,' he said proudly. 'Grandpa was a lawyer and merchant. Served as a Pennsylvania delegate to the Continental Congress in the 1780s. And those aren't just any portraits there, boy. Those are Peales my grandpa commissioned.' The name rolled off the master's tongue. 'Yes, sir, Charles Wilson Peale, the same fellow who'd painted the founders of the republic—Hancock, Washington, and Jefferson.'

"The master then placed his hand lightly on my shoulder and led me over to an enormous desk. He pointed to a small wooden case on the right-hand side and said, 'Be wary now, boy. It's okay. Lift the lid there and see what's inside.' So I carefully opened the case and discovered a superb pair of .58-caliber dueling pistols, with long octagonal steel barrels and highly figured walnut stocks. Besides the pistols, there were a number of accessories: a pistol powder flask, a flint wallet, and even a bullet mold.

"The master picked up one of the guns, rubbed his fingers back and forth slowly along the top of the barrel, and reminisced, 'These really bring back memories.' .

"'How's that?' I asked.

"'Oh, some years ago I had to defend my honor. Hard thing challenging a close friend to a duel and then killin' him outright with a shot through the heart.'

"'What happened?' I probed.

"And even hearin' his answer at thirteen, I've never forgotten it nor how coldly and nonchalantly he answered. 'He'd impugned my mastery of classical philosophy,' he said.

"Think of it. Killed his friend, not for impugning his character but his mastery of philosophy!"

Uncle Billy pulled his watch from his vest pocket, checked the time, and politely urged Burns to pick up the pace a bit. "No offense, sir. The stories about your youth are fascinating. But it's getting late and I've got to get up real early to milk the cows. They just won't wait. So how about getting us closer to now—how ya ended up here in the first place."

Burns laughed heartily. "I understand, sir. No offense taken. My Mama always said I had the gift for gab. . . . So, let's see. Well, I followed in the footsteps of my grandfather, father, and uncle and attended West Point. Became a junior officer in 1860, but resigned the followin' year to take a commission as a captain in the Confederate cavalry.

"And it wasn't long afterwards, I had my first taste of action. Fought on the front lines at Bull Run in Virginia. Met our P.G.T. Beauregard there. Won't go into details but ended up spendin' time there with the general and his men. And let me tell you, he was angry! Bangin' on his field desk and screamin' at the top of his lungs about the sloppy intelligence he was gettin' out of Richmond. He calmed down some, surveyed all of us standin' there in his tent. He gritted his teeth and wished aloud, 'I'm convinced now I just can't rely on 'em for solid information. Yes, sir, I need my own men collectin' fresh information behind the bluebellies' lines.'

"And before you could say 'jackrabbit,' there I was steppin' forward, and without thinkin', I was offerin' the general my services. And before you could say 'boo,' there he was acceptin' my offer and orderin' me behind Union lines in middle Tennessee."

"Now we're getting somewhere!" Uncle Billy exclaimed. "Keep going, Burns! Keep going!"

Feeding off Uncle Billy's enthusiasm, our guest leaned forward and quickly picked up the thread. "So, workin' with forged credentials under a false name, I managed to crack General Halleck's security. Became a bodyguard. But after a lot of hard work, found out it was pretty much a dry hole. Couldn't get my hands much on anything operational—anything that'd be useful to General Beauregard."

"What'd ya do then?" I asked. I was riveted.

"Well, I did what any good spy would do: got a message to the general tellin' him the little I knew and then askin' for somethin' else to do—for somethin' closer to the action. And it sure wasn't long till the general was raisin' the stakes, raisin' 'em real high this time."

"What do ya mean?" Uncle Billy asked. "What'd Beauregard say?"

"He told me in code to try gettin' close to General Grant, who'd moved out of Kentucky and was raisin' hell along the Tennessee River." Burns then sat back in his chair and proudly announced, "And I got the job done too. I managed to catch on as a bodyguard for a brigadier general under Grant's command."

"Did ya learn anything this time?" Uncle Billy asked.

"Sure did. Got some real good information to pass along—Grant's force strength and his location. Got the word to our General Floyd at Fort Donelson—you know, the fort near Nashville—and it wasn't long after that, I moved down the Tennessee with the Brigadier General. Ended up in a tiny place along the river, a town you folks probably never heard of. Pittsburg Landin', it was called. We met up with Grant there."

Without mentioning Robert or any of his exploits, Uncle Billy simply responded, "I wouldn't bet on our not knowing the Landing, Burns. We pretty much know every nook and cranny in western Tennessee. If I'm not mistaken, it's a little north of Corinth. Corinth, Mississippi."

"I'll be damned! How in the world?"

"Never ya mind. Just get on now with your story."

"Well, let's see. Gettin' that close to Grant allowed me to pass along up-to-the-minute intelligence to General Beauregard, who was amassing rebel troops in that very Corinth, Mississippi, you just spoke of. Ya see, the general was planning an all-out strike on Grant's position at the Landin', which he indeed carried out in early April of '62.

"Followin' the Battle of Shiloh as we like to call it in the

South. It's confusin' 'cause the bluecoats call it the Battle of Pittsburg Landin'. . . . Anyways, followin' the Fed victory at Shiloh, I rode with the brigadier general down to Corinth. Grant had ordered us to pursue and destroy the retreatin' Confederate troops. Now I don't like to brag or anything but General Beauregard gives me some credit for delayin' the Feds long enough for our boys to clear out all their supplies and artillery before our showin' up in Corinth."

As soon as Burns began mentioning battles, Uncle Billy became completely engaged in his story. "So after Shiloh and Corinth, where'd you go? What'd you do next?"

"After Lincoln's boys took Fort Donelson, Shiloh, and Corinth, the Fed generals felt the real threat now lay no longer in pitched battles with the rebels, but with insurgents like Forrest, Ferguson, and the like. So I was ordered to Nashville in May of '62. Became a bodyguard for Andrew Johnson. Ya see, Lincoln had appointed him military governor of Tennessee to be in charge of future reconstruction and handlin' the rebel insurgency.

"So I'd been there workin' in Nashville for a short time, when I became privy to some Fed directives related specifically to Bedford Forrest, whose cavalry had just captured Murfrees-boro. Believe the town's some thirty miles or so outside Nash-ville, where we were stationed with Governor Johnson. Yes, sir, the Feds were now beginnin' to feel the rebel heat. Murfrees-boro was just gettin' too damn close to us in Nashville."

"Did ya get the word out to the Wizard of the Saddle?" Uncle Billy asked.

"Yeah, I sure tried, sir. Tried passin' the word to Forrest

through an intermediary. Would meet the fella in the back-room of a safe tavern near the state capitol buildin'. But I'm convinced now he was a double agent working for that Fed spy, Pinkerton, or one of his boys. Wasn't long after I started meetin' with him, I noticed I was being left out of Johnson's strategy sessions. And it wasn't long after that I got the feelin' I was being followed every time I left headquarters."

"Did Governor Johnson or anyone else ever confront you about the meetings at the tavern?" I asked.

"They sure were about to, but—"

Uncle Billy jumped in. "About to, Burns?"

"Yeah. About to. But I didn't give 'em the chance. Ya see, as I was returnin' home to my boardin' house, I noticed a number of fellas loiterin' out front and on the stoop. I sus-pected the game was up. Figured they were Pinkerton's boys settin' a trap."

"My word, Mr. Burns, what'd ya do then?" Rachel asked eagerly.

"Well, I backed away, Miss. Ducked into the alley behind the boardin' house. Climbed a fence on the far side of the stable out back and worked my way around to a side window. Crawled in and quickly saddled my horse, opened the door facing the alley, and rode out past the capitol buildin'.

"I kept lookin' back but didn't see anybody trailin' me. Started to turn north toward Kentucky but thought the Feds would check on my family up there the first thing. Next I thought about headin' due south but thought the Feds would telegraph ahead—workin' the theory I'd flee south to friend-lier territory. But I finally decided to head out this way, west toward the Tennessee River. I figured I could meet up with some old contacts, lie low for a spell, and then make a bee line south toward true Confederate sympathizers."

By now we were all sitting on the edges of our seats and chimed in simultaneously, "So where'd ya go? What ya do next?"

"Since there was a full moon, I rode west on the back roads and kept ridin' till daybreak. Planned to hide out with my horse off the trail in the thick underbrush durin' daylight and then ride on after dark. In fact, I actually made it over the Warreth River, circled Bellville, and almost made it to Charlotte before it was too light to carry on. And then luck'd have it the sky was clear and the moon full for a second night. So sometime around seven o'clock I mounted and rode northwest around Charlotte and then hightailed it through Maysville after midnight, assumin' the Feds wouldn't be patrollin' an out-of-the-way place like Maysville."

"I'm not so good with maps," Mama said. "Never heard of this Maysville. . . . Were you still headed out this way—headed west?"

"Sure was, ma'am. Actually ridin' southwest out of Maysville, headin' straight your way. And in fact, almost reached the Nashville-Memphis Road just before dawn."

"You stopped again at daybreak?" I asked.

"Yeah, had to. Woulda run into Feds ridin' the main highway. So I surveyed the area and found a dilapidated shed some hundred yards off the back road. Thought it safe to hide there durin' the day. Also thought I might find some old forage for my horse. And it turned out okay stayin' there in the shed.

Had only one scare. Heard some shoutin' and dogs barkin'. Figured the Feds were out lookin' for me, but luckily they never picked up the scent.

"I got a little shut-eye after my scare. Slept till nightfall, then saddled up and merged onto the main Memphis Road tryin' to make it past Warfield and south over the Duck River before daybreak. . . . Unfortunately, had another well-lit night. Ya see, the full moon was my friend on the back roads lightin' the way. But the moon was now the enemy, so to speak, makin' it a lot easier for the Feds to recognize me on the main road."

"Ya run into anybody?" Uncle Billy asked.

"I rode the first five miles without seein' a soul; but then about ten miles west of Bell's Furnace, I spotted a small cavalry detail approachin'. My first thought was to turn tail, but then somethin' in me said, 'Take the challenge. Bluff your way through it.' I pulled on the reins and stopped as eight of the Feds formed a blockin' line across the road. Their lead officer then moved out from behind and slowly approached."

"Were you scared, Mr. Burns?" Rachel asked.

"Not so much scared as payin' close attention to everything goin' on around me. Figured if things got bad, I could make a run for it, lay low in the saddle and dodge their fire."

"Go on, go on. Tell us what happened next," Uncle Billy demanded.

"So this Fed officer rode up and started askin' questions: 'Who are you?' 'Why you out here in the dead of night?' 'What are you up to?' And bein' honest with you folks here, I really didn't know how to answer. Didn't know whether he'd been tipped off by a telegraph message; if he was suspicious of my Kentucky drawl; or if he thought I was just nervous and bein' evasive. But I sure got the feelin' he wasn't buyin' what I was sellin'.

"The officer turned and ordered one of his troopers to join the interrogation. I just sensed there was goin' to be trouble. And all the while the cavalryman was ridin' up to join us, I was lookin' around for a way out. Noticed a small openin' between two of the Feds, the space the approachin' trooper had just vacated. I figured I better make a move, so I spurred my horse and raced through the opening headed west.

"The soldiers shouted, 'Halt! Halt!' But I just kept ridin', stayin' low in the saddle. Bullets whistled past my head. I just couldn't shake 'em. They seemed to be closin' in for the kill. And just after crossin' a small bridge, my mare collapsed under me. The bastards—forgive me, ladies—the bastards had shot my horse out from under me. I landed hard, but luckily my horse hadn't rolled over on top of me. As the bullets whizzed by, I scrambled on all fours over to the underbrush, crawled up a small incline, and stretched out behind an outcroppin'.

"I lay still as death. Heard the leader shoutin', 'Hold your fire! Spread out! He couldn't a gotten far.' My heart was poundin' and I was sweatin' like a stuck pig. Imagine that—sweatin' buckets on a cold November night. And I was breathin' hard too. Had to concentrate on not wheezin'. It'd give me away. And over the next few minutes their voices became increasingly faint; but I didn't dare move a muscle for fear they'd left a trooper posted nearby to snare me, if I let my guard down. I continued hearin' their muffled voices for another ten minutes or so, and then everything became quiet.

"I lay there behind that outcroppin' all day listenin' to the few brave crows that hadn't been driven farther south by the deepenin' cold. I was thankful I had my greatcoat, that it hadn't rained or snowed, and that I hadn't heard a soul all day long. I decided to make my next move after dark. I was extremely thirsty. Knew I had to find a stream to keep my strength up. And then perhaps find a barn or a farm buildin' where I could hide out until the Feds' pursuit cooled way down.

"So after scurryin' for several hours through dense underbrush borderin' the main road, I stumbled on a shallow creek, savored the clean, cold water as I had never before, and then decided to abandon the thicket for the creek bed, where I could walk upright and cover more distance seekin' shelter. The partially frozen creek meandered for a mile or so through a forest of hickories, oaks, and pines and then curved southward into an open field bounded by orchards.

"When I stopped to rest, I spotted an old trail cuttin' through a field. I decided to follow it a ways to see where it led and spied your farmhouse sittin' pretty up on the far hill. After climbin' the rise borderin' the highway and seein' no one approachin' from either direction, I raced across the road and ran up behind the log cabin below your farmhouse. And I believe this is where you, Thomas, and Uncle Billy make your entrance into the story."

Burns paused and then made his pitch. "I want to thank you folks for your southern hospitality. And I'll make only one request of you: as brethren of the South, permit me to stay here on the farm until it's safe for me to cross the Duck River and get on down to N'Orleans. In the meanwhile, I could help with the chores as long as I stay back a ways from the highway. I'm sure you understand."

I immediately looked over at Uncle Billy for his reaction. Uncle Billy just sat there for a minute silently stroking his chin. He then transferred Burns's revolver from his thigh up onto the tabletop and passed judgment. "As a Dixie gentleman, I wouldn't mind sharing a room with you for a spell, Mr. Burns." Uncle Billy then turned to Mama and Grandma and concluded, "I don't think his brief stay here could do us any harm."

I turned toward the ladies to gauge their response. Rachel was smiling broadly.

14

THE SHORT NOVEMBER days passed quickly into weeks, and then it was Christmas Day. Uncle Billy had gone home to be with his family. And knowing he was there with Beth produced continuous waves of guilt and envy, wishing he were here and I there.

Burns was still with us, waiting for the right time to safely resume his escape to New Orleans. His southern charm and calm demeanor had allowed him to easily mesh into our family routine, and he had been very helpful completing odd jobs Uncle Billy had assigned him. I even think for Mama his presence had taken some of the sting out of Robert's long absence. But as with any guest staying on for an extended period, I began wondering if the right time would ever come. Burns appeared increasingly more comfortable with his new station in life, and I noticed he was finding ways to spend more time with Rachel, who seemed happier now than she had in years.

While going about my chores, I'd find the two of them together collecting the eggs, trimming a shoulder outside the smokehouse, or fetching fresh water from the well. I believed my sixteen-year-old sister had become infatuated with the older, attractive Burns, but I assumed he, as an adult and a soldier, understood the protocol and would handle their relationship honorably. And up until now Burns appeared to be handling himself as a gentleman in every respect.

As was our custom over the past few years, Israel and I went hunting early Christmas morning and dressed out five squirrels for our traditional yuletide meal. And when we sat down for dinner, Grandma asked us to bow our heads and reflect for a moment on our blessings despite this time of war, Father's death, and Grandpa's illness. Before bowing her head, she offered up a few examples for our consideration: we had a place to sleep; we weren't going hungry; we had each other; and we had our health. After a minute of silence, Grandma asked Israel to say his traditional Christmas prayer, which he delivered adding special thanks this year for Mr. Burns, who had been helping us out with all the daily chores.

When we had finished another of Mama's incomparable meals, Grandma and I carried a heaping Christmas plate over to Grandpa in the front room. We found him dozing with his head slightly turned to the left and his beard settled against his red flannel gown. The windows were a muted December gray. Grandma approached him quietly, gently stroked his silver hair, nuzzled against his cheek, and whispered for him to wake up. But as he often did, he jumped and began screaming at the top of his lungs, ordering an arcane battle maneuver generously laced with blasphemies inappropriate for this festive, holy day.

Grandma finally managed to calm him enough to interest him in the Christmas meal. She'd raise a rounded spoon to his lips, say "open wide," and then scrape the edge of the emptied spoon across his mouth to remove any excess that hadn't already fallen into his beard. I could only think of melancholy

Jacques and Grandpa's arc from infancy to war hero and now back again, knowing the place for the first time:

> All the world's a stage,
> And all the men and women merely players;
> They have their exits and their entrances;
> And one man in his time plays many parts.

As she lifted one spoonful after another to Grandpa's lips, my dear grandfather stared through us and mumbled incessantly about the war. Twenty minutes into the feeding, Israel cautiously entered, nodded, and said softly, "Happy Christmas, Grandpa." The old man shuddered, looked directly at Israel, and ordered him to come near. Israel approached the rocker, gently lowered his head against Grandpa's wiry beard, and whispered, "I love you, Grandpa." The gruff warrior replied coherently, "I love you too, Israel. I'll ever regret takin' you to Warfield that day, the time we stopped in at the blacksmith's shop to shoe the horse. I'm sorry. Please forgive me. I wouldn't have hurt you for the world."

Grandpa raised his head, stared blankly again through Grandma and me, and reassured General Pickett that Longstreet's colors were still secure. Everything was silence except for the ticking of the antique clock. As Israel slowly backed away, Grandma lovingly patted her husband's arm and offered a heartfelt benediction. "All's forgiven here and in the hereafter, dear." The enigmatic, timeless man in the moon beamed while proclaiming a quarter past three.

15

SEVERAL TIMES A year John Mashburne would ride out from town to exchange information about the war. His son, Will, and my brother, Robert, were part of the "Warfield contingent," who trained together at Camp Yellow Jacket, received promotions to second lieutenant, and then served together in Memphis guarding the highways and rail lines supplying the river city.

After that first tour of duty, they followed similar paths for a while, first northward to Forts Henry and Donelson and then southward to Shiloh near the Mississippi line. But after that great battle on the Tennessee, they were assigned to different cavalry commands operating in different theaters. While Robert joined Forrest's guerrillas in western Tennessee, Will rode with Morgan's raiders throughout Kentucky, laying waste to Federal depots and supplies.

After repeated displays of gallantry, the young officers received promotions to captain and became leaders of their own forces conducting cavalry strikes throughout Federally occupied Tennessee—Will to the east of Nashville and Robert to the west. Comparing notes with Mr. Mashburne, we were able to identify many of the guerrilla commanders working the state: Hinson, Napier, Dawson, and McNairy in the west with Robert and Champ Ferguson, Hamilton, Carter, and Hughes in the east with Will.

"If I knew then, Thomas, what I know now, I'd a waited a day or two before riding out here," Mr. Mashburne declared as he stood on the top step brushing snow off the shoulders of his outer coat. "You see, the cold just plays hell with my rheumatism."

"Well, hurry on in here, Mr. Mashburne!" I replied while extending my hand to help him up over the last step. "Everyone's inside huddled around the stove. They'll really be happy to see you, pleased you made a trip out here even in the dead of winter."

I quickly hung Mr. Mashburne's coat in the hallway to thaw and then rushed him into the dining room to warm up.

Mama was the first to spot our guest. She immediately stood up and extended her arms. "Well, will y'all look at what the cat's drug in. It's really good seeing ya, John."

"Likewise, ma'am."

Uncle Billy got up and extended his hand. "You look like ya need some warming up, John. Come on over here and take my chair by the stove."

"And I'll get right to work stirring ya up a hot toddy for sippin' while we chew the fat," Mama added.

Rachel peered in from the kitchen to see what the commotion was all about. "Oh, hello, Mr. Mashburne. Good to see ya. Grandma and I are out here whipping up some cayenne cornbread sticks for lunch. Mama says they'll help warm us up in this freezing weather."

"Oh, I remember 'em, Rachel," Mr. Mashburne replied.

"Your mama's sure got that one right. Last time we had 'em out here they 'bout set my hair on fire."

Burns, who had opted for Father's hand-me-downs rather than his freshly washed uniform, stood up and cleared his throat to draw attention his way.

"Oh, I'm sorry. John, this is Mr. Burns," Uncle Billy said. "And Mr. Burns, this is John Mashburne, an old friend from Warfield. His son, Will, was a schoolmate of my older nephew, Robert."

"Pleased to meet you, Mr. Burns," Mr. Mashburne said. "What brings you to our neck of the woods?"

"Ah, business, sir. Business," Burns answered and then added, "Been stayin' here a spell with these kind folks before headin' on south to N'Orleans." Burns then glanced over at Rachel, smiled, and turned back toward the rest of us again. "And if you folks don't mind, no disrespect intended, I'd like joinin' the ladies in the kitchen. Ya see, I've a hankerin' for cookin', and I'm always on the lookout for somethin' special, somethin' new, and it sounds like those cayenne sticks are right up my alley."

"No offense taken, sir," Mr. Mashburne replied. "What Mama, Uncle Billy, and I have to say would probably bore you anyway."

Once Burns had disappeared into the kitchen, Uncle Billy leaned over toward Mr. Mashburne and whispered, "Have a lot to tell you about this fella, but now's not the time. Long and complicated. Best suited for a visit later this spring."

Mama returned with the promised whiskey and softly suggested Mr. Mashburne immediately share any personal stories while Mr. Burns was out of earshot.

"Yes, tell us, what's the news bringing you out this way in the dead of winter?" Uncle Billy asked in a lowered voice.

"A couple of things: the latest dispatch from Will and some news just crossin' the wires this mornin'." Mr. Mashburne pulled some folded papers from his pocket and adjusted his reading glasses. "But before beginnin' with Will's latest, think it's best I give y'all a little context—help you get the drift of what's really goin' on."

Mama, Uncle Billy, and I shrugged, wondering what Mr. Mashburne had in mind. Uncle Billy then turned to our guest and encouraged him lightheartedly, "If you think the context's necessary, John, but please get right on into the news then. We're anxious to hear what's been going on."

"I promise to keep it short and sweet. Well, you folks know I served with Grandpa in the Mexican War, so you can take my word for it—sometimes ya have to read between the lines when you're dealin' with soldiers. I remember on the one hand wantin' to impress folks with my own exploits, while on the other hand wantin' everyone to know how all the credit was bein' showered on troops in rival units. It's just natural for soldiers to complain, to feel unappreciated, and especially when conditions are as unbearable as they've been for most of this winter. So keep all this in mind as you hear what Will has to say."

Mr. Mashburne glanced down at Will's letter, scanned the first page, and began paraphrasing what he had just read. "Will says over in eastern Tennessee where he's fightin', the Confederate infantry spends all its time in camp drilling, eating, and getting fat. He assures me this isn't the case with the cavalry units, which patrol day and night protectin' the slumberin' foot soldiers from slaughter in their warm tents. He says cavalrymen don't receive anywhere near the attention or praise they deserve. He emphasizes—actually underlinin' his words here—he says, 'There are no ladies, no top-level generals, no brass bands, no waving flags or parades honoring our service.'

"In fact, he says, the cavalry has been 'saddled'—that's his mocking play on words—has been 'saddled' with the undeserved reputation of fightin' around the edges of major engagements and makin' brief raids into enemy territory. He complains that the foot soldiers sit in their cozy camp listenin' to the sounds of distant cavalry skirmishes. He writes, 'The infantrymen don't realize that, yes, it may only be a hundred cavalrymen total on both sides shootin' at each other, but some of us are dyin' while others are havin' their arms and legs ripped from their sockets.'"

Mr. Mashburne paused to reload. He scanned the second page and continued his summary: "Will says he and his men carry their wounded and dead away on horseback and quickly bury the fallen as honorably as they can in shallow, unmarked graves. He emphasizes with the underlining again that neither the widows nor the world knows how bravely these guerrillas fought and sacrificed everything. He says they get no glory because they died skirmishing up at the front.

"He ends the letter describing the sacrifices he and his men make every day that's above and beyond the fighting and the dying. He says when they aren't attacking, they serve on outpost and picket duty, waiting alone at highway junctions, or riding through thick backwoods and bramble, and in either case, exposed to the most severe weather with no campfires to warm them—soaking rains, freezing temperatures, strong winds, and heavy snows. Says he's had numerous men with frostbite this winter and had one hero who froze to death in his saddle."

Mama gasped, "My good Lord, John!" And then turning toward Uncle Billy, she expressed an alarming afterthought. "If this is happening to Will, you just know it's gotta be happening to our Robert, too."

Uncle Billy leaned in. "I think you've been a bit harsh in your judgment of Will's comments, John. Sounds like he has every right to be complaining about conditions and the lack of respect he and his men are getting from higher-ups."

"Well, given it's my own boy doing the complaining, Uncle Billy, I'm bending over backwards trying to be objective. Perhaps I'm being a bit too critical, but back in the day, Grandpa and I went through a lot and sure did our own share of complaining. . . . I'll just leave it to you folks to draw your own conclusions about conditions."

After a few seconds of reflective silence, Uncle Billy changed the subject. "While I'm sure we all agree the most important dispatches are always the ones about our own flesh and blood, but ah, I believe you said you also had general news just crossing the wires this morning. Ya wanna fill us in?"

"Lincoln's finally issued his rumored proclamation, formally declaring Negroes free and clear."

"Apply everywhere, John . . . including Tennessee?" Mama asked.

"Politicians worked out a compromise. Doesn't apply to the border states and here in Tennessee."

"Well, that's comforting for folks in these parts," Mama said.

"On the surface it sure looks that way, but . . ."

"But what, John?"

"It's already started."

"What's started?"

"Already hearing reports of Negroes running away from the farms and plantations, headed straight to Nashville or Memphis where a lot of Fed troops are stationed. The runaways are seeking help from Lincoln's boys."

"Ya see there? Ya see the hell he's putting us through?" Uncle Billy exclaimed angrily. "And if ya wanna be straight up about it, his proclamation has nothing to do with freeing the slaves. In my opinion, it has everything to do with politics and winning his damned war! That's right—politics and winning his war, as simple as that!"

"I don't understand, Uncle Billy," Mama said. "How's the proclamation gonna help Lincoln win the war?"

"Helps the bluebellies two ways. First, draws Negroes away from farms supplying goods to rebel troops and, secondly, encourages the freed and runaways to join the Feds on the battlefield fighting the rebs!"

"Looks like y'all are gonna be in the same stew," Mr. Mashburne suggested. "I mean with Bella and Israel."

"Don't think so, John," Mama replied.

"Why's that?"

"Ya see, some time ago when the rumors started flying about a proclamation, Uncle Billy suggested we go talk to

Bella, see how she felt about staying on here even if there was a proclamation."

"What'd she say?"

"Well, I pretty much asked her point-blank," Mama said. "She smiled, rushed over, and gave me a big hug. Said she and Israel weren't going anywhere. Said we were family, had a warm place to call home, had no guarantees elsewhere of a job or income, and besides, had no way of knowing how a new family would take to Israel. But she said the main reason for staying, said it was God's will. He wanted her and Israel to live out their lives here with all of us on the farm."

Grandma came into the dining room and walked over to where we were huddled around the potbelly stove. "Excuse me for interrupting, but lunch is ready. So y'all get over to the table and get settled."

"Thanks for the thought, Grandma, but I believe it's best I be heading out. It's gonna get dark fast today, seeing there's no sun."

"Nonsense, John," Grandma replied. "You'll have plenty of time to get home before dark. And besides, I just know that once you hear the menu, you won't resist." Grandma now assumed the role of mature seductress, lowering the pitch of her voice and lengthening the vowels in her drawl. "Fried chicken . . ."

Mr. Mashburne thrust his arms in the air feigning resistance. "Now stop that!"

Everyone laughed as Grandma continued tempting Mr. Mashburne. "Boiled potatoes swimming in butter . . ."

Our guest waved his arms good-naturedly. "Stop it! Now stop it, I say."

"Black-eyed peas . . ."

Mr. Mashburne lowered his chin onto his chest smiling embarrassedly as Grandma finished with a flourish. "Rachel's cayenne cornsticks, and topping it all off with your favorite sweet, John, fresh-baked apple pie. Ya see, even the heavens are telling you to stay. We baked your favorite dessert this morning and didn't have an inkling you'd show up on our doorstep today. So whatdaya have to say now, John? What-daya have to say?"

Before the vanquished fellow had a chance to respond, Mama, Uncle Billy, and I were all tugging at his arms moving him in the direction of the dining room table. And as it turned out, we were really happy he stayed because he regaled us with the latest Warfield gossip gleaned from an unimpeach-able source, the all-knowing, all-telling Mrs. Mashburne. Mama was the only one of us who dared interrupt his nar-rative. She alternated between encouraging Mr. Mashburne to take another helping and asking him what else he needed. He would smile, jokingly reply all he needed was just a little more time, and then gleefully dive back into Warfield's murky waters without missing a beat.

So after a fine meal with "good people and good compa-ny," as Grandpa used to say, Uncle Billy and I escorted Mr. Mashburne out to his horse; wished his son, Will, good luck; said our sincere "so longs"; and then watched our good friend ride out to the highway and turn westward into a shifting Jan-uary wind.

16

THERE'S AN OLD adage in the county—"hard winters make for early springs"—and that was surely the case in '63. Only weeks after Mr. Mashburne wrote telling us he had practically frozen to death riding home from the farm, we were all outside in our shirtsleeves doing our routine chores. At Saturday dinner Uncle Billy announced that since the winter weather had broken, he would ride home for a couple of days and would return the following Tuesday. We teased him about missing church, and he responded that we all needed worship a lot more than he did. The next morning we saw Uncle Billy off and then headed out to Mrs. Booker's parlor.

I woke up the following morning with a lot of energy. I attributed my renewed spirit to our early spring weather. Grandpa used to say, "Springtime lubricates the mind and the joints." So feeling well oiled and completely motivated, I decided to repair the fence bordering the hayfield between our house and Sugar Grove School. I rolled out of bed, dressed, and hurried down to the kitchen for a couple biscuits and some strong black coffee. After saying so long to Mama and Grandma, I walked down to Bella's cabin to fetch Israel. As I passed the buckeye tree, I could hear Bella's voice flowing out through the small, open window:

Jubilee, Jubilee

O, my Lord!

Jubilee, Jubilee!

What is the matter with the mourners?

O, my Lord!

The Devil's in the Amen corner,

O, my Lord!

Jubilee, Jubilee!

When Israel had finished his hearty breakfast, we strolled over to the toolshed to collect the wood splitter, axes, and saws. Along the way we saw Rachel and Mr. Burns in the barnyard; she shouted they were going to open the hen house and muck out some stalls. Yes, Mr. Burns was still with us, with little apology, and his trip to New Orleans appeared to be a much more distant prospect every day. While Rachel was thrilled and Grandma rarely seemed to notice, Mama had finally begun grumbling about how much food the soldier ate.

Israel and I worked well into the afternoon; we guessed it was getting close to three o'clock. It was strenuous work, but we both enjoyed our resurrection from the long, hard winter. We cleaned the mud off our tools in a nearby brook and started home on the path closest to the woods. As we crossed the dirt road leading up to Anderson's farm, I spotted a couple embracing just off the trail. My mind didn't want to accept what my eyes were seeing. It was Rachel and Burns. She was facing the path while Burns had his back to us.

Rachel must have seen us approaching; she tried shoving Burns away and shouting, "No!" Even as she became more insistent, Burns still didn't seem to understand why she had suddenly begun responding so negatively to his advances. When Israel and I got within several yards, I yelled, "Stop!" Burns loosened his grip, and Rachel finally succeeded in pushing the soldier backward toward us. As the space between them widened, I could now see the top of my sister's dress was hanging down around her waist. I instinctively turned away but heard Israel growl and drop his axe. I whirled back around just as Israel jumped Burns from behind and violently twisted his neck from side to side. I became ill hearing the horrible cracking and snapping of bone and sinew.

Burns never screamed and became limp instantly. Israel finally released his hold and let Burns crash to the ground. He stood there over the soldier for a moment, stared into Burns's open eyes, and then raised his clenched fists into the air. Rachel threw herself onto Burns's body and began wailing. I hooked Israel's arm, slowly but forcefully moved him away, and sat him down on the flat edge of an outcropping. He began moving from side to side and muttering, "You hurt sister. . . . You hurt sister."

I rushed over to Rachel, put my arm around her, and gently tried to lift her head off Burns's motionless chest. She resisted and screamed, "Let me be!" I backed off and leaned against an old stump, trying to gain enough composure to devise a workable plan. After ten minutes or so, I moved back over to Rachel and put my arm around her again. She was still lying across Burns's chest and quietly sobbing. I whispered, "Rachel, you've gotta collect yourself. . . . You've gotta be strong. . . . We have to get you back to the house."

I gently tugged at her shoulders, and this time she offered no resistance. I returned the sleeves of her dress to her shoulders, then turned to Israel and said, "Collect all the tools here and put 'em back in the shed. And while you're there, grab two long shovels and bring 'em up to the house around back, you hear?"

"Yes, sir, Mr. Thomas. Israel hears."

When Rachel and I reached the back porch, I began shouting out for Mama, but there was no answer. I then went from room to room and finally found her and Grandma mending shirts on the front porch. Mama looked up from her sewing and explained cheerfully, "We're out here mending and taking advantage of the spring air."

I didn't respond, which caused her to look up again. "What's the matter with you, boy? You look like you've seen a ghost. You coming down with something, Thomas?"

I collapsed into the rocker next to her recalling the conflict I'd felt as a young boy—struggling to confess to a horrific transgression while hoping she could make things better, hoping she would get me out of the mess I was in.

She reached over to feel my forehead. "You running a fever, boy?"

I instinctively pushed her hand away. "It's not like that, Mama. It's . . . it's Burns."

"Burns? What's wrong with him? He sick?"

"Worse than that," I replied.

"Worse than that? For heaven's sake, boy, get it out!"

"He's . . . he's dead, Mama." Grandma stuck herself with her needle and cried out in pain. Mama gasped. "Oh my God, what happened?"

I gave them a brief account without sharing the more disturbing details. I next explained the situation with Rachel, also without disclosing the more unseemly nature of her relationship with Burns. I told them what I planned to do. They agreed and promised to hurry down to Bella's cabin and relay the dreadful news.

I ran up the back stairs to Burns's room, where I collected his few possessions: his greatcoat, shell jacket, antique pocket watch, and a buckeye, which I assumed Rachel had given him on one of their walks. I rushed back down the hallway stairs, out the door, and onto the forest path where we had left Burns's body. I stopped behind the smokehouse and shouted for Israel, who immediately came running.

When we got back out to where Burns had fallen, I asked Israel to help me drag the body farther into the woods. Burns looked as if he were sleeping. Rigor mortis hadn't begun to set in; his finger and knee joints hadn't flexed. I knew we had to find a place to bury him far enough away from the path and Anderson's road, but the farther we dragged him into the woods, the more ledge and outcroppings we encountered.

We finally decided on a site and began digging through the small boulders the best we could. After about a half hour of shoveling, I was already exhausted; but because of Israel's strength and experience trenching at Fort Henry, he continued digging and lifting the heavy rocks out until he had managed to create a respectable, albeit shallow grave.

I folded Burns's jacket and laid it across his chest, stuffed his old watch into his right pants pocket, and then covered his head and torso with the greatcoat. We carefully lowered him into his grave and began placing the larger rocks back into the hole around and directly on top of his body. We then filled in the remaining spaces with the loose clay; spread some small branches and leaves over the slight earth mound; asked Burns for forgiveness; and headed back to the toolshed. After we'd stowed the shovels, I sent Israel down to the log cabin to be with his mother.

I lay awake most of the night dreading the difficult discussion I knew I'd be having with Uncle Billy the following afternoon. And when I saw his wagon approaching the next day, my heart sank. I walked slowly down to the barnyard to meet him and to help unharness the mare. I asked him about his visit home and how Beth was doing, and he replied that everyone was doing just fine now after having recovered from a bad case of fever and the shivers. I didn't dare broach the subject of Burns until Uncle Billy had enjoyed his long-anticipated lunch and Grandma and Mama had joined us at the table to help lay out our new and more challenging world.

Uncle Billy listened impassively as I related what had happened while he was away. When I'd finished the abridged version of Burns's "accidental" death, Uncle Billy sat silently for a moment, took a deep breath, and then surprised us all with a "thank you" for effectively handling a very bad situation. Uncle Billy said no one could have anticipated Israel's mistaken perception of what he was witnessing. So he thought we'd done the right thing as far as burying Burns in the deep woods with all his belongings. He also believed there was little risk now of anyone coming onto the property and snooping around, since no one had been seriously pursuing the Confederate spy over the past few months. And he emphasized that from now on, no one here knew anything about a Mr. Burns or his whereabouts.

17

THE WEATHER CONTINUED to be mild the rest of February. I spent most of my time consoling Rachel, doing my routine chores, and counting the days until spring planting season came around again. Thankfully, Master Hudson would be returning to help us, and he and I would surely continue our vital quest.

As I thought about his upcoming visit, I admit I felt some frustration knowing I couldn't disclose Burns's death despite its ironic relevance to our ongoing discussions. But during these last weeks of February, the most difficult part of my day was continuously discouraging Rachel from visiting Burns's hidden grave and leaving handwritten pledges of everlasting love.

It was now the first Wednesday in March or what Mama and Grandma would call "wash day." It was also Grandpa's birthday. Mama said her back was acting up and asked me to fetch some buckets of water for the washhouse kettle. As I slogged back up the rise with my overflowing buckets, I heard hoofbeats on the highway. I watched carefully as the mounted troops stopped and then turned onto our entry road.

I set the pails down and walked over to the buckeye tree. I could now see they were Feds, which eased my fears concerning a potential problem with the Confederate, Mr. Burns. Uncle Billy, who was shelling corn in the barnyard, also saw the horsemen entering the property and hurried over to join me under the buckeye tree.

It was an unusual sight, one I'd never seen before around here, a combination of white and Negro soldiers on horseback. The three white officers and a black sergeant dismounted and approached us. As they neared, the ranking captain extended his hand and said, "Good morning, gentlemen."

"A fine morning, I say," Uncle Billy replied in a friendly tone. "How can we help you?"

"I'm Captain Gray, sir, US Corps of Engineers. This here's Lieutenants Burrows and Carrier, heading up our coloreds who are out here protecting us engineers." The white captain then turned to the Negro noncommissioned officer standing to his right and introduced him. "This here's Sergeant Dixon, our acting liaison dealing directly with our coloreds there."

"Nice meeting y'all," Uncle Billy responded perfunctorily and then persisted in his original line of questioning. "So what brings you boys out our way today?"

"Looking for crossties."

"Crossties?"

"Yes, sir, crossties, and plenty of 'em, for the new Nashville & Northwestern Railroad. Laying track from one end of the county to the other, running alongside the main highway out front there. So, ya see, we're scouring the neighborhood lookin' for locals willing to deal, and you fellas look like you could fit the bill."

"Ya might have that right, Captain. But on conditions."

"Ya name 'em, sir."

"No permanent contracts."

The captain eagerly jumped in. "That's fine with us."

"Another stipulation . . ."

"Yes, sir, go ahead."

"Must look like y'all are making us sell. Ya see, Captain, I've heard of other folk around here admitting to long-term deals and they wound up dead. Guerrillas killed 'em."

"We understand, sir."

"So being clear, Captain, forced and one-off sales only."

The officer smiled slyly, extended his hand, and replied, "Absolutely clear, sir. We can work on that basis with you time and again. . . . And let's see now if I can sweeten the pot a bit."

Uncle Billy smiled. "I'm all ears, Captain."

"Well, if you gentlemen agree to cut the timber of our choosing and then y'all make the ties and stack 'em, we could see paying y'all a lot more for your labor."

"How many ties ya talking about, Captain?"

"Some thousand or so, sir."

"Looks like we have ourselves a deal after dickering on the price."

"I know y'all will be pleased with our offer. Top dollar! . . . Y'all see."

After handshakes all around, I leaned back against the buckeye tree, sighed, and mumbled to myself, "With all the planting and farming this spring and summer along with the added timber work, looks like Master Hudson and I won't be spending much time together pursuing our quest."

The captain turned and addressed Sergeant Dixon.

"Order the troops to dismount. Tell 'em the folks here won't mind 'em filling their canteens at the well house. And then order 'em to stand down under the tree here. We're gonna walk the forest line with these gentlemen, select our timber, and draw up a plan of attack."

Uncle Billy, the Feds, and I then walked up the rise and out onto the path running between the smokehouse and the dense woods. Uncle Billy and I escorted the Feds as they moved back and forth several times along the forest line between the Anderson entry road and the back of our smokehouse. More than once Lieutenant Burrows praised the quality of the hardwoods we'd be harvesting for their railroad project.

As we turned a final time at the Anderson road, I saw Lieutenant Carrier stoop down and pick something up. He studied the object carefully and then approached Captain Gray. The junior officer handed the item to his superior and whispered something that Uncle Billy and I couldn't make out. The captain then gave the lieutenant an unintelligible order, and Lieutenant Carrier quickly departed, heading back toward the farmhouse.

Captain Gray walked over to where Uncle Billy and I were standing and asked, "Y'all seen any Union soldiers on your property lately?"

We glanced at each other, and Uncle Billy answered truthfully, "Ne'r a hide nor hair, Captain."

The Fed responded, "Well, let's head on back for now."

When we reached the washhouse, the junior officer re-appeared carrying several rolls of paper. He handed them to the captain, who immediately began scanning the documents, which appeared to be long lists of soldiers' names. After several minutes, he looked up and asked Uncle Billy, "Would you mind giving Lieutenant Burrows and me a brief tour of your house? We're just following a long-established protocol," he continued apologetically. "I'm sure you understand."

Knowing we had to comply, Uncle Billy smiled warmly and replied, "Gentlemen, y'all are always welcome in our home." The captain nodded in acknowledgment and then motioned for us to follow him back to the house. As we neared the side entrance, a tidal wave of fear spontaneously rushed through me—what if I'd left something behind that belonged to Burns?

After entering through the hallway door, the captain pointed to the stairs and said he wished to start with the top rooms and work down. I jumped in to explain Grandpa's condition and his confinement to the front room. The senior officer responded they would have to inspect the room but that they would be sensitive to Grandpa's situation. After Uncle Billy led the two officers upstairs, the Feds split up; the captain went into Burns's room and Lieutenant Burrows into mine.

After a tense fifteen minutes, the officers rejoined Uncle Billy and me in the hallway. The captain next asked to visit the downstairs rooms; and again, Uncle Billy led the way, deferentially cautioning the men about the narrowness of the stairs. I followed the trio down, feeling much more relaxed now that we had passed muster in Burns's chamber. The Feds started their downstairs inspection by briefly surveying the back porch, the kitchen, and the dining room. I then unlocked the front room, where we fortunately found Grandpa sleeping soundly. The captain entered quietly, stood just inside the door, scanned the room for no more than a minute or two, and backed out into the hallway, signaling it was all right to close and lock the door.

We next headed down the hallway to Grandpa's old room, which some years ago had become Mama and Rachel's bedroom. As the four of us approached the door, I noticed something unexpected was happening. My normally relaxed, jocular Uncle Billy appeared to grow increasingly agitated. The captain knocked on the closed door, and after receiving no response, he slowly opened it and shouted, "Anyone here?"

When no one answered, both soldiers entered the bedroom to look around. They seemed to be walking the fine line between conducting a thorough, professional examination of the room and infringing on the ladies' privacy. After a cursory inspection of the ladies' closet, Lieutenant Burrows walked over to Mama's writing table, and assuming there would be nothing embarrassingly personal in the antique desk, he opened the drawer, peered in, and pulled something out.

As the lieutenant called his superior over to the desk, Uncle Billy slouched back against the doorframe. The Feds conferred quietly for a moment, and then Captain Gray turned and held out a revolver. "Can either of ya tell me where y'all got this government-issued Colt?"

Uncle Billy answered hesitantly. "It's . . . it's complicated. But shooting straight with ya, Captain, out of the kindness of our hearts, we took in a rebel sympathizer for a spell. The name's Burns and was dressed in a Fed uniform."

Captain Gray stared at the gun and then replied, "I'm sure y'all understand. This'll require a further inspection of the property."

"We understand, sir." Uncle Billy's voice quavered as he spoke.

The captain walked out onto the wraparound porch and called out to Sergeant Dixon. "Get your men over to the side of the house," he said, "and wait there for instructions." The officer returned and asked us to follow him outside. We joined the Negro troops near the washhouse, and the captain led all of us back out onto the forest path headed for its intersection with Anderson's road.

As we walked along, Captain Gray asked Lieutenant Carrier to show him exactly where he'd found the object that had launched their initial inquiry. And just before we reached the Anderson junction, the junior officer stopped, pointed over to the side of the path, and said, "Right here, sir. This is where I found the gold eagle button."

The captain then lined the cavalrymen up side-by-side facing the forest and ordered them, "Walk slowly now up through the woods there. Ya see anything peculiar, give a shout to Sergeant Dixon. Is that clear?"

"Yes, sir!" they roared in unison.

The troops had been walking up the rise for only a few minutes when one of the Feds shouted for the sergeant to come over to his position near where we had buried Burns. And after conferring with the cavalryman, Sergeant Dixon yelled down to the three officers. "Y'all better get up here right away!" They rushed up the hill and converged on the spot where the sergeant and the cavalryman were standing.

When they had finished their inspection, the captain walked back down the hill and said to Uncle Billy, "We're gonna need some shovels right away."

"Not a problem, sir. We store 'em in the barnyard shed. Thomas and I'll run down and get 'em."

"No, you boys sit tight. I'll send my men." And after ordering two of the cavalrymen to fetch the tools, the captain walked over to confer with his subordinate officers. They stayed to themselves, talking, until the troops returned with the long-handled shovels. The captain then led his soldiers back up the hill. All Uncle Billy and I could do was watch uneasily as the Negro troops dug up Burns's body. Some of the onlookers began gagging as the repugnant odor wafted up from the deteriorating corpse. Some near the shallow grave began shouting a description of the horrific scene to the rest of the cavalrymen waiting farther down the hill. "Pullin' him up now. Fed soldier, rotting, swollen, maggots around the eyes."

Captain Gray then asked a private to search the body for papers. There were none, but the soldier did find the antique watch in Burns's right pants pocket. He handed the watch to Lieutenant Burrows, who inspected it carefully and located tiny hinges at the bottom of the back case. He removed a penknife from his pocket, pried open the back cover, and motioned for the captain to come over to see what he had discovered.

After reading the inscription the lieutenant had found inside, Captain Gray pulled the rolled documents from his coat pocket and began scanning the list of names, glancing back and forth several times from the timepiece to the papers. He then walked down to where Uncle Billy and I were waiting and declared, "We have a real mystery here. Your Burns fellow, the 'rebel spy' as you call him, had a pocket watch on him belonging to a James Albert Parker. And lo and behold, a Lieutenant J. A. Parker appears here on my list of troops reported as missing in action. Says he was twenty-four years old. Height, five feet seven inches. Eyes dark. Reported missing after Captain Webster's colored troops were attacked by guerrillas south of Warfield. Now, gentlemen, we have some serious questions to address. For starters, how did our Lieutenant Parker get from the battlefield to your farm? How did he end up dead? And who buried him here on the hill?" Uncle Billy and I just stood there silently, listening and wondering now whether there was ever any truth to Burns's heroic battle history, his elaborate spy story, and the valiant escape from Nashville.

After ordering the troops to properly reinter Lieutenant Parker's body, Captain Gray said, "Let's head on back to the house for now and see if we can solve this mystery."

18

W̲HEN WE REACHED the dining room, Captain Gray asked Uncle Billy, "So tell me, sir, who all lives here on the farm?"

"Well, let's see, besides me and Thomas, there's Grandma and Grandpa, you know all about him. Then there's Thomas's mother and his sister, Rachel, and then there are our two . . . ah. . . slaves—I mean, ah, free slaves—Bella and her son, Israel. Believe that's everyone, Captain."

The Fed turned to me and said, "How about ya fetchin' all the folk and bringin' 'em back here so we can have a chat around the table here."

I spent the next fifteen minutes or so collecting everyone. When Mama and Grandma had seen all the commotion with the Feds, they abandoned "wash day" and went down to the barnyard to choose a hen for supper. Bella was in her cabin preparing lunch for Israel, and Rachel was up at the shaded cemetery gate staring in at the faded names on the mossy headstones. As I located each of them, I described the reason for the meeting, and they immediately left for the house. But when I told Rachel it had to do with Burns, she recoiled and refused leaving the cemetery until I convinced her she had to attend for the sake of the family.

Upon returning to the dining room, I reported I had found everyone and said they would all be arriving shortly. And within another fifteen minutes, Uncle Billy, Grandma, Mama, Rachel, Bella, Israel, and I had all taken seats on one side of the dining room table facing the three Federal officers. The lieutenant said he wanted to start at the beginning, when we first met James Albert Parker. Uncle Billy took the lead and described Burns's spontaneous appearance on the farm in November. He repeated Burns's history, which the spy had so vividly related at that very table, and emphasized we allowed him to stay with us because we were Christians, not because we were sympathizers with the rebels or their cause.

Lieutenant Burrows next turned to Mama and requested she tell them what happened from November until the Fed's death. Mama provided an almost minute-by-minute account of the approximate ninety days Burns lived with us, except for the growing relationship between Rachel and the Confederate spy.

When Mama had completed her account, Captain Gray responded, "One thing truly mystifies me, Ma'am. Lieutenant Parker was reported missing in action after the attack in November just south of Warfield. You said he appeared here about that time and he lived here with you for about three months. So what was his motive? Why didn't he return to his troops? Any ideas? . . . Anyone?"

Everyone on both sides of the table turned to Uncle Billy, expecting him to provide a plausible answer; and after several uncomfortable moments, he tried unsuccessfully framing a diplomatic response to a very sensitive subject. "Gentlemen,

I've been thinking about this ever since you said our Burns was a Federal officer, whose troops were attacked near Warfield. No offense to anyone here, but I can only fashion one explanation, if he was Parker and not Burns. He had to have become frightened during the battle and just scurried away, living to fight another day."

Lieutenant Carrier jumped in. "With all due respect, sir, I find that offensive. For one thing, Lieutenant Parker was on the missing in action roll, not on the deserters list. And even more importantly, sir, I served with the good lieutenant at Fort Donelson, in General John A. McClernand's division. So I just know James Albert Parker was serving as the junior officer in a well-respected company—I just know the lieutenant would never have deserted his colored troops in the heat of battle even if surrounded by ten thousand rebels!"

As the Fed offered his rebuttal, his face reddened, his jaw became set, and his expression grew increasingly sinister. "So let me try another explanation on you," he continued. "Perhaps you folks are supporting the guerrillas around here. You know they call this Warfield area 'the hornet's nest' or 'secesh heaven.' Isn't it likely that Lieutenant Parker somehow managed to escape the rebel trap, became disoriented, and ended up here on your farm? . . . Isn't it possible you could've been holding our Lieutenant Parker prisoner at the behest of rebel outlaws?"

Everyone on our side of the table knew it was time to remain silent. Trying to restore civility to the proceedings, Captain Gray spoke in soft, almost apologetic tones. "We're not accusing anyone of anything. We're only trying to get the facts about the lieutenant's last days here on the farm. So that brings us to a critical question. How did Lieutenant James Albert Parker die? Anyone want to tackle that one?"

We all remained silent and avoided staring directly into the captain's face. He asked the question again, this time more firmly. And still, none of us responded. "All right then," he said at last. "I'm gonna ask each of you one more time. Look directly at me. Tell me what you know. And if y'all don't want to cooperate, there'll be consequences for the lot of you. I don't wanta be a bastard, but I can be, and these fellas can testify I've been one in the past. So tell me now, how did Lieutenant Parker die?"

Every time he'd asked a question, Captain Gray looked across the table toward Uncle Billy seated at the far right end on our side; but perversely, this time, and only God truly knows the reason why, the Fed turned to the far left end and directed this most difficult question to Israel. "So, boy, tell me, how'd Lieutenant Parker die?"

Israel looked down mumbling something under his breath. Realizing Israel was at least attempting to say something, the captain repeated his question, using a more relaxed tone. "Now, boy, it's okay. Tell us, how did Lieutenant Parker die?"

And this time, everyone sitting at the table heard clearly Israel's response: "He hurt sister. The man hurt sister."

The lieutenant continued the questioning. "So, boy, did you hurt him back? . . . It's okay. Tell me, did you hurt him back?"

Israel answered softly, "I hurt him back, I hurt him back."

At this point Uncle Billy interrupted to launch a vigorous defense of Israel's actions. "Gentlemen, please. Please allow me to explain what happened here. You can clearly see the boy ain't right. A horse crushed his skull when he was twelve.

He continued growing, but his mind stopped. Ya see, I was away from the farm on business, but Thomas here says Israel saw Mr. Burns and Rachel there sparking on the forest path where y'all found the button. Israel took Burns's advances as an attack on her, so he charged Burns from behind, snapped his neck, killed him in an instant! We swear to ya, that's how it happened, how your Parker and our Burns died."

The room fell silent. I looked over at Rachel, who had turned deathly pale and begun crying. The captain then asked everyone on our side of the table except Israel and me to step out of the dining room but to stay close by. The Fed next instructed Israel and me to exchange places with Sergeant Dixon, who had joined the meeting late and taken a seat over by the potbelly stove. The Fed officers at the table stood up to stretch their legs before proceeding.

When they reconvened, the Feds split up into two groups and moved to opposite ends of the table—Lieutenant Carrier and Sergeant Dixon at the end nearest the window and Captain Gray and Lieutenant Burrows at the other end, near the center of the room. So we now had four Feds, two at each end of the dining room table, sitting in judgment on Israel. I could understand most of what was being said. While Carrier and Dixon were recommending strict adherence to the law with severe punishment, Gray and Burrows were advocating leniency given the circumstances.

A strange feeling came over me. I was back in Master Hudson's schoolroom standing up with my arms outstretched and my palms cupped as weighing pans. And now here we had another balance scale—our dining room table the balance beam and the Feds seated at each end, the weighing pans. I wondered aloud, "Which argument will win the day and tilt the scale?" But as the deliberation continued and became increasingly heated, I conjured up a more sinister vision. I could now see the interloper's thumb moving back and forth along the thick pine beam. So who or what would control the outcome here? Would it be the weight of the arguments or the arbitrary whim of an indifferent, intervening force?

The tribunal debated for almost an hour with the harshest language booming from the end nearest the window. The Negro sergeant was especially concerned about the message clemency would send to their colored troops and to the locals living in and around the hornets' nest. "If the colored troops here see a black man walkin' away unpunished after killin' a white officer, who himself had commanded colored cavalrymen, they'd think we're not serious about adherin' to military code. Consider what that'd do to morale.

"And as for the locals, they'd see our leniency as just another example of applyin' a double standard, bendin' over backwards for colored criminals because they'd lived so long in bondage. The locals would see our action as based on color rather than the law. Stop to think about it. Wouldn't they be in their rights to see us as hypocrites?"

When Sergeant Dixon finished his argument, Captain Gray scanned the room and asked, "Further comments? A rebuttal?" But all was silence.

The captain then turned and said politely, "Thomas, take the boy there and wait outside. I think we have all we need for now."

As Israel and I exited through the hallway door, everyone crowded around to learn what had happened after they had left. I explained the intense struggle that ensued between the factions at either end of the table and expressed my opinion that a final decision about Israel hadn't been made yet but was certainly imminent. They then resumed their vigil in the side yard near Grandma's kettle. Uncle Billy smoked a rare cigarette; Grandma paced and prayed; Mama tried consoling Bella, who was swaying and beseeching the Almighty for her son's deliverance; and Rachel peered into the bare branches of the antique lilacs searching for ciphers foretelling the outcome of the trial.

Another twenty agonizing minutes passed, and finally the Feds filed out through the hallway door. Captain Gray walked over to Uncle Billy, who was sitting on the washhouse steps. "I hope you understand how difficult this has been, given the boy's capacity and everything. I'm truly sorry, but we have no leeway. We have to follow military code and the established law of occupied Tennessee. You see, despite the motive, the boy confessed. We all heard it. There's no ambiguity here. There's no question of guilt or innocence. And both the code and the law require punishment of death by hanging. I'm sorry. I assure you we'll carry out the sentence with the greatest care and decorum."

Uncle Billy launched a counteroffensive. "For God's sake, man, has the war robbed you of your humanity? Forget your code. Forget the law. Heaven knows this is wrong. The boy here acted spontaneously. He didn't know what he was doing. I'm not even sure he knows he killed somebody or understands what death really is. Believe me, Captain, this is not about our losing a Negro. It's about you killing a child in a man's body. You'll all have the blood of an innocent on your hands. You'll all burn in hell!"

Growing both embarrassed and offended, the captain interrupted Uncle Billy's impassioned appeal and warned him, "I understand your feelings, sir, but don't carry this too far. Don't make a spectacle in front of your folk and our colored troops. Listen closely now, the decision was a compromise. We could have taken this a lot further, and we'd have been well within the bounds of military code and Tennessee law. Ya see, sir, being honest with ya, if we wanted to we coulda ordered all of ya executed. All of ya were willfully complicit in Lieutenant Parker's murder. You may not have killed him, but y'all sure as hell knew what happened and ya hid the truth from us. Is that clear, sir?"

"Yes . . . very clear, Captain."

"Okay then, let's just get this over and done with. Tell me, where do y'all store the hay wagon?"

"In the main barn, at the far end."

Grandma, Mama, and Rachel began sobbing. Bella became hysterical, falling to her knees, flailing her arms helplessly, and shouting out repeatedly, "O, sweet Jesus, spare my boy." Reacting to the grim, wrenching scene he'd created, Captain Gray turned to me and said, "Best ya get the ladies away from here for now, perhaps to the cabin out front."

After escorting Mama, Grandma, Rachel, and Bella to the log house, I quickly eased away and joined Uncle Billy and Israel, who were sitting on the front lawn just up the rise from the buckeye tree. As I watched several Feds head off to fetch our wagon, my heart sank. For the first time I'd lost all hope the captain would have a last-minute change of heart. I was now convinced the Feds were serious and had every intention of carrying out their sentence.

As a roulette ball on the gambler's wheel, my mind raced from one random thought to another and finally settled on the befitting need that Grandpa see his beloved Israel a final time. I slipped my arm around Israel's shoulder and said, "Ya know, today's Grandpa's birthday. We should go pay him a visit." Uncle Billy leaned forward and looked past Israel at me. He didn't say anything. He just sat there nodding an affectionate, proud approval of the thought behind the suggestion.

Israel and I walked up to the house. I got the key down from the wall; unlocked the door; and cautiously entered the front room. I could see Grandpa clearly. He was bathed in a late-afternoon shaft of brilliant spring sunlight, wide-awake and conversing with the forever-jovial man in the moon. He was telling the wise old fool one of his oft-repeated stories about his last few heroic days in Mexico before returning home for good. I moved over to the side of the room and motioned for Israel to approach the rocker. Israel then leaned over the old warrior, quizzically touched the burn marks on Grandpa's left arm above the restraining bandage, and said haltingly, "Happy birthday, Grandpa. I love you." Unfortunately, on this day of all days, Grandpa wasn't there in the room with us. He shouted repeatedly, "Death to Saint Patrick's Battalion! Hang Saint Patrick's Battalion!" I shuddered and reflexively tugged at Israel's arm, signaling it was time to go. As I slowly shut the door behind us, Grandpa stopped screaming just long enough to hear the indomitable heartbeat of his mahogany long case clock.

When we returned to the front yard, I was shocked to see preparations were almost complete. And then the disturbing discoveries came in waves—the colored troops had not only requisitioned our hay wagon, but our mare, our harness, our rope, and even one of Mama's burlap bags to carry out their contemptible deed. The soldiers had parked the wagon down under our special buckeye tree, yes, the very wagon Father was driving when he had the fatal accident. I heard one of the Feds ask another, "Ya count the coils when ya made the noose?" His companion nodded and answered, "Ya have to. Checked 'em twice—thirteen coils, no more, no less. That means bad luck for the wearer, but good luck for all of us." When I heard them say "thirteen," I remembered Burns's tale about the "good luck" mansion in Kentucky with the thirteen rooms, windows, and stairs, and concocted a bizarre theory that Israel's death with the thirteen coils was the mansion's way of avenging Burns's murder and the house's previously spotless reputation.

I looked over at Israel. I was convinced he had no idea what was about to happen. He was completely engaged in watching the soldiers' actions and listening to their banter. The captain approached Uncle Billy and said preparations were now complete and that Israel should perhaps visit with his mother for a few minutes. I walked down to the log house with Israel where I could hear Mama, Grandma, and Rachel inside, still trying to comfort an inconsolable mother about to lose her only child.

I couldn't muster the strength to enter, so I remained outside over by the well. Everything was silent until Captain Gray approached, knocked firmly on the door, and announced, "Israel, it's time to go." As the door swung open, I could see Bella down on her knees, hanging on to Israel's legs for dear life. And it was only after several agonizing attempts to free himself that he managed to gently break his mother's desperate grasp and follow the captain out to Father's wagon parked beneath the buckeye tree.

After conferring with Lieutenants Carrier and Burrows, Captain Gray asked Israel to jump up on the wagon bed. Sergeant Dixon was there waiting to pinion Israel's hands with thick cord and bind his feet with a leather strap. Following protocol, the captain asked Israel if he had anything to say. Israel didn't answer but oddly began singing a verse he'd learned from the county Negroes while trenching up at Fort Henry:

> Rise and shine,
> And give God the glory, glory.
> Rise and shine,
> And give God the glory, glory
> For this year of Jubilee.

When the lyric trailed off, Sergeant Dixon pulled the burlap sack down over Israel's head and ceremoniously positioned and tightened the thirteen coils under Israel's left ear. The rope between Israel's neck and the large buckeye branch was now sufficiently taut to produce a quick, pain-free death.

Sergeant Dixon hopped down and positioned himself so

the soldier sitting up on the wagon bench could clearly see his signals. The sergeant then slowly raised his arm and whipped it downward across his chest. The driver yanked the reins and whistled loudly. Our mare reacted immediately, lurching forward and ripping Israel out the back of the wagon bed. As he spun rapidly counterclockwise at the end of the rope, his body simultaneously moved in small circles from side to side under the thick buckeye branch, cruelly mimicking the hidden movements of the escapement, gears, and pendulum inside Grandpa's imposing clock.

I believe the captain's assessment was accurate. Israel died painlessly the moment his feet left the wagon bed. We were prepared for anguish and horror, but the jester refused to entertain the rabble. There was no gruesome display this time, no dancing at the end of the noose, no movement. No, not even the slightest twitch.

About five minutes after the hanging, a trooper climbed out onto the large branch and cut the rope as three others stood below and eased the body to the ground. Captain Gray approached Uncle Billy and me and said that given the circumstances, he'd return tomorrow to negotiate a fair price for the crossties. The Feds then quickly mounted, rode out to the main highway, and headed west toward Warfield, leaving their dazed, whirlwind victims standing silently amidst their repulsive handiwork.

After the cavalrymen disappeared beyond the first curve, Uncle Billy slipped the noose and burlap bag off Israel's head. Fortunately, for Bella's sake, Israel's eyes hadn't popped, and there were no deep rope cuts around the neck or chin. The

Feds had eased Israel down onto his right side with his knees slightly curled up toward his chest. When Uncle Billy repositioned Israel's body, stretching him out flat on his back, I spotted the same small object that I'd watched fall from Israel's relaxed grip as the soldiers lowered him down. I didn't say anything. I just picked it up and put it in my pocket. I vowed to return it to Bella when I had the chance.

Uncle Billy turned to me and said, "Thomas, run over to the Andersons'. Explain what happened. Ask them to do a favor—ride to Warfield for us and request a coffin of Mr. Patrick and a sermon from Pastor Reed."

By the time I returned from the Andersons', Bella, Mama, Grandma, and Rachel had joined Uncle Billy under the buckeye tree. Bella was sitting braced against the wide, gray trunk holding Israel in her arms, stroking his hair, and whispering, "Why, Jesus? Why?" This sacred assembly peering into the face of a young, sinewy man pressed against his mother, wouldn't include the customary Caspar, Melchior, and Balthazar bearing gifts. No, this wasn't the alpha, but the omega. This was Joseph, the honorable counselor, and the women who the gospels say watched from afar with their aloes and myrrh. This was another Pietà, another innocent whose fate was sealed by crossties.

I slowly approached Bella, stooped down, and returned the whittled, antique infant Jesus that Israel had clutched until the very end.

19

Pastor Reed stared at the flames well into the flickering night, trying to forge a sermon explaining the inexplicable. Yet I believe he did not make a final decision about his remarks until turning onto our entry road the following morning and discovering his prayers of support for his eldest daughter's family had already begun to be answered. A number of folk had arrived to help out, including Master Hudson and several neighbors whom the aging pastor could see hard at work on the hill preparing Israel's final home.

We expected as many attendees for Israel's service as we had had for Father's, and the protocol would be eerily the same. The neighbors, relatives, and church members began arriving hours before the eleven o'clock memorial, each bearing the usual abundance of delicacies sufficient to feed the five thousand. When the undertaker, Mr. Patrick, had finished preparing the body, we carried Israel's coffin into the dining room and placed it near the open windows to ensure a strong, continuous March ventilation.

As the funeral hour approached, mourners filed past Grandpa's locked ward into the dining room with some spilling over into the hallway and into Mama's narrow kitchen. Bella sat in the front row flanked by Mama and Grandma. As on other solemn occasions, Mr. Anderson provided a stirring invocation, and Master Hudson led us in several of Israel's favorite spirituals, including "Children, We Shall All Be Free," "Walk Together, Children," and "Children, Go Where I Send Thee."

Pastor Reed then moved over in front of the open casket and began his funeral sermon. "Our text today is from the second book of Samuel:

> And David's child was very sick. He therefore besought God for the child; and David fasted, and lay all night upon the earth. And the elders of his house arose, and went to him, to raise him up from the earth; but he would not, neither did he eat bread with them. And it came to pass on the seventh day that the child died.
>
> And the servants of David feared to tell him; for they said, behold, while the child was yet alive, we spoke unto him, and he would not hearken unto our voice; how will he then vex himself, if we tell him that the child is dead? But when David saw that his servants whispered, he perceived the child was dead; therefore he asked them. And they confirmed that indeed his son was dead.
>
> Then David arose from the earth, washed, anointed himself, changed his apparel, came into the house of the Lord, and worshipped; then he came to his own house; and when he

required, they set bread before him, and he did eat. Then said his servants unto him, what thing is this that thou hast done? Thou didst fast and weep for the child, while he was alive; but when the child was dead, thou didst rise and eat bread.

And he said, while the child was yet alive, I fasted and wept; for I said, who can tell whether God will be gracious to me that the child may live? But now that he is dead, why should I fast? Can I bring him back again? No. I shall go to him, but he shall not return to me.

After finishing the hopeful passage, the good pastor closed his Bible, gazed into the mourners' eyes, and spoke directly from the heart. "This sacred text provides two important lessons. The first, that the Lord requires us to be resilient, to carry on even after suffering the most horrific of losses. And the second lesson, that we will only be away from our loved ones for a short time. While they'll never return to us here, we'll go meet them soon in the Promised Land.

"A few minutes ago we sang several spirituals dear to Israel's heart. One of them in particular, 'Walk Together, Children,' emphasizes those important lessons we find in the second book of Samuel. Please refer to your handout now and read along with me:

Walk together children.

Don't you get weary.

Sing together children.

Mourn but never tire.

There'll be a great camp meeting in the
Promised Land.

"To conclude our service this morning, I'm going to ask Master Hudson to lead us in reprising 'Walk Together, Children.' It will serve as Israel's final message to all of us here today." And then as was his custom at the close of every sermon, Pastor Reed recited a passage from Saint Paul's letter to the Philippians: "Finally, brethren, whatsoever things are true, whatsoever things are honest, whatsoever things are just, whatsoever things are pure, whatsoever things are lovely, whatsoever things are of good report; if there be any virtue, and if there be any praise, think on these things."

As the mourners filed out to escort us to the burial plot, Bella, Mama, Grandma, Uncle Billy, Rachel, and I began reliving the final moments of Father's funeral not so very long ago—the wrenching final farewell . . . the resounding, baritone benediction . . . the hollow thuds securing the pine coffin . . . the respectful, caring pallbearers . . . the seldom used, ceremonial funeral door . . . the fifty-yard path near the budding lilacs . . . and finally the familiar evergreen cemetery gate.

After offering the final gravesite prayer, Pastor Reed led the mourners back to the house for a muted, albeit bountiful feast for kings. Mr. Anderson, Uncle Billy, and I stayed behind to oversee the final re-grading of the burial mound. When the work was finished, Mr. Anderson presented us with a hand-made wooden cross for Israel's grave. He had thoughtfully and profoundly inscribed a handwritten message along the transverse beam: ISRAEL HAS CROSSED OVER TO THE PROMISED LAND.

We planted the temporary marker in the fresh, moist clay at the head of the plot and offered up a brief, simple prayer asking God to spare Israel's soul. Uncle Billy thanked Mr. Anderson and said he'd suggest Bella chisel this eloquent epitaph into Israel's permanent marker. And after one more silent prayer, we exited the cemetery, leaving Israel in the constant care of our other family already waiting patiently there on the western hill.

As we neared the farmhouse, a thick, billowy cloud gradually obstructed the early spring sunlight, casting a distinct charcoal shadow diagonally across the farm. We were all so struck by this spontaneous, dramatic effect that we tracked the dark line's progress from our stand of timber, out to the main road, and then over a pack of bluecoats rounding Warfield curve.

We watched the cavalrymen halt at the front gate, peer in at the large crowd amassed on the front lawn, and then turn around and head back toward Warfield. As they rode away, the Feds respectfully raised their hats as if to say, "We will not intrude with our talk of business." They would return another day to negotiate a fair price for railroad ties.

Uncle Billy and Mr. Anderson split off toward the dining room, and I continued on around back to the worn stone step, which had become a hermitage during difficult times. Israel's sanctioned murder had revived my youthful speculation on whether childlike adults such as Israel were allowed into heaven. Over the years I'd heard ministers dance about the scriptures without achieving certitude, at least not to my mind. They quote Saint Matthew: "Then were there brought unto him little children, that he should put his hands on them, and pray; and the disciples rebuked Him. But Jesus said, 'Suffer little children, and forbid them not to come unto me; for of such is the kingdom of heaven.' And he laid his hands on them and departed thence."

I have read of scholars who interpret the passage as proof children go to heaven because as adults with accountability, we must become as children again—innocent, pure, and trusting, like Israel. And then again, theologians contend Psalm 24 proves dying children go to heaven: "Who shall ascend into the hill of the Lord? Or who shall stand in his holy place? He that hath clean hands and a pure heart; who hath not lifted up his soul unto vanity, nor sworn deceitfully." The psalmist's depiction of who may enter heaven, they say, essentially describes a childlike state.

These arguments have always seemed to me to sidestep the issue. But Pastor Reed's memorial text that day from II Samuel came close to resolving my youthful uncertainty about innocents in heaven. "But now he is dead, wherefore should I fast? Can I bring him back again? No. I shall go to him, but he shall not return to me." David believed he'd see his young son in heaven.

With this new clarity, I felt I was now living up to Saint Paul's message: "When I was a child, I spake as a child, I understood as a child, I thought as a child; but when I became a man, I put away childish things." It meant closure to an open question from my youth, making room for headier ideas. You see, Master Hudson, Beth, and I were quickly moving beyond these youthful concerns to far more dangerous, probing examinations involving divine motive, suffering, and even the indefensible massacre of innocents.

After Israel's funeral the residents of the farm spent the rest of the year laboring and healing. We worked from sunrise to sunset six days a week planting, weeding, and harvesting; caring for the animals and repairing fences; cutting our timber; and making crossties for the Feds' new railroad tracks. The hard work helped us keep our minds off the horrific events of the past February and March. Staying busy and the passage of time were like the curative sap that had already begun sealing the deep gash in the buckeye branch where the Feds had tied our rope.

The unfortunate irony was that I saw more of Master Hudson that year than ever before, but we spent far less time together pursuing our quest for "Why?" The Confederate Burns haunted us from the hill overlooking Anderson's road, and his legacy grew by one during the next Christmas season, when our Rachel gave birth to a healthy son, whom she named Joseph.

The following spring right at planting season, I was in the barnyard oiling harnesses when I heard a soft whistle over by the side gate. It was Robert, whom we hadn't seen for well over a year. We gave each other a firm hug, and I held him out at arm's length to get a good, long look at my prodigal brother. He had aged; and the sparkle in his eyes had been replaced with worry and despair. His uniform was quite muddy and his bright red hair and beard unkempt. I asked him how he was doing, and he responded with a disjointed admonition that I couldn't repeat to anyone what he was going to tell me this afternoon.

I escorted him over to the stalls, where we unsaddled and fed his mare. I asked him if he was hungry, and he said he had already taken a ration. Since it was still fairly early in the day and he really wanted to talk privately, I suggested we go out through the side gate and up along the forest path, where we could find a spot to sit down and speak at length without interruption.

As we moved along the back path, I reported all that had happened here, while he was away: Burns's arrival, Parker's death and burial, cutting timber to make crossties, the Feds' inquisition, Israel's massacre, and the birth of a new nephew, Joseph. Any other time these revelations would have launched him into an exhaustive battery of increasingly specific questions. But he didn't engage at all that day. He just ambled along, staring at the ground directly in front of him.

I stopped midsentence and pointed to a ledge far enough off the path to ensure privacy. Robert sat down, removed the dog-eared, leather notebook from his left breast pocket, flipped through the extensive entries, and began describing the last harrowing eighteen months.

"To be honest with you, Thomas, it'd take me days to report the many raids we conducted over the past year and a half: Burnt Bridge, Rising Sun, Hatchie Bottom, Wood Springs, the Iron Works, Nonconah Creek, Island 10, Double Bridge, Galloway Switch. No, sir, no one can say Robert's Raiders didn't take it to the Feds—ripping down telegraph lines, burning supplies, picking their troops off one at a time. . . .

"But, brother, all that seems so distant now, so long ago, so small compared to what's happened in the past few days. . . . But I have to back up a bit to set the stage for the whole story, and suffice it to say, during that entire period of raids and skirmishes, I was passing notes back and forth with other guerrilla commanders and General Forrest's overall command.

"But late last month General Forrest ordered a face-to-face meeting of all his west Tennessee cavalry leaders. We were to meet up on the Kentucky-Tennessee border near Union City. I arrived late Saturday morning at General Forrest's bivouac and spent a couple of hours before the meeting exchanging stories with other unit commanders whom I'd rarely seen over the past year. Well, exactly at the designated hour of three, General Forrest returned from a reconnoitering across the state line. The general dismounted, vigorously shook our hands, and invited all of us into his large headquarters tent.

"He first thanked us for serving and then explained why he'd called a face-to-face meetin'. He said ever since returning to western Tennessee earlier this month he'd been angered by well-authenticated instances, repeatedly brought to his notice, of 'rapine and atrocious outrage upon noncombatants by the garrison at Fort Pillow.' He said a delegation from Jackson had even petitioned him to do something about the Fed outlaws."

I broke in to let Robert know we'd heard similar stories. "Uncle Billy's talked about it at dinner. Nothing happening around here, mind ya, but in places west of Warfield. Uncle

Billy got wind of it last time he was in town. Folks really upset having soldiers harassing citizens, especially if, like they say, colored troops are causing much of the trouble."

"Well, according to the general, y'all were hearing it about right. He told us the garrison's force strength was a battalion of whites, commanded by a Tennessean, Major Bradford, and a Negro battalion under a Major Booth, who also commanded the fort. The general said many of Bradford's men were deserters from the Confederate army and the rest 'entertained a malignant hatred toward our soldiers, families, and friends.' He explained that under the guise of searching the west Tennessee territory for weapons and rebel soldiers, Bradford and his outlaws had 'robbed our citizens of their cattle, horses, mules, clothes, beds, plates, money, and anything else of value; and to top it all off, the bluecoats had publicly called the wives and daughters of southern soldiers disgusting, obscene epithets.' General Forrest added he had learned that even the families of many of his own men had been 'grievously wronged, despoiled, and insulted.'

"He then ended our meeting with an order to reconvene with all our troops just west of Jackson at nine o'clock sharp on the ninth—that's right, just last week. The general said we were going to employ our combined forces in the 'summary suppression of the evil and grievances.' We were going to attack and capture this Fort Pillow some forty miles north of Memphis."

Robert paused to check his notes and then continued: "Well, by April 10, all our forces had arrived near Jackson. The battle plans were drafted and our horsemen well on their way westward. And by eight o'clock on the morning of the twelfth, our sharpshooters had begun firing down on the bluebellies from the hills overlooking the compound. About an hour or so later, McCullough's men captured two rows of abandoned barracks just south of the fort, which the Feds had missed burning before retreating inside the walls. And don't ya know, our boys used these cabins as shields and fired round after round directly into the Fed positions. Afterwards, the sharpshooters smiled while telling us it was just way too easy—like shooting fish in a barrel."

"What were ya doing while all this was going on?" I asked.

For the first time all afternoon, Robert managed a faint smile while allowing the suspense to build. "Sitting in my saddle . . . watching from a hilltop."

"Why'd ya crack a smile just now? There's more to it. Tell me. What were ya doing?"

"You're not asking the right question."

"Well, what is it then?"

"Who was watching with ya?"

"Okay then, brother, who was there watching with ya?"

Robert replied wistfully, "Well, there was General Forrest, his chief of staff, and . . . and my second in command."

"Amazing, sitting there with General Forrest! . . . What is it they call him? The Wizard?"

"The Wizard of the Saddle."

"Could ya really see much from up there?"

"For sure. We had good field binoculars, but ya really didn't need 'em. The fighting wasn't that far off. And ya won't believe it but the general had three horses shot right out from under him, two of 'em killed outright and a third wounded. I'll never know how the Feds missed my mare and me, being right there beside him. And, brother, ya never saw greater acts of courage. When the horses collapsed, the general'd just get up, dust himself off, and order up another mount. Proudest day of my life, Thomas, being right there beside him as he barked out the orders, helping him climb back up in the saddle on his new mounts. . . . And then, in the blink of an eye, it all turns to shit, the same goddamn day." Robert's face darkened as he spoke. "It all turns to shit, going from pride and living a dream to shame and hoping no one ever learns I was ever anywhere near Fort Pillow. All this happening in minutes, learning in an instant that what ya been up to for going on four years in the name of honor is wasted—isn't what ya think it was. Isn't real."

"What happened, brother?" I asked. I had not seen such a turn in him since we were boys. "What made ya change your mind so suddenly about the war?"

"I'm getting ahead of myself, Thomas. I wanna tell you the whole story, unburden myself. I have to tell ya everything. I don't dare trust anyone else with knowing what I know."

"Go on then, Robert. Say what ya have to say. I'll keep quiet and just listen."

Robert began flipping through his notebook again. After finding the passage he was looking for, he took a deep breath and continued his account of Forrest's raid on Fort Pillow: "When the last of our commanders had reported in, sometime early in the afternoon, General Forrest pulled some maps from his saddlebag, pored over 'em, and calmly declared to me and the chief of staff, 'Boys, we got 'em now. Ya see here? We got 'em blocked on three sides and their backsides are rubbin' up again' the Mississippi River. No chance of hiding now. No chance of running. . . . Bradford and Booth have to know this. So, Robert, I want ya to ride down to the fort, white flag and all. Tell the majors we're expecting a surrender—unconditional—otherwise, they'll be hearing from all of us real soon.'

"Next thing I know, I'm riding down the hillside toward the fort waving a piece of white muslin on a stick. As I neared the fort, all the shooting stopped. The Feds opened the front gate, took me to a bunker serving as their command post, spoke with both Bradford and Booth. Polite tension. They were all business, and after listening to the general's message, they stepped aside to talk and returned with a request for an additional hour to consider General Forrest's demands. Well, as I rode back I was wondering how the general would react to their delaying. But didn't take long to find out. He gritted his teeth and snarled, 'Ya tell 'em straight up, they have twenty minutes, and if they don't accept our terms, then I can't be held responsible for the consequences if we're obliged to storm the place.'

"And back I went with my muslin flying. Delivered the message and then waited at the gate for the Fed response. About fifteen minutes later a colored trooper handed me a folded note, which I immediately carried to General Forrest, who had by now dismounted and found a perch on an outcropping at the edge of the bluff. Not being privy to the contents, I remained in the saddle watchin' for his reaction. At first he didn't say anything. He just kept sitting there staring at the note. But after the longest minute in my life, he exploded. Crushed the Fed response in his right hand and boomed out to his chief of staff, 'Ready the force for an immediate, simultaneous attack! . . . Deploy a semicircle stretching from one end of the hillside to the other! When I give the order, direct a crescent of fire down on 'em! We'll teach these bluebellies our patience has limits! Is that clear, sir?'

"'All clear, General!' And with that the chief of staff saluted and raced off to deliver the order.

"When I started peeling away to let my boys know what was going on, the general raised his gloved hand and motioned for me to stop. 'Ride back there to your men, Robert, but tell 'em I'm holding 'em in reserve for now. Then get your tail back up here! I wanna keep ya close by, just in case things start getting out o' hand.' So I immediately flew down the hill to inform my Raiders; charged back up the rise; and got back up to the hilltop just as the general ordered the bugler to sound out the signal to attack!"

When Robert paused again to review his notes, I broke my promise. I couldn't hold back any longer. "Sounds like you boys were about to lower the boom," I said. "Give 'em what they deserved."

He looked up from his journal and gazed into my eyes. I immediately sensed I'd upset him. I could see the pain. And as I soon learned, it was not the interruption per se but the comment, the thought itself, that had cut him to the quick. He shook his head and whispered, "No one on earth, brother— Fed or no Fed—deserved what they got that day. Just wait. You'll see. . . ."

He paused to find the thread and then continued his narrative: "Our sharpshooters opened with a blistering fusillade. The Feds were effectively pinned down and couldn't offer much resistance. The bugler continued sounding the charge; and next our main forces, lookin' like some giant gray wave rolling off the hillside, topped their parapets and spilled over into the fort. And I wanna tell ya, the Feds—both black and white—immediately turned tail and started running down a steep embankment toward the Mississippi. Guess they were thinking a Fed gunboat patrollin' off shore there was gonna help 'em somehow. . . . But give 'em their due, some of their riflemen stopped, turned around, and fired at our boys in hot pursuit. And then it was back to running again, racing toward the trap we'd set for 'em at the riverbank. Ran right into the meat grinder. Came under heavy close-range fire from Anderson's men to their south. So the Feds turned north and came under an even more deadly crossfire from Barteau's troops waiting at the mouth of the Coal Creek ravine. No other way to describe it. It was a meat grinder, chewing 'em up and spitting 'em out.

"Seeing their flag was still waving over the fort, General Forrest ordered me to fetch my men and follow him down off the bluffs. It was strange, Thomas, ya could hear every boom and rifle shot up where we were. But once we'd reached the flatland below, you'd hear a *pop . . . pop . . . pop* once in a while. Otherwise, all you'd hear was our hoofbeats sploshing in the swampy floodplain outside the front gate. But one thing's for sure: no one was firing at us, no one from inside the fort. And it wasn't long till we found out why. We rode into an abandoned garrison, ne'er a soul inside."

"With no one to fight or round up, what y'all do then?" I asked.

"I'll tell ya the first thing the general did. He rode over to the officer barracks on his fourth horse of the day and respectfully lowered that huge flag ya could see waving in the river breeze from atop the bluffs. He then ordered me to ride down where our boys were fighting along the riverbank, talk to our officers behind the lines to see if a cease-fire was in order."

"Ya take anyone with ya?"

"Coupla fellas who'd been with me from the start—boys I could trust to do as directed and keep their noses clean. Ya see, the general'd given me strict orders to stay back and out of the fighting. So my lieutenants and I headed down toward the beach where the battle continued raging. Wasn't what we expected, though. There was shooting all right, but also a helluva lot of brutal hand-to-hand fighting. Feds and Rebs slashing away at each other's throats with bayonets, splitting heads wide open with their rifle butts, bloodcurdling screams drowning out the rifle volleys just up—"

Robert stopped suddenly, stared at the partially obscured path below, and began shaking his head. It was as if his mind had been racing along ahead of his words; that it had reached a gut-wrenching spot in the narrative just seconds before his words got there; and that his emotions just shut the account down midsentence. His hand holding the notebook began trembling. I slid over from my side of the ledge and put my arm around his shoulder. "It's okay if ya wanna stop now. I understand, Robert. Perhaps you'll wanna go on later."

He shook his head. "No, no. It hurts. It really hurts. But the pain'll help with the cleansing, help me get my mind right again. Scoot back on over there now and I'll go on."

"Ya sure?"

"Sure, brother. Scoot on over now."

Robert took several deep breaths and then doggedly continued his story. "I wanna tell ya, Thomas, with all that throat slashing and head splitting going on, I didn't think the slaughter could get any worse. But it wasn't long until the fighting really got outta hand—ugliest I'd ever seen. In an instant, our boys pissed away a heroic victory. . . . Right before my eyes, saw Negro troops dropping their rifles and running up to our men. Fell to their knees, stretched their arms to the heavens, and begged our troops, 'Have mercy, have mercy on us.' Our boys ordered 'em to their feet, waved their rifles at 'em. I thought to scare 'em, give 'em something to remember before picking a fight with us again. But no, Thomas, our boys opened up on 'em. Shot 'em all right where they stood praying for mercy."

"Maybe what ya saw was isolated. Ya know, just a small number of bad apples losing control."

"Crossed my mind, brother, but after all the fighting stopped, my lieutenants and I walked the battlefield from one end to the other. Found a lot of Negro soldiers shot through the temple at close range. Ya could see the powder around the holes in their heads. And that's not the half of it. Saw other Negro troops who had been driven into the cabins surrounding the fort and burned alive. . . . The way it looked to me, it had to be deliberate. And to top it all off, during the night after the battle, I kept hearing random gunshots coming from the pen where we were holding the rest of the prisoners of the Sixth Heavy and the Second Light Artillery.

"As we walked along viewing the carnage, neither of my lieutenants uttered a single word. They were as much in shock as I was. I could see it in their eyes—the pain, the disappointment. They'd not only seen what I'd seen but had read it the same way. And reliving the nightmare over and over again, none of us slept that night. While pacing outside the fort's barracks not too long before dawn, I could see my lieutenants sitting in there at a table sharing corn liquor, vainly trying to erase the memories of that awful day."

"How long did ya stay at the fort?"

"Wanted to get out of there as soon as possible, limit the damage to my Raiders. So the following morning I moved 'em east toward Jackson and then on over to Grave's Bend on the Duck River south of Warfield. That's where I left 'em to ride over here. I knew I had to talk to someone and you were the first person came to mind, brother. I knew you'd listen. I knew you'd understand. . . .

"Ya see, this wasn't what I signed on for so long ago now. This Fort Pillow was not Grandpa scaling the wall. Where was the heroism? The glory? The honor? Or the majesty in all the slaughtering? No other way to put it. It was evil fighting evil. And then what about my hero, General Forrest? The question here shouldn't be 'Did anyone inform him what was going on outside the fort?' No, the more severe, cutting questions would be, 'Why didn't he know what was happening?' and 'Why didn't he stop the killing?' I'll never know for sure if the general actually knew of the atrocities or not, but I do know as the leader of the overall attack on the fort, he should've known and should've halted it immediately.

"I could now say, 'Enough is enough; this is not who I am or what I believe.' This was the opposite of the heroic deeds Grandpa had described time and again. But how could I quit now? I feel a strong affinity to my men. They've sacrificed so much for our cause and for me personally. How could I live with myself walking away from these brave horsemen? The guilt would be even stronger than what I'm feeling now having just witnessed such unspeakable malice and cruelty."

Robert's voice trailed off into thought as he slipped the small leather notebook back into his breast pocket next to Mama's rosewood cross. I moved back over beside him and stretched my right arm around his back and patted him con-solingly. I needed to let him know that despite his display of vulnerability, he was still my beloved older brother and we'd fight through his horrifying hell together.

Several silent minutes passed, and then Robert looked over and flashed a faint smile. "We'd better get up to the farmhouse. I can only stay the night. Gotta get back to my Raiders."

When we entered the kitchen, Mama spontaneously screamed and cried. She wiped her greasy hands on her long yellow apron and ran over to give her eldest child a warm embrace. She sensed something was sadly different about Robert this time. But as Mama always did with us children, she immediately began rationalizing her initial negative impression. Robert was just tired. There wasn't anything here that sound sleep and a little of her home cooking couldn't fix.

Robert's brief stay this time was similar to his other visits. Mama did indeed prepare a great dinner in his honor, and he faithfully described his heroic exploits from Burnt Bridge to Rising Sun and then on to Galloway Switch. But he ended his personal report this time at Jackson, only days before the inexcusable incident at Fort Pillow.

There was, however, one substantive difference about Robert's visit this time. Despite doing most of the talking about his latest exploits, he was no longer the center of attention. He had abdicated the title to his infant nephew, Joseph, who always smiled and never knew a stranger. As Robert spoke and Rachel looked on with proud approval, our youngest, giggling member was passed gracefully and swiftly around the dining room table, stopping occasionally and briefly to bounce on an accommodating knee.

The following morning, I escorted Robert down to the barnyard to saddle his mare. I didn't know what had brought it about—whether it was just having been home among loved ones, or telling me about Fort Pillow, or getting sound, uninterrupted sleep, or the prospect of returning to his troops, or even closely cuddling his affectionate nephew—but Robert's old spirit appeared to have been restored. I actually heard him whistling one of Grandpa's old military tunes while enjoying a warm bath in the washhouse before breakfast.

After fetching his horse, Robert and I exited the barnyard through the side gate and walked up the path running behind the smokehouse. He and I met the family there again; and we were still the same number of people as before, but this time one child had incomprehensibly been substituted for another.

We said our sincere good-byes and then watched our Robert slowly ascend the rugged switchback trail that would take him back to his admiring men at Grave's Bend just miles beyond Slaughter Hill.

After Robert vanished in the greening thicket, Uncle Billy, Mama, Grandma, and Bella chose to congregate in the path to review Robert's stay. As usual, Mama was the chief instigator and driver of the topics for their ad hoc meeting. "How did he look to you?" "Ya think he enjoyed his meals?" "Did he get enough to eat?" "Wasn't it great seeing how he took to the baby?" "Wonder what he thought about all that'd happened around here?" And when Rachel sensed where the conversation was headed, she excused herself and moved away, cradling Joseph in her arms. I knew where she was headed—going on out the path to spend time with the boy's mysterious father and perhaps thank him for the continuous joy their son had brought into her life.

I then turned to the west, walked out to our burial ground, and draped my arms across the sturdy cemetery gate. As I peered in at Israel's small marble marker, the tapered headstone became the fulcrum for another balance scale. First, the colored troops had promoted Israel's death and callously performed his execution. But the dreaded thumb capriciously appeared on the beam and began sliding away from them. And on the first anniversary of their massacre of an innocent, avenging rebels screamed near Memphis, "Kill the last damn one of 'em colored troops," and the Confederates assiduously set about their sanctioned mission, blasting and immolating their pleading Negro petitioners.

20

EVERY HAMLET, VILLAGE, and town along the seventy-eight-mile stretch from Nashville to the Tennessee River was abuzz with the prospects of seeing the influential gentlemen who would be passing through that very day. Even Uncle Billy, Mama, and I had gotten caught up in the commotion and planned on driving to Warfield for the grand ceremonies. In his role as teacher, Master Hudson had made a special request of Uncle Billy to transport the students from Sugar Grove School to this historic spectacle, the likes of which none of these young folks had ever witnessed before and most likely would never have a chance to see again.

The official opening of the Nashville & Northwestern Railroad had finally arrived, and there would be a special ceremony in Warfield that afternoon replete with dignitaries, speeches, soldiers, and military bands. So all of us from the farm and Master Hudson's school piled into the wagons and headed west for this homegrown entertainment.

When we arrived at the depot early in the afternoon, the crowd had already grown to over five hundred, including most of Warfield's citizenry and many of the inhabitants of the small surrounding communities. The town fathers had ordered copious amounts of bunting for the large buildings, the depot, and the freshly erected speakers' platform standing in an open field near the tracks. We quickly hitched the wagons and rushed to a vantage point between the rails and the stairs leading up to the colorfully decorated platform. Uncle Billy said we would all have a very good view of the engine pulling into the station and also an up-close look at the famous politicians passing by to climb the steps to the rostrum.

The telegraph wires between Nashville and Warfield must have been coordinating the activities. At precisely fifteen minutes of two, Federal drummers rapped rhythmically on the rims of their polished drums and ushered four horse-drawn caissons and cannon from Captain Terry's First Kansas Battery onto the large field immediately to our left. Exactly fifteen minutes after that, we heard the first throaty blasts from the unseen engine's whistle, and then we spied the front of the imposing locomotive rounding the gentle curve a quarter mile up from the depot.

Everything about the engine was big—the square reflective headlamp, the pointed cowcatcher, the curved "wagon top" boiler, the four bright-red driving wheels, the churning silver coupling rods, and the tall Radley and Hunter balloon stack belching massive quantities of gray smoke up into the air above the slowing train. A husky uniformed guard sat in a small iron cage atop the cowcatcher between a pair of fluttering Federal flags.

The engineer pulled back on the Johnson bar, threw the locomotive into reverse, and stopped the engine perfectly just yards beyond the depot platform. After setting the handbrake on the tender, the fireman climbed up onto the brimming mound of hardwood to get a better view of the impending ceremony. The conductor jumped down from one of the passenger cars and began positioning sets of wooden stairs below the coach steps to ease the dignitaries' exit from the train.

As the locomotive quieted, we could hear the brass band discoursing patriotic and enlivening airs. A Federal officer, Captain Phillips, climbed down from the train and shouted orders for his troops to join him on the platform. Captain Phillips's storied Company C of the Tenth Tennessee Infantry was directly responsible for security that day on the ceremonial train, around the depot, and in the open field at the speakers' platform.

Captain Terry then signaled a salute, and the four cannon fired sequentially three times each, engulfing half the audience in thick black smoke because of an unruly wind. Captain Phillips waved his right arm with a flourish, and the buglers attached to his regiment struck up a stately fanfare announcing the appearance of Nashville's influential gentlemen.

And then one after another the smiling dignitaries stepped down from the train, shook numerous hands lining the path to the speakers' platform, and gestured broadly as they mounted the stairs to the rostrum far above the friendly, admiring crowd. Years later, many of us still remember attending the legendary gathering, but none of us could honestly recall one memorable line from any of the speeches by Governor Andrew Johnson, Comptroller Joseph S. Fowler, or His Honor the Mayor of Nashville, John Hugh Smith. But I must admit I was proud to tell everyone from that day on that His Excellency the Governor looked directly into my eyes, smiled, and vigorously shook my hand as he made his way to the speakers' platform.

While standing amidst the pageantry on that cloudless spring afternoon, little did we know or understand the darker implications of the mechanical beast's invasion into our western wilderness. While the Feds viewed their laden gondolas and boxcars as vital shipments supplying a strategic military hub in Nashville, the rebels viewed the overflowing trains, the lengthy railway bridges, and the elaborate eighty-foot-tall wooden trestles as rich potential targets for ongoing, deadly guerrilla attacks.

Almost as soon as the festivities ended, the Confederate assaults began. These early rebel strikes were all very similar. If the guerrillas were not burning the wooden bridges or trestles, they were raiding the trains themselves. The marauders would capture Union track repairers and force them to draw the spikes from the crossties to make the rails loose. The rebels would then lie in wait in the thick bramble on the sides of the track bed. The first train in the morning may pass through without derailing but would be subject to repeated rounds of bullets, which occasionally severely wounded or killed a brakeman, fireman, or conductor dreaming on one of the narrow bunk beds in the caboose.

The second train was usually not as fortunate as the first. The locomotive would hit the loosened track, derail, and slide over on its side along the track bed. The guerrillas would swarm onto the train and strip everyone of whatever watches, money, or other valuables they were carrying that day. The insurgents would then axe holes in the engine boilers and ignite the brimming boxcars and flatcars loaded with iron arriving from the Pittsburgh mills.

And then a third train would approach, loaded with sawed timber from a nearby mill. The marauders would ride up to the train and begin pumping bullets into the engine, tender, and boxcars. All the Federal hands on board would instinctively jump from the slow-moving train, attempting to save their lives and possessions; but they would usually end up in the grasp of their wily attackers watching the thousands of cords of wood going up in smoke. And to conclude a successful day, the rebels might also burn a section foreman's house, the log dwellings of Negro laborers, and thousands of cords of wood piled up at various railway sections along the route back to their outlaw camp.

About a month following the festive ceremony, I witnessed one of these lightning raids firsthand, while playing hooky from school all week to help weed the family garden. I was alone, as Uncle Billy was in the far western field tending to the cattle. It was about eleven o'clock on a Friday morning. First, I heard the sharp whistle blasts and then the loud clanging of the engine bell. But something was different. I sensed the locomotive was slowing, and then I heard the loud screeching of the driving wheels spinning into an emergency reverse. As the engine sounds faded, the gunshots began. *Pop, pop, pop,* silence, echo, *pop, pop,* silence, echo, echo, *pop, pop;* and then the shouting began. I scrambled over to the garden fence, where I hoped to find cover and perhaps still see what was going on.

I spotted the engine sitting sideways across the tracks, still firing large volumes of thick smoke out of its balloon stack.

At first, I didn't see anyone, but then I discovered three men running across the highway onto our property. The rifle and pistol shots rang out again. The three men stopped, squeezed off several rounds from their Navy Colts, and then resumed running across our hayfield between Anderson's road and Sugar Grove School.

When the gunfire stopped, I saw two men with rifles run out from between the boxcars, cross the highway, and crawl under the split-rail fence onto our property. The first three men turned, began shooting again at their pursuers, and then split up, with one of the rebels running toward our woods and the other two headed straight for the Sugar Grove School. I was shocked; I thought the two Confederates would run on into the woods beyond the schoolhouse. But they climbed the steps and went inside. The two Federal guards continued advancing cautiously through the open field toward the building, somewhat relieved, I'm sure, that there were no windows on the highway side allowing the rebels to track their moves or take some long-distance shots at them.

When the bluecoats opened fire again, shooting randomly into the side of the frame building, I realized they didn't know they were firing into a schoolhouse. There were no signs on the property or on the building itself announcing "Sugar Grove School." Once I understood what the Feds didn't know, my heart began racing as I catalogued all the bad things that could now go wrong. In my mind's eye, I could see poor Master Hudson inside the school trying to calm the twenty or so children who must have been horrified at having fallen into the hands of outlaws and hearing rifle shots whizzing past their heads and crashing into the far wall.

But as my anxiety grew, I heard the welcome hoofbeats of Federal cavalry troops riding up the highway. They passed my location and headed on up toward the wreckage as one of the two Federal pursuers left his partner in the field and began chasing the horsemen. And it wasn't long then before I heard them riding back down the road toward my position. They hitched their horses to our fence, climbed over, and began advancing en masse toward the nondescript wooden structure.

When they got within fifteen yards of the building, the Fed troops fanned out into a semicircle partially ringing the exterior. I couldn't believe what was happening. I watched in horror as the officer raised his arm and waved the troops into deadly action. The fusillade ripped into the thin walls; I could see large, smoking chunks of wood flying off the surface. I jumped up from my lair and thought of screaming, but something told me to stop. I could immediately become a new target for the Feds' blind aggression. How then could I advance on their position to inform them the guerrillas had taken refuge in a one-room school? If they saw me running toward them, I would get shot on the spot. How could I save Master Hudson and the children, whom I knew he was bravely trying to protect inside?

As I crouched behind the garden fence trying to devise a workable plan, the hostage situation became even more threatening. I watched several Feds run over to our woods and return with armloads of thick, dry brush. The soldiers figured if they couldn't shoot their way in, they were going to burn the rebels out. They spread the old vines, sticks, and leaves beneath the building, which Grandpa had built on two-foot pillars. The officer gave the signal to light the scattered brush and motioned for the rest of his troops to assume prone firing positions with their rifles aimed directly at the closed door.

As the flames licked up the front wall, my thoughts oscillated between hope and despair. Perhaps Master Hudson and the children weren't in the schoolhouse just now; maybe they had taken one of their excursions down to Trace Creek to study the spring flowers emerging near its banks. And then the pendulum would swing the other way, and the burning structure would become Master Hudson's raging Peloponnesian pyre.

As I contemplated the possibilities, the door swung open violently and the rebels rushed down the steps with pistols firing from both hands. When they turned to their left and started running toward our woods, Federal sharpshooters dropped both guerrillas almost simultaneously. The cavalrymen then rose and moved very slowly toward the wounded or dead marauders. The school was now totally engulfed in flames, and a section of the roof closest to the highway collapsed, sending dense smoke and intense sparks flying up into the tall pine trees. And then my deepest fears were confirmed; the light easterly breeze carried the unmistakable stench of burning flesh. People had indeed died in this intentional conflagration.

As I reached for my handkerchief to cover my mouth and nose, I heard someone scrambling up behind me. It was Uncle Billy, who had heard the shots and come running from the distant field. I breathlessly explained what the Feds had done. I then suggested we stand up, wave my handkerchief, and shout that we meant no harm. Uncle Billy instinctively grabbed my arms to hold me down, fearing I might spontaneously begin acting on my recommendation.

He shook his head and whispered some pointed questions. "What if the Feds want to hide what really happened here? What if they want to blame their atrocity on the rebels? What if they find out you've seen everything? What if they just kill us to keep their brutality a secret? . . . No, Thomas, let's make a quick retreat through the garden, fetch the wagon, and ride back up the road toward 'em acting as if we didn't know anything about what was going on. It'll give us a good chance to find out about the children without getting ourselves shot in the process."

Since the young corn wasn't up enough to provide cover, we crawled half the length of the garden and then scurried the rest of the way in a crouched position. We then hurried down the rise to the wagon, climbed aboard, and headed east on the highway toward the wreckage and the smoldering schoolhouse. We stopped where the cavalrymen had tied their horses, climbed down, and hitched the wagon to the fence.

A Fed soldier standing in our field a relatively safe distance from the foul air spotted us and shouted out, "Ya boys have any business in the neighborhood?"

Uncle Billy didn't take the caustic bait and responded in his friendly, down-home manner. "We own the property here, sir. In fact, our patriarch built the schoolhouse up there. One of our seasonal helpers is the headmaster and everyone in these parts sends their children there to school."

When Uncle Billy mentioned the word "schoolhouse," the trooper turned to stare at the ruins and remained fixated on the smoldering shell all the while Uncle Billy was talking. As the soldier continued staring at the building, Uncle Billy asked, "Any idea how many mighta died in the fire up there?"

Without turning around, the soldier responded distractedly, "No. No way of tellin' yet. Still too hot to get in there and look around."

Uncle Billy made his pitch. "Since we own the property here, sir, ya be so kind as to escort us up to have a word with your officer in charge? . . . Perhaps help him sort through all this."

At first the Fed didn't respond, but finally he turned around and replied, "Guess it can't do no harm. Come on up and follow me."

"Much obliged, sir," Uncle Billy drawled.

As we approached the officer, Uncle Billy extended his hand and then in a relaxed manner explained who we were and why we had a strong interest in what had just happened up there at the schoolhouse. While visibly shaken to learn it was a schoolhouse he and his men had just torched, the senior officer, to his credit, described the incident pretty much as I'd witnessed it. He didn't try to cover up anyone's actions. He emphasized they had no idea it was a school. The building certainly didn't look like one, with only one small window on the right side. And besides, there was no signage anywhere declaring the structure a school. As Uncle Billy and the Fed continued their conversation, I became increasingly impatient. I still didn't know what had happened to Master Hudson and my twenty classmates who had ventured out to school that bright, cloudless morning with no expectation they were about to die.

Several more agonizing minutes passed before Uncle Billy finally broached trying to get inside to examine the ruins. The officer agreed we might as well get on with the ghastly task. I again placed the handkerchief over my face and passed through the scorched threshold into an unfamiliar, familiar setting. Quickly scanning the smoking debris, I didn't see anyone at first and thought perhaps Master Hudson and the children had in fact taken that spring excursion down to Trace Creek. But as I surveyed the room more carefully, I spotted a child's body in the southeast corner, which had been least affected by the fire. And then I discovered two . . . three . . . four other first-year students curled up as if asleep, untouched by the flames. Next to these dead innocents lay a partially charred adult, frozen in a final protective act of unconditional love. I shuddered at the sight. I stumbled out of the ruin, collapsed beneath a tree, and buried my head in my hands.

After regaining my composure, I muttered, "But where are Master Hudson and the rest of the children? Have they been completely consumed by the fire?" With still no answer to those questions, inspecting the debris had done little to ease my fear for their safety. It was only much later in the day I was relieved to learn Master Hudson and the remaining students had "luckily" taken ill the day before with a strong, highly contagious bout of the grippe. Only Master Hudson's assistant teacher, Miss Owings, and a few "lucky" students had escaped the virulent illness and dutifully marched to school that awful Friday morning.

Since the Feds had earlier requisitioned the only church building in Warfield, the town fathers offered the open lot next to the depot as an appropriate site for a countywide memorial for Miss Owings and her five young students. The Feds' central command for western Tennessee erected a large mess tent near the new speakers' platform to protect the grieving families in case of bad weather.

The subdued gathering sang "Savior, Like a Shepherd Lead Us," as close friends and relatives carried the six pine coffins up the center aisle and gently placed them on a hastily constructed dais at the front of the tent. Warfield's mayor offered a moving invocation. And after the attendees sang "Blessed Assurance," Pastor Reed stepped before the diminutive coffins and cleared his throat. "The text for today's memorial service is from II Kings:

> And Elisha said, what then is to be done for the Shunammite woman? And Gehazi answered, verily she hath no child, and her husband is old. And Elisha said, call her.
>
> And when he had called her, she stood in the door. And Elisha said, about this season, according to the time of life, thou shalt embrace a son. And she said, nay, my Lord, thou man of God, do not lie unto thine handmaid. And the woman conceived and bore a son at that season that Elisha had said unto her, according to the time of life. And when the child was grown, he said unto his father, my head, my head. And the

father said to a young lad, carry my son to his mother.

And when he had taken him, and brought him to his mother, he sat on her knees till noon, and then he died. . . . So she went and came unto the man of God at Mount Carmel. And it came to pass, when the man of God saw her afar off that he said to Gehazi, his servant, behold, yonder is that Shunammite. Run now, I pray thee, to meet her and say unto her, Is it well with thee? Is it well with thy husband? Is it well with the child? And she answered, It is well.

Pastor Reed surprised me that day with his choice of text for the funeral. I thought he would surely revert to the inspirational scripture from II Samuel, which he had used so effectively during Israel's memorial service. But in fact, he had chosen another fitting text, one that recommended the anguished parents accept God's inscrutable will and adopt the Shunammite woman's response to the sudden death of her only child. Though we are told "her soul is vexed within her," she still maintains that "It is well," that it is well with her soul.

After a final prayer, the pallbearers collected the six caskets from the low altar and carried the innocents outside, while the mournful congregants stood singing a familiar, prayerful hymn:

Abide with me; fast falls the eventide;

The darkness deepens; Lord with me abide.

When other helpers fail and comforts flee,

Help of the helpless, O abide with me.

They loaded the six coffins on to six flatbeds. And then, holding the Bible in his left hand and raising his right into the muted afternoon light, Pastor Reed offered a heartening benediction from St. Paul to the church at Philippi: "Rejoice in the Lord always: and again I say, rejoice. . . . Be careful for nothing; but in every thing by prayer and supplication with thanksgiving let your requests be made known unto God. And the peace of God, which passeth all understanding, shall keep your hearts and minds through Christ Jesus, our Lord." As Pastor Reed lowered his arm to his side and bowed his head, the six wagons began six journeys to six plots, where six families faced incalculable suffering in their own way.

Before the tragedy at Sugar Grove School, I privately estimated eighty percent of the civilians in the district had tired of war and would accept peace on almost any terms. Most of the merchants and farmers in our county appeared to be ready to return to their allegiance and to the restoration of civil authority under the old government. But the Fed's massacre of the innocents swung the pendulum back in the opposite direction, toward a renewed willingness to vigorously support the insurgency and avenge an unspeakable slaughter.

The Federal command for western Tennessee realized the damage that had been done to relations and to gaining wholesale acceptance for Reconstruction once the war was over. Attempting to defuse the situation and hopefully mollify the citizenry, the central command first held an inquest and then something of a show trial, which they opened to the public. The officer swore he and his troops didn't know they were torching a school and that they were only trying to send a clear message to the "hornet's nest" that guerrilla warfare wouldn't be tolerated around here. He sincerely apologized to the bereaved families and said he and his men would never intentionally harm a child under any circumstances.

The upshot of the military proceeding was the officer received a demotion in rank and was transferred along with his cavalry unit to Louisville, where they became foot guards patrolling arguably the safest city in the South. The Warfield citizenry perceived the sham military proceedings for what they really were, simply a ruse to divert attention from at best the Feds' gross incompetence or at worst their unfathomable cruelty.

Only days after the mock trial ended, the white colonel for the Thirteenth US Colored Infantry received orders to deploy his regiment along the Nashville & Northwestern Railroad from Johnsonville to five miles east of Warfield. They were replacing the dishonored cavalrymen and significantly upgrading Federal supply-line security. The first complement of Negro troops arrived along our track section within six weeks of the tragedy; and the culture of these new units appeared to be much more supportive of the citizenry in and around Warfield. In fact, two of the field officers, a white lieutenant colonel and a major, rode onto our property, introduced themselves to Uncle Billy and me, and politely asked permission to bivouac some of their Negro troops in our second forage field across the highway. And then it wasn't too long after the regiment's arrival that an impressive noncommissioned officer began frequenting our farm bearing gifts for the baby Jesus.

21

UNCLE BILLY CALLED a family meeting around the dining room table to discuss supporting Master Hudson until we could find a way to rebuild the Sugar Grove School. Mama had been looking forward to moving upstairs to Robert's room to give Rachel and Lil Joe a little more space, but she certainly agreed with the rest of us that Master Hudson needed all the help we could provide him, especially given his current mental and financial state. So Mama, Grandma, Rachel, Uncle Billy, and I unanimously agreed to invite Master Hudson to come live with us and work on the farm for at least the rest of spring and summer.

Since the schoolhouse burned, Master Hudson hadn't been the same. He continually haunted the ruins, walking among the burnt timbers and murmuring to himself. He only spoke once with me about the deep sense of guilt he felt having survived while Miss Owings and five of his students had perished. He described how hard it was falling asleep; and then even on those rare occasions when he managed to do so, he would hear bloodcurdling screams rising out of searing, hellish flames.

He said he couldn't concentrate on anything for any length of time and had lost all interest in being with people.

He added that every time he sees children now, his mind flashes back to the school, imagining the absolute horror Miss Owings and the students must have felt, crouched in the corner of the schoolhouse as the bullets ricocheted and the intense fire consumed the thin pine walls.

Several weeks after Master Hudson moved in, I was down in the barnyard patching holes in a leaky water trough. I heard a whistle and looked up from my stool. I could only see the crown, brim, and leather band of a rebel hat topped with an ice-blue plume. I jumped up and began moving toward the side gate. I could now see it looked a lot like Robert with his red hair and beard, but it wasn't my older brother. This cavalry officer was shorter and somewhat heavier than Robert. He was carrying a worn leather satchel draped over his left shoulder, sported two Colt revolvers wedged beneath a wide leather belt, and held the reins of two horses, one of which was Robert's latest mare.

As he passed through the gate, the cavalryman shook my hand firmly, looked directly into my eyes, and said he was truly sorry for what he had to report: Robert was dead.

Although my heart began racing, I didn't dare betray my manhood with any outward display of emotion. I had to appear stoic in this warrior's presence. I numbly led the officer over to the clean stalls, where we unsaddled the horses, watered them, and fed them fresh hay. I then guided him out the back gate and headed for the tree line far from the main road. We took a seat on the same outcropping Robert and I had used earlier to discuss Fort Pillow. With my insides shaking, I calmly asked the officer, "Tell me now, sir, how'd my brother die?"

The rebel removed his sweat-stained cavalry hat and replied, "We all noticed a big difference in Robert after we captured Fort Pillow. He started drinking a lot more. His spirits would change in an instant, swinging wildly from pickin' fights with a trooper or two to happily chasing every woman within twenty miles of Grave's Bend. He became totally unpredictable. Ya didn't know from one minute to the next. . . .

"Anyway, it was during one of these binges that he got into a serious fistfight with one of our junior officers; they were fightin' over a pretty young thing—a widow with two small children. She lives over near New Zion. Well, the fight pretty much ended in a draw with both men bleedin' from the mouth and nose. But the war between 'em raged on into the next week. Finally, matters, as they say, reached a tippin' point. The junior officer mocked Robert's manhood. So your brother felt he didn't have a choice now, felt he had to throw down the gauntlet, challengin' the young officer to a duel.

"So followin' the Code Duello, each man chose a second. This junior officer picked his brother-in-law, who also rode along with us, and your brother chose me to be his assistant. Following the code's requirements, the brother-in-law and I immediately tried easin' the situation, but neither man would have anything of it.

"Given the circumstances, his second and I agreed the 'meetin'' would take place at nine o'clock the followin' mornin' in a field about a hundred yards from our tents at Grave's Bend. We further agreed to load one round in each of the revolvers, position the men at twenty paces, and drop a handkerchief to signal the time to fire. We ended our negotiation with a pledge of secrecy. No one else in camp would know anything about the meetin' before it took place.

"Well, the next mornin' I woke Robert at seven and made sure he had a good breakfast. Your brother was sober and calm—focused—more like the old Robert. We eased out of camp a few minutes of nine and walked the hundred yards to the agreed-upon field. The junior officer showed up about five minutes later, and bein' honest with ya, he seemed sad and a tad bit nervous. Again, following the code, I approached the brother-in-law and asked him to inquire of the junior officer if there were any possibility of resolving the situation peacefully. The second returned in no more than a minute or two sayin' there couldn't be a resolution . . . and there'd be no backin' down.

"So we loaded a single bullet into each duelist's Colt, walked the men out to their assigned positions, and stepped back from the line of fire. I raised the designated handkerchief above my head, counted to three, and let the bright signal drop from my hand. Captain Robert raised his pistol well above the junior officer's head, fired his only round up into the tree branches, and then slowly lowered his empty revolver back to his side.

"The junior officer began shakin' noticeably. He raised his pistol parallel to the ground and squeezed the trigger. The bullet struck Robert in the left side of his chest. He pitched forward to his knees and collapsed facefirst into the soft mud. I ran over to Robert, turned him over, and cradled him in my arms. His eyelids were partially closed, and bright blood trickled out the left side of his mouth. He coughed and then whispered, 'Bury me here with my fallen brothers. Say nothin' of this to my grandpa. He'd be ashamed of . . . ' Your brother closed his eyes, heaved his chest, and faded away.

"Between their meetin' and now, I thought of several things I have to say. Robert didn't die leadin' a cavalry charge, but I wanted you to know that his Raiders believe your brother still died a hero. He didn't want to take the young man's life, so he clearly fired his only round up into the trees, and I'm suspectin' he hoped the junior officer would follow his own brave lead. But things didn't work out that way. Too much anger had built up in that boy's heart to see what your brother had just done for him.

"To his credit, the brother-in-law helped me carry Robert over to our provisional cemetery and stayed to help me shovel out a respectable grave. And then after searching Robert's pockets for possible effects, I buried him honorably there at Grave's Bend just as Robert had requested with his final breaths. Before ridin' over here today, I searched your brother's tent for any other belongings I thought you or your family might want to keep as mementos. I placed everything I thought valuable in my satchel here or in your brother's saddlebags."

The cavalryman opened his large leather satchel and carefully removed Robert's beloved stag hat decorated with a deep purple ostrich plume. The rebel next cautiously pulled out Grandpa's old bowie knife he'd used in the Mexican War, Robert's Navy revolvers, and his crocodile bandolier bristling with more than fifty rounds of ammunition. He then draped Robert's saddlebags across his knees and unlatched the brittle leather straps. He placed his hand inside the left pocket and slowly drew out Mama's polished rosewood cross. Next to the cross he placed the worn, dog-eared notebook that Robert had referenced so many times while regaling us with his heroic exploits well into the night. But the small leather diary was so different now. As the cavalryman explained, the fatal shot missed the rosewood cross, passed completely through the thin notebook, and penetrated Robert's chest just above the heart.

He then turned to the other leather pocket and pulled out a checkered muslin shirt, which had been loosely rolled to protect a valuable item. The rebel carefully unwrapped the shirt and held up the carved Balthazar that Bella had given Robert on one of his first visits home from the war. The walnut torso, the cattle-bone legs, and the horsehair turban looked as they did when Robert had packed Bella's gift that morning under our buckeye tree. The only difference was the moveable arms were no longer down at Balthazar's sides but were stretched far above the wise man's head.

The cavalryman said he had to be getting back to Grave's Bend. I carefully placed the cross, the diary, and Bella's wise man back in the saddlebags and then packed Robert's hat, his revolvers, and the bandolier under my left arm. I shook the rebel's hand firmly and thanked him for all he had done for Robert and for returning the keepsakes to the family. I escorted him back to the barn, where he hurriedly saddled his horse. I led him up the trail behind the smokehouse, thanked him again for his efforts, and watched him slowly climb the demanding switchback trail just as Robert had done so many times before.

I managed to get into the house, up the stairs, and into my room without anyone seeing the contraband or me. I closed my door and collapsed across the bed, trying to assimilate what I'd just heard. I knew mourning the loss of a brother I'd grown to respect would have to wait until after I'd delivered the horrific news that Robert was dead. After a few more moments to gather my thoughts, I made my way downstairs. I found everyone congregated in the kitchen waiting for supper to be served. "I know this is unusual," I said, standing in the doorway, "but I have to ask y'all for an immediate family meeting in the dining room. It's important, and I think Master Hudson and Bella should be here too."

After everyone had sat down around the table, I took several deep breaths and solemnly announced, "I got some really bad news just now. Robert . . . Robert's died a hero." Mama, Grandma, and Rachel gasped and began crying. Uncle Billy and Master Hudson just sat there silently shaking their heads. Bella began swaying in her chair and repeating, "Oh, Jesus, sweet Jesus."

When the room quieted in shock, Uncle Billy asked, "Thomas, how'd ya find this out?"

"Well, I finally got around today to patching those holes in the trough I'd promised to fix last month, and while I'm out there, this rebel cavalryman appears at the side gate carrying Robert's effects and leading his mare. Before I could say anything, he offered his hand and his condolences, said he'd been told Robert died a hero. Being in shock and everything, I didn't say a word. I just motioned for him to follow me. Took him out on the forest path—you know, away from the

Feds patrolling the highway. Sat down with him and then after catching my breath, I asked him to tell me everything he'd learned about Robert's death. I told him I knew everyone here would want to know how it happened."

Uncle Billy looked over at Mama, who had buried her head in her hands and was sobbing. "Ya gonna be okay with all this right now or ya wanna wait for a time?"

Without raising her head she whispered poignantly, "It's my own flesh and blood. I have to know. Better the truth now than waiting and dredging up nightmares . . . speculating."

Uncle Billy turned and signaled for me to continue.

"Y'all remember the last time Robert was home he described a whole lot of raids—Rising Sun, Hatchie Bottom, Knob Creek, and the like. Robert's winning ways brought him a lot of fame around here, but also got the attention of the Feds. As high up as the military governor himself in Nashville—ya know, Andrew Johnson. The rebel today said he'd heard the Feds put a bounty on Robert's head, ordered search-and-destroy missions, going after Robert and the 'hornet's nest' around Warfield in a big way. Said Johnson's top general handpicked seventy cavalrymen from the Fourteenth Tennessee and Thirteenth Independent Cavalries to carry out the governor's orders.

"After entering the county, the Feds met up with a couple 'home guards,' who said they knew where the 'rebel bushwhackers' were hiding out near Tumbling Creek. These fellas became paid guides leading the bluecoats some twelve miles or so over to the junction of Indian and Tumbling Creeks, where the Fed captain divided his forces, sending half his men reconnoitering across Indian Creek and the other half riding down the Tumbling.

"And when those thirty-five Feds reached the far side of Indian Creek, Robert gave the signal, and all hundred of his Raiders charged from the woods slamming into the Feds' side. Robert managed to split 'em in two and began killing the ones who were retreating into the woods planning to circle back and recross the stream. About fifteen minutes into the skirmish, Robert sensed the other Feds from the Tumbling were closing in fast and ordered a hasty withdrawal westward toward Humboldt.

"Over the next couple of days, Robert's Raiders and the Feds continued clashing. The Raiders would flee, set up an ambush, attack, retreat, and then set up another trap for the Feds. The Raiders were using back roads and switchback trails, which ran westward and parallel to the Memphis Highway from Warfield through Camden and Huntingdon to Burnt Bridge not too far from Humboldt. Robert felt his constant bleeding of the Feds over the last two days had sufficiently weakened 'em to allow an all-out attack, an ambush at Burnt Bridge the following day." I paused, looked over at Uncle Billy, and asked, "Think I should go on?"

Uncle Billy turned to Mama. "Ya want Thomas to keep on going?"

Mama murmured, "Yes, son, go on . . . go on."

Uncle Billy nodded for me to continue.

"Well, let's see then. It was about nine o'clock the next morning when Robert intentionally allowed the pursuing Feds to catch up to his rear guard and chase him and his men into a little box canyon with limestone cliffs rising some two hundred feet above the canyon floor. By the way, I remember Robert describing this Burnt Bridge to me once before on one of his trips home. I recall the conversation because Robert's description was so strange. One minute he was talking about how easy it would be to set ambushes there and then the next minute he was describing the beauty of the mountain laurel, the fern, the hemlocks, and the abundance of eagle and elk— everything thriving in this paradise. And then he ended his description of the box canyon saying if he had his druthers, he'd be buried there some day near the horsetail waterfall. . . .

"Anyway, the Feds took the bait and stormed into the canyon with only one way in and one way out. Robert deployed his men behind a thick bramble, allowing these bluecoats to blindly pass and continue on toward the steep cliffs blocking any chance of their escape. When Robert felt the Feds had reached the dead end, he ordered an all-out attack. But as luck, or someone, or some*thing* would have it, a second Fed cavalry unit was passing by and heard the shots ring out. Up to that point Robert's Raiders were getting the best of the trapped bluecoats. That's till the other Feds showed up and sandwiched the Raiders between the two Union forces.

"Apparently Robert didn't panic. He remembered Bedford Forrest's words when the general and he had faced a similar tight spot at the battle for Fort Donelson: 'I'm determined to cut my way out of here. I promised many of these boys' parents I'd look out for their sons the best I knew how. And now I'd rather have their bones bleachin' on the sides of the hills than have 'em captured and carried north to rot in prison-pens in the dead of winter.'

"So with a slashing, two-edged saber in his left hand and a blazing Navy Colt in his right, Robert tried rallying his troops to break the Feds' stranglehold. But as Robert charged into the thick blue wall, a Fed officer fired a single shot into Robert's chest. He fell forward, grabbed his horse's mane, and managed to stay in the saddle. But when his men saw what'd happened to him, the fight went out of 'em. They lowered their guns and surrendered.

"The Feds apparently tried saving Robert, but he was bleeding too badly. After he died, one of the Fed junior officers, originally from our own county, said he knew Robert and asked permission to collect his belongings and return 'em to friends, when his regiment passed back through Warfield. Permission was granted, and then once all our heroes had been collected, the Feds and the remaining Raiders jointly dug a common grave and buried Robert and his fallen men at his beloved Burnt Bridge."

"And how did this fella you met today get Robert's things?" Uncle Billy asked.

"He said that the junior officer had passed Robert's effects to a family on the far side of Warfield with instructions to return the items to Robert's loved ones. This family in turn passed them on to the fella I spoke with today, who knew Robert and knew where we lived."

"Where'd ya put Robert's things?" Uncle Billy asked.

"Got 'em up in my room. Didn't want to show 'em till we all talked. Should I run up and get 'em now?"

Uncle Billy turned to Mama. "Should Thomas fetch Robert's effects?"

Mama looked up and nodded.

"Okay then," I said. "I'll be right back."

I hurried up to my room, pulled Robert's belongings out from beneath the bed, and quickly returned to the dining room. When Mama saw Robert's sweat-stained hat with the ostrich plume, she began sobbing again. Uncle Billy put his right arm around Mama and began patting her lightly on the shoulder. I laid all the effects on the table and began instinctively handing out each item to the person whom I believed was the appropriate recipient. I first passed Robert's cavalry hat over to Mama and then handed the two Navy revolvers and bandolier to Uncle Billy for safekeeping. From the left pocket of Robert's saddlebag I removed the brownish rosewood cross and returned that to Mama also.

And before pulling the next belonging from the pocket, I asked permission to keep the memento for myself. When I removed the damaged notebook from the saddlebag, Mama quickly turned away and buried her head on Uncle Billy's chest. I apologized to Mama and quickly stuffed the diary in my leather vest. I then opened the right pocket, carefully removed the checkered muslin shirt, and unrolled it to reveal the wood-and-bone Balthazar. As I handed Bella the statue, I told her the wise man was one of Robert's favorite possessions.

Grandma, who hadn't said a word up to now, began speculating about the meaning of the unspoiled cross and the bullet-ridden diary. But you could tell Uncle Billy wasn't about to dwell on religion today. He pushed back from the table and said, "I've gotta check on that cow, see if she's dropped the calf yet."

I also excused myself. I wanted to sit alone on the familiar back step and whisper again to the starry night. "To some, I guess, I've committed an evil act. But the most important thing was reporting that Robert had died. . . . In the long run it didn't really matter how he died. I didn't invent Robert's last days out of embarrassment. No, it was out of a love I'd never known until Robert left home and I'd met and lost Beth.

"Why destroy my brother's reputation when he couldn't withstand the cowardice and brutality many of the rebels displayed at Fort Pillow? If he'd never seen the atrocities, would he have begun drinking and womanizing? No, that's not who he was. He was trying to ease the pain, the loneliness, the deep sense of betrayal. Grandpa and the cavalry'd meant everything to him.

"And after all that Mama's been through, heap the truth on top of an unimaginable despair of losing her son? Do you gods really care that I wove a story to protect Mama from even more pain? If so, why? Haven't you caused enough suffering? I acknowledge I don't have the power to retaliate against your cruelty. But I sure as hell can deflect your warring thrusts with a heroic tale of courage, honor, and resolute love.

"And then there's Grandma's conventional explanation of the cross and the diary. But I see it differently. Robert was carrying both in his left breast pocket. The bullet missed the cross. Does it mean faith can't protect us from your outrageous acts? But, yes, the bullet did rip through the notebook. Is this your way of showing your disapproval of Robert's military actions, or is it your devious attempt to invalidate his pages—to trick us into believing he wasn't recording facts but inexcusable lies? . . .

"And what are we to make of Balthazar's raised arms? Did Robert raise them over the king's head after Fort Pillow? Had the wise man become a doomed, pleading member of the Second Light shot in the temple at point-blank range? Or had Balthazar become all mankind? If so, are his arms raised in prayer, in adoration, or in supplication for our pain to end?

"But perhaps I'm being too cynical and broad in my interpretation. Could the figure just be a message to Bella? Were you gods admitting she'd suffered enough for now? Is the return of the statue and the restoration of her incomplete nativity a positive sign, a hint that a force will enter her life and fulfill the prophet's promise that 'she'll have her strength renewed, that she'll mount up with wings as eagles and not be weary?'"

22

As August aged into autumn, a springlike rebirth arrived on our farm. The gods had stowed their fire and declared a rare Sabbath. Hopeful fronds pushed up through the cracked red mud. The flames had passed; a revival had begun. Master Hudson spent less time now at the charred schoolhouse; Rachel made fewer visits to update Burns; and Lil Joe had found a father. All the signs of healing were now there—smiles, long walks, gazes, nuanced phrases, selfless favors, and furtive embraces behind the barn. Lil Joe had become the unintended catalyst accelerating their love; the cradled infant would extend his plump arms, grasp their caring hands, and flash an approving smile.

So October became a blessed month for me; my fellow pilgrim had asked my sister to marry him. The three questions facing our excited family were where should we hold the ceremony, when should we celebrate the wedding, and then, whom should we invite? The first question was easy to answer. Since we no longer had a church building, we'd have the ceremony on our front lawn.

The second question actually related to the third. Everyone agreed we should invite the Reverend and Mrs. Hudson, who lived over in Somerville near Memphis. We knew it'd take some time for Master Hudson's parents to make arrangements and get here. The Reverend would need to find a replacement for his Sunday services, and the date would also depend on Mrs. Hudson's current condition. Master Hudson told us recently he'd received word from his father fearing his wife's dropsy was getting worse. And when we finally decided on All Hallows' Eve, Uncle Billy added some of his odd humor to the discussion. He said we could also invite everyone sleeping up on the hill because the thirty-first was the day the boundary dissolved between the living and the dead.

After resolving the easy questions, we confronted the more difficult, political question of whom to invite. Master Hudson and Rachel repeatedly said they wanted a very small ceremony; but as usually happens with weddings, invitees multiply as quickly as field mice. During our conversations at the table, we'd agreed to invite the Reverend and Mrs. Hudson, Pastor Reed, who would officiate, Mrs. Reed, Father's cousins, and our close neighbors, the Andersons. But by the time the wedding rolled around, the guest list had quadrupled.

Pastor Reed was the primary culprit for the increased participation. A week after the nuptial announcement, the minister rode out to the farm and requested permission to invite everyone worshiping in Mrs. Booker's parlor. Since none of us in the family had attended church the week before, we didn't know what had transpired during that service.

I later learned from a friend the real reason everyone at Mrs. Booker's attended the ceremony and the reception. When Pastor Reed announced Rachel and Master Hudson would be getting married, there was apparently an audible

gasp among the worshippers followed by a loud, long murmuring. Pastor Reed said he thought everyone should attend,
not because Rachel was his granddaughter but because it was
the Christian thing to do.

In fact, he crafted his weekly sermon around the text of
Mary Magdalene in Luke:

> Now one of the Pharisees invited Jesus to have
> dinner with him, so he went to the Pharisee's
> house and reclined at the table. When a woman
> who had lived a sinful life in that town learned
> that Jesus was eating at the Pharisee's house,
> she brought an alabaster jar of perfume, and as
> she stood behind him at his feet weeping, she
> began to wet his feet with her tears.
>
> Then she wiped them with her hair, kissed
> them, and poured perfume on them. When
> the Pharisee who had invited him saw this, he
> said to himself, "If this man were a prophet,
> he would know who is touching him and what
> kind of woman she is—that she is a sinner." Je-
> sus answered him, "Simon, I have something to
> tell you."
>
> "Tell me, teacher," he said. "Two men owed
> money to a certain moneylender. One owed
> him five hundred denarii and the other fifty.
> Neither of them had the money to pay him
> back, so he canceled the debts of both. Now

which of them will love him more?" Simon replied, "I suppose the one who had the bigger debt canceled."

"You have judged correctly," Jesus said. Then the Lord said to her, "Your sins are forgiven. Your faith has saved you; go in peace."

Pastor Reed acknowledged that Master Hudson only occasionally came to church, and Rachel hadn't been to services since she became pregnant with Lil Joe. He defended his granddaughter, saying she stopped coming to church because of her embarrassment and uncertainty of how the congregants would treat her. Young Rachel was simply afraid. Pastor Reed encouraged the worshippers to celebrate the marriage of two lost souls who'd been "wandering in the wilderness." He concluded his sermon asserting that attending the wedding and showing outward signs of love and acceptance would go a long way to bringing these lost sheep back into the fold. And after Pastor Reed ended his remarks, the members praised his sermon and assured the relative-minister they'd willingly attend the wedding on All Saints' Eve.

Another unexpected wedding guest was our new acquaintance, the remarkable Sergeant Basanater, who'd never met a stranger and could lift your spirits from the darkest depths. This noncommissioned officer had arrived with the first complement of Negro sentries bivouacked in our second forage field across the highway. While on guard duty one searing July afternoon, the Sergeant noticed Bella sitting quietly on a rock wall in the shade of our buckeye tree. He thought she was merely resting from the scorching heat; he had no way of knowing the history of the place.

When he finished his shift, the officer walked over, smiled broadly, and introduced himself to Bella. It was only several days later that the persuasive Sergeant Basanater came calling and telling us his inspiring story: "I've always said that by knowin' where someone's been, you've a pretty good idea where they're goin'. My mama and papa were from Ethiopia. How they got here is a sad, shadowy tale.

"My father was a local chief in a small village in the west. Several weeks after my parents married, African traders attacked my father's village and abducted all the young inhabitants, including my parents, my two uncles, and an aunt. You see, the Americans and Europeans didn't capture and enslave people. They purchased their slaves from the Negro traders. The white folks were restricted to several ports on the west coast of Africa, while the Negro traders roamed the interior roundin' up our people to exchange 'em for money and guns.

"Mama said everyone abducted from their village was chained, yoked, and shackled for the difficult journey from Ethiopia to Nigeria. Some of Mama and Papa's friends and relatives died from the heat, hunger, and exhaustion during their forced march across the continent. Some even killed themselves out of despair. Others died at the hands of their Negro captors for refusin' to continue the journey. When Mama and Papa finally reached the Nigerian port, they were fortunately auctioned off to the same white dealer. Other captives weren't so lucky; when they were left unsold, their

Negro captors quickly beheaded them in full view of the marketplace crowd.

"Mama also explained their auctioning was only the end of the beginning. There was still the six-week voyage across the Atlantic in the ship's stinking hold with five hundred branded slaves. She said they sat under grated hatchways between the decks in filthy cells three feet high. The space was so small they sat between each other's legs with no chance of standing, lying down, or even changing positions day or night.

"But Mama said the most painful part of the journey came at the end, when she and Papa were put up for sale separately at the Charleston market. After auctionin' off Papa to a rich master, the white traders put Mama up for bid. Before the auction started, Papa begged his new South Carolina owner to buy his wife. When the actual sale began, Papa's master kept his word and bid on Mama, but eventually he lost her to a higher bidder. Mama later said they both cried, and my father prayed they'd meet again someday in heaven.

"It wasn't long after my parents were separated, Mama suspected she was pregnant. She was right. Mama'd carried me across the African continent and the Atlantic and all the way to South Carolina. . . . So I was born later that year, and Mama and I stayed on the Carolina plantation a long time—all the way up until I turned twenty-five. That's when we were both sold to a Tennessee speculator, who in turn sold both of us to a plantation owner in Franklin—ya know, on the outskirts of Nashville.

"Three years later, Mama died of the fever; and I stayed on with my owner until the Union army took control of middle Tennessee early on in the war. I then felt a callin' to leave my master and join a new military unit in Nashville, the Thirteenth US Colored Infantry Regiment. In November '63, after trainin', I was surprised—and bein' honest with ya, a bit disappointed—our five hundred men didn't get the orders to join the fight but to come out here to western Tennessee and build a railroad. So I spent half my time drivin' spikes and the other half guardin' the fellows laying the ties and the rails.

"And after finishin' construction on the Nashville & Northwestern line in May '64, we all stayed on to provide security around Johnsonville. But after that incident up the road there at the school, some of us were reassigned to your track section here. And that's how I ended up seein' Bella under the buckeye tree and how she led me to your house and your hospitality."

The room fell silent. We all just sat there shaking our bowed heads with mixed emotions. While we were shocked and embarrassed hearing a firsthand account of the unimaginable cruelty the Sergeant and his family had suffered at the hands of traders, we were equally struck by his courage to forgive the past and look to the future for a better life. After a few awkward seconds had passed, Uncle Billy rose from his chair, approached the Sergeant, and extended his hand, signaling our family had just grown by one.

23

THE MAGICAL DAY finally arrived, and the gods smiled on Rachel and Master Hudson, blessing them with a brilliant autumn morning. Everyone on the farm rose early, had a hearty breakfast, and dressed in their Sunday best. According to plan, Pastor Reed and his wife came early to rehearse the wedding. Mrs. Booker's contingent and the Anderson family arrived en masse. And a half hour before the ceremony, Sergeant Basanater walked up the entry road leading a stout mule harnessed to a mysterious covered wagon.

When the soldier steered the mule to the right of the buckeye tree, we could clearly see the message emblazoned on the side: "James G. Coughlin, U.S. Photographer, Department of the South." Sergeant Basanater halted the mule, and two well-dressed men jumped down from the wagon bench. The Sergeant then introduced Mr. Coughlin and his assistant, Mr. Choate, and announced he was purchasing a couple of wedding photographs as a gift for the family.

The Sergeant explained the Topographical Branch of the Department of Engineers had hired Mr. Coughlin to run the army's photographic operations, including photo-duplication of maps, plans, and other materials and the compiling of official military portraits. As part of his "documenting sites and subjects as assigned" duties, Mr. Coughlin had been ordered to photograph the Thirteenth US Colored securing the new track sections between Johnsonville Depot and McKenzie. So the Sergeant asked Mr. Coughlin to do him a big favor while he was working here, and the photographer generously complied.

As the wedding party and guests positioned themselves on the front lawn for the ceremony, Mr. Coughlin and Mr. Choate began hauling the bulky camera and tripod out of the photographer's wagon. The smiling bride and groom then said their vows, kissed, and sauntered down the rise arm-in-arm to the buckeye tree, where Mr. Coughlin and Mr. Choate were positioned to capture the happy day.

Mr. Coughlin arranged the wedding party, focused the camera, and urged his assistant to hurry out with a wet plate before it dried. Mr. Choate rushed out from behind the wagon and quickly placed the plate holder in the camera. The photographer told everyone to smile, removed the lens cap for five seconds, and then replaced it. The assistant then rushed the exposed plate to his mobile darkroom at the back of the wagon, where he immediately developed, fixed, and rinsed the plate. Having completed this involved process, Mr. Coughlin and Mr. Choate sensitized, exposed, developed, fixed, and rinsed a second family heirloom.

When we had a chance to examine the photographs, we noticed several peculiarities, two of which we could easily explain. First, Master Hudson was holding a young child in his arms for his wedding pictures. Second, Grandpa's head had blurred in both exposures. Since it was a warm day and a special occasion, we'd carried Grandpa's rocker out to the front porch. And all during the wedding and the photography session afterward, Grandpa jerked his head from side to side and made only low guttural sounds, since he'd now forgotten how to speak.

But the third oddity was baffling. In both pictures, a fiery light could be seen over Mama's face, and neither of our photographic experts could explain it. We were standing under the buckeye tree with no apparent light dappling the wedding party. Mr. Coughlin apologized profusely, saying he would've taken another picture at no charge had he brought additional plates along on the wagon.

To end the awkward moment and demonstrate there were no hard feelings about the defective photographs, Uncle Billy cheerfully invited Mr. Coughlin and Mr. Choate to join us for refreshments. They accepted and enjoyed the rest of the festivities as much as we did. And after sampling every dessert on the sideboard except Mrs. Hunter's special key lime pie, Mama excused herself and spent an hour transferring her belongings from the old bedroom she shared with Rachel to her new home upstairs with all the memories and the ghosts.

The afterglow from the nuptials lasted exactly a month to the day. At the end of November Bella walked into the kitchen with tears streaming down her face. Mama rushed over and hugged her. "Lord, what's the matter, Bella?"

"The Thirteenth Colored's been called to Nashville. They're expectin' a rebel attack on the capital. The Sergeant says he has to leave tomorrow mornin'." So at a solemn dining room table that evening, Uncle Billy offered an eloquent prayer asking God to protect Sergeant Basanater from harm and to "strengthen Bella during her upcoming Christmas season of worry and despair."

I must admit, the gods fooled me this time. I thought for sure they'd begun unpacking their fire; but Sergeant Basanater returned unscathed to Bella at the beginning of February '65. And after an incomparable welcoming feast, we all sat around the dinner table listening to the Sergeant's account of the heroic defense of Nashville.

"As you know," he began, "we boarded the Nashville & Northwestern on the thirtieth, and when we arrived in the city that evenin', we joined the Second Colored Brigade under a Colonel C. R. Thompson. The rebels began arrivin' from the south on the second and established positions facin' our men entrenched on the outskirts. There was a rumor floatin' about that their general wouldn't attack us, because he didn't want to take another beatin' like the one he'd just gotten down the road in Franklin. And lo and behold, that rumor turned out to be true. The rebels were takin' a defensive stand, waitin' for us to attack 'em. Well, we finally got the word we'd attack on the fifteenth. Our Colonel Hatensteine said the Thirteenth would be held in reserve in a second line over on the Confederate right flank.

"So the followin' mornin' at six o'clock sharp, our boys attacked their right side and kept 'em penned down there the rest of the day. The main attack on the rebel left launched after daybreak. And by the afternoon that attack on their left flank had pushed the rebels back a fair piece, all the way back to the Granny White Turnpike where our boys ceased fire and bivouacked for the night. And once we let up the pressure the rebels immediately began settin' a new defensive line extending from Shy's Hill all the way down to Overton's Hill.

"While our Thirteenth didn't see any real action the first day, we saw all we wanted the second afternoon. Colonel Hatensteine ordered us over to the foot of Overton's Hill, over on the rebels' right flank. At high noon our boys in the first line charged up Overton's but were pushed back into our regiment waiting in reserve at the bottom of the hill. The colonel then gave the order for us to charge. As I ran up the rise with my bayonet fixed, I heard bullets whistlin' past my head and then makin' these awful thudlike sounds as they ripped into my closest friends. Well, a dozen or so of us actually climbed the rebel parapet and stood there for an instant, frozen, starin' into the rebels' eyes and sharin' a mutual fear of dyin' there that afternoon on that hill.

"We tried holdin' our ground on Overton's but got pushed back to the bottom of the rise. A little later in the afternoon, other Union regiments attacked the rebels from three sides on nearby Shy's Hill and finally forced 'em to break and run. We then pulled ourselves together and ran back up Overton's Hill, and by the grace of God, this time we took it.

"As we sat bloodied and exhausted at the crest of the hill, our commandin' officer came by and praised us, recognizin' many of us were fightin' for the first time but that we'd bravely stormed the strongest defenses on the entire rebel line, fightin' alongside veterans of Atlanta, Stone's River, and Missionary Ridge. He then concluded his speech sayin' we 'inexperienced warriors had vied with his old soldiers in bravery, tenacity, and deeds of noble daring.'

"Well, the next mornin' we got orders to chase the retreatin' rebels, but the cold, heavy rains mired us down, and their infantry was gettin' good cover from their cavalry under this fella, Forrest. But we kept pushin', kept chasin' 'em, all the way down into Alabama, and we didn't let up until Christmas Day.

"By the fifteenth of January we'd all returned to Nashville and gotten the good news we'd be headin' back out here to start guardin' the Nashville & Northwestern again. And so it is by the grace of God and your strong prayers I've come back home again."

I anxiously looked over toward Uncle Billy to gauge his reaction to the Sergeant's personal account of a decisive Union victory at Nashville. But Uncle Billy had already risen from his chair and was extending his hand to the brave soldier. He said, "Welcome home, Sergeant. We're all happy you made it back to us safe and sound."

The Sergeant then moved slowly around the table, giving each of us a long, firm hug.

24

MIRACLES DO HAPPEN. Only months later we finally persuaded Uncle Billy to attend Easter services in Warfield. Well, we really couldn't say that for sure because we didn't really know what had changed his mind. Perhaps it was the great news burning the Warfield wires that Lee had surrendered at Appomattox and the war was over; or the structured military persuasion of Bella's new beau; or the good-natured prodding from a rejuvenated Master Hudson; or just Uncle Billy's personal wish to spend a little more time holding Lil Joe on his knee. We'd never know his true motivation for sure; it was just impossible interpreting his sly smile.

We all dressed, congregated under the buckeye tree, and piled into the wagons for the journey to Warfield. It was a quiet, overcast day. Everyone was going to church except Mama; she said she'd stay home with Grandpa and work on the Easter meal. On the way to the services, we passed several companies of Union troops; they were not raucously celebrating their recent victory. The continuous fighting, the blasted landscape, and the sheer suffering of the citizenry had stripped the soldiers of any joy. As far as I could see, the only feeling they had left was a sense of exhausted satisfaction that they had endured and were going home.

After Master Hudson led us in two rousing resurrection hymns, Pastor Reed rose and moved to the front of Mrs. Booker's overflowing parlor. Something was different; something was wrong. This wasn't the Pastor Reed of Easters past. He appeared ashen and shaken. He began his homily with some very inauspicious lines: "Brothers and sisters, I've some news that's as dark and disturbing as those threatening clouds you see out the windows there. Sorry to say . . . President Lincoln was shot in the head while attending the theater last night and died early this Easter morning."

There were audible gasps in the room followed by anxious murmurings. After quieting us down, Pastor Reed continued, "I didn't want to say anything before services began. I thought it'd be a distraction; but by telling y'all together, I could perhaps help you focus on how to react to the news and how these events might relate to Jesus' death and resurrection, which we celebrate today.

"When I heard the troubling news, I decided to change the text for today's service. I've chosen the book of Matthew:

> Now from the sixth hour of daylight, about noon, there was darkness over all the land unto the ninth hour of daylight, about three o'clock. And at this ninth hour of daylight, Jesus cried with a loud voice, saying, "My God, my God, why hast thou forsaken me?" And straightway one of them ran, took a sponge and filled it with vinegar, and gave it to Jesus to drink. Jesus cried out again with a loud voice and yielded up the ghost.

And, behold, the veil of the temple was torn in two from the top to the bottom; and the earth did quake, and the rocks split; and the graves were opened; and many bodies of the saints arose. Now when the centurion and they that were with him saw the earthquake and those things that were done, they feared greatly, saying this truly was the Son of God.

"Brothers and sisters, no matter what we may have thought about the president or his policies, we must admit this was a cruel and unjust act, which I'm truly afraid will bring more suffering to all of us down here in the South. So we have an important question to ask and then to answer—how should we as Christians react to the bleak news? Well, the Bible teaches us we should respond now just as strongly and resolutely as we have throughout the tribulations of the past few years. The gospel teaches us we'll survive these earthly trials and the sun will one day shine on us again. And when we die, we know we'll all be resurrected just as the Lord was, and we'll be with him in the bright heavens at the right-hand side of God.

"And how again did the scripture describe the time of the crucifixion? It says, 'From the sixth hour of daylight, about noon, there was darkness over all the land unto the ninth hour of daylight, about three o'clock.' But oh, how different the weather was on that resurrection day! How'd the scriptures describe that glorious morning? . . .

"Well, in the gospel according to Mark we read: 'When the Sabbath was over, Mary Magdalene, Mary the mother of James, and Salome brought spices so that they might go in to anoint Jesus' body. Very early on the first day of the week, just after sunrise, they were on their way to the grave and they asked each other, "Who will roll the stone away from the entrance of the tomb?" But when they looked up, they saw that the stone, which was very large, had been rolled away. As they entered the tomb, they saw a young man dressed in a white robe sittin' on the right side, and they were alarmed. "Don't be afraid," he said. "You're looking for Jesus the Nazarene, who was crucified. He has risen! He is no longer here."'

"So Saint Mark reports that that first Easter had a beautiful sunrise unlike the dark Friday just days before. Brothers and sisters in Christ, the weather for the crucifixion and the resurrection were symbolic of what was happening at that moment on those days, but the difference in the weather, between the crucifixion and the resurrection, serves as an emblematic promise that we too will see the sunshine again, both here on earth and in the blessed hereafter."

Pastor Reed paused and signaled Master Hudson to lead the congregation in an appropriate final gospel hymn, "Rise, Shine, for Thy Light Is A-Coming":

> O, rise! Shine! For thy light is a-coming,
> Rise! Shine! For thy light is a-coming,
> O, rise! Shine! For thy light is a-coming,
> This is the year of Jubilee.

O wet and dry I intend to try,

My Lord says He's coming by and by,

To serve the Lord until I die,

My Lord says He's coming by and by.

Because of the fierce storm marching through Warfield from west to east, we couldn't leave immediately for the farm. We stayed on at Mrs. Booker's; spoke about the discouraging events of the last few days; and consumed a few of her light refreshments. The strong winds finally passed, and the sun filtered through the diminishing rain, pinning a rare brilliant double rainbow on the still dark eastern sky. So we finally left for the farm a little past three o'clock, and as with the morning trip to Warfield, we encountered several staid groups of off-duty bluecoats milling about, quietly chatting and smoking their clay pipes and stubby, black cigars.

When we rounded the last curve before home, everyone in the wagons gasped. "God, oh my God." Uncle Billy and Sergeant Basanater, who were driving the wagons, whipped the reins and whistled for the horses to race toward the farm. Lightning must have hit either the barn or the dreaded wagon shed and started a massive crescent of fire lashing the sky and arcing about the barnyard from the fence before the toolshed to the gate a little past the barn. Uncle Billy and the Sergeant stopped the wagons beneath the buckeye tree and began running toward the gates of hell to try saving some of the structures and the helpless livestock.

Master Hudson and I rushed up the rise toward the house to

check on Mama and Grandpa. We flung open the hallway door and shouted out for Mama. There was no answer. I screamed again and still no answer. Master Hudson and I next set about searching each of the rooms. He took the upstairs, and I started downstairs in Grandpa's old room. No one was there.

I hurried around to the dining room, where the windows were open, the lace curtains were waving in the stiff winds, and the rain had puddled on the floor. I shouted again . . . and still no answer. I ran into the kitchen, where Mama had apparently been preparing our Easter dinner. The corn had been shucked, the lettuce washed, and the ham ready to go into the oven but the room was empty. I ran out onto the back porch and then outside toward the smokehouse. I shouted again and still no answer. I rushed back to the hallway entrance, where I met up with Master Hudson, who said he'd found Grandpa sleeping alone in the front room . . . but still no sign of Mama.

We then raced down to the barnyard to let Uncle Billy know Mama was still missing. As we approached the corral, Uncle Billy and the Sergeant turned away from the intense flames and motioned for us to wait for them on the other side of the fence. When Uncle Billy walked up to us, he just lowered his head and said, "I'm sorry, Thomas. There isn't a damn thing we can do."

"It's okay, Uncle Billy, toolsheds and barns can be rebuilt."

Uncle Billy shook his head. "No, Thomas, that's not what I meant. It's your Mama. . . . There isn't a damn thing we can do."

"Is she trapped?" I asked, my fears quickly rising. "For God's sake, we have to get her out of there! We can't just let her burn up!"

When I instinctively started toward the fire, the Sergeant stepped in the way. "It's not a good idea, Thomas. Uncle Billy's right. We saw your mama. There's nothin' any of us can do right now, not until the fire dies down."

As I began moving toward the barn again, Uncle Billy grabbed my shoulders, shook me, and shouted, "Listen to me, boy! There's nothing we can do. Your mama's gone."

Once their words registered, I moved up as far as the barnyard fence and draped my arms over the gate. I'd never felt pain like this before, standing there, helplessly watching the flames consume one structure after another, and knowing my mama had been in there suffering. Suffering just as Miss Owings and my schoolmates had. My heart was breaking. I took several deep breaths to ensure my voice was steady before turning to Uncle Billy. "What was she doing down here in the storm? . . . All the windows are open in the dining room, and there's rain all over the floor."

Uncle Billy kept staring ahead into the flames. "She must have spotted smoke rising down here after a lightning strike. She knew the barn was a tinderbox—the stored hay, dry timbers, and everything. She was down here trying to get the animals out of their stalls."

"Ya think so, Uncle Billy?"

"I'm sure of it, Thomas. The Sergeant and I saw her for just a brief moment. She was trying to drag a new foal out of its pen after freeing the mare. The fire was burning so hot that the loft and then the roof collapsed on 'em. When the smoke thinned a bit, enough to where I could see in again, Mama and the foal had disappeared. I'm really sorry, Thomas."

When we finally turned away, Uncle Billy asked Master Hudson to saddle one of the horses and ride into Warfield to let Pastor Reed know of his daughter's death and to request another casket from Mr. Patrick, the undertaker. We didn't know how to proceed with the services. We thought it best we wait until we heard back from Pastor Reed. We were sure he wouldn't want to conduct a funeral for his own daughter.

We held Mama's funeral on the Tuesday after Easter, and I believe everyone in the county was there. At eleven o'clock we all gathered in the hallway, kitchen, and dining room, where we had positioned Mama's closed coffin beneath the large open windows. Unfortunately, I overheard Mr. Patrick explaining to Mr. Anderson why we had to forego the customary viewing. The undertaker said there was not much of Mama left; and what little there was had fused with the week-old colt she was trying to save. Mr. Patrick said he did the best he could to separate Mama and the foal, but he was sure a great deal of the colt ended up in the pine coffin with Mama's remains.

After Master Hudson led us in singing two of Mama's favorite hymns, "Mercy Is Boundless and Free" and "God Will Take Care of You," Pastor Reed's old friend, a Reverend Lyons, from the Cumberland Church in Benton County, moved to the front of the room to the right of Mama's casket.

Unlike Pastor Reed, who could throw some extra logs on the fire, the Reverend Lyons was a gentle, soft-spoken cleric. He chose to emphasize Mama's loyalty to her family, her friends, and the Almighty. His text was from the Old Testament, the book of Ruth, which describes Ruth's unwavering loyalty to Naomi, her mother-in-law: "Now Elimelech, Naomi's husband, died, and she was left with her two sons. They married Moabite women, one named Orpah and the other Ruth. After they had lived there about ten years, both of Naomi's sons also died. Then Naomi said to her two daughters-in-law, 'Go back, each of you, to your mother's home. May the Lord show kindness to you, as you have shown to your dead husbands and to me. May the Lord grant that each of you will find rest in the home of another husband.'

"Then Orpah kissed her mother-in-law good-bye, but Ruth clung to her. And Ruth replied, 'Do not urge me to leave you or to turn back from you. Where you go I will go, and where you stay I will stay. Your people will be my people and your God my God. Where you die I will die, and there I will be buried. May the Lord deal with me, be it ever so severely, if anything but death separates you and me.'"

The Reverend closed his Bible, signaling Master Hudson to lead us in a final hymn, "The Rainbow Round the Throne":

> When the clouds hang dark and heavy,
> And the rolling surge we hear,
> When no earthly power can shield us,
> From the storm that most we fear,
> O 'tis then our Father's presence,
> To the trusting heart is shown,
> In a bright and glorious vision,
> Of the rainbow round the throne.

After the services, we carried Mama's coffin up the path past the blooming lilacs to her shaded plot on the hill. Reverend Lyons raised his right hand and offered a benediction from Psalms, which I believe was meant more to comfort all of us than it was to say farewell to Mama: "God is our refuge and strength, a very present help in trouble. Therefore we will not fear, though the earth be removed, and though the mountains be carried into the midst of the sea; though the waters thereof roar and are troubled, though the mountains shake with the swelling thereof."

As everyone migrated to the dining room after the burial, I walked alone across the highway, passed the bivouacked Union troops, and sat alone on Jacob's anointed pillar in Bethel staring out into the afternoon forage field where even the air was tinged with green. I didn't want to be anywhere near the dining room or the kitchen that afternoon. I'd expect to see Mama checking the bread in the oven, replenishing the myriad bowls on the antique sideboard, or kindly encouraging folks to have another helping, since they weren't "splurging" every day. I just had to be alone for a while. For the first time in my life, I felt unanchored from everyone and everything. They were all gone now—Father, Mama, Robert, and Israel. The gods had laid waste to a generation . . . both for the country and for me.

When I was sure all the attendees had left, I returned to the lighted farmhouse and sat on the front porch with my resurrected pilgrim, who spoke very plainly now about our quest. "I thought Reverend Lyons gave a good sermon today," Master Hudson began, "praising all the caring acts your mama'd done for everyone over the years. But he sure didn't answer our 'why' question, did he, Thomas? . . .

"You and I started out talking about Moses, the Massacre of the Innocents, Caledonia, the Napoleonic Wars, and asking ourselves, 'Why would a loving God allow such cruelty, dissembling, and human suffering?' But over the past several years it's become personal for you and me: your grandfather, your father, your mother, your brother, Israel, my mama, Miss Owings, the five innocents at the schoolhouse . . . Got me to thinking. Maybe we should now push beyond 'why?' to 'what if?'

"We've always assumed there was a capricious puppeteer controlling the strings behind the curtain, but what if we stepped behind the screen and saw there wasn't anyone there? . . . I wonder, would that be more frightening than believing there are gods who sometimes bless us while reserving the right to destroy us at any time?

"By pushing past Dante and Shakespeare to 'why did the gods allow these things to happen?' we've excused the marionettes' actions because we're blaming their masters, the puppeteers. In our carnival we've accepted the shocking, the absurd, the outrageous. We've permitted the puppets to say and do almost anything they've wanted to, just because we've stipulated it's not their fault. Since the supreme puppeteers control the marionettes, we exonerate our human puppets, granting them absolution.

"But ya know, Thomas, in a perverse reading of Shakespeare, Cassius could be right: 'The fault, dear Brutus, is not in the stars, but in ourselves.' Perhaps our hell never really had anything to do with the heavens or the gods, just chance and inhumanity. And if this were true, then how can we make life tolerable? How can we face this unpredictability and human cruelty? . . . As we discussed during one of my early visits, it's strange how the source of our suffering might just be our path to salvation. We have each other."

Master Hudson paused. It was getting very late. I suggested he rush in to Rachel and Lil Joe and give them a big hug. And as he quietly stepped into Grandpa's old room, a brilliant meteor arced the diamond sky, dodging the fire in Aries.

25

AFTER MAMA'S DEATH, I decided to leave the farm and write about hell rather than continue living in it. But before speaking with Uncle Billy about my intentions to go away to school, I walked up to the family plot and said my good-byes to Father, Mama, and Israel. I assured them I wasn't abandoning them and that they'd always be with me, woven among my warmest memories.

I waited until the spring planting was over and then asked Uncle Billy if we could take a walk out back and discuss the future. The acrid odor of brimstone still lingered in the spring air. I felt guilty about wanting to move on, and so I opened our difficult conversation with a rehearsed pitch. I began by highlighting the neighbors' generous offer to hold a barn raising during the summer; moved on to Hudson's decision to live on the farm permanently with Rachel and Lil Joe; and concluded with Sergeant Basanater's open desire to opt out of the army and move in with his new love, Bella.

The thrust of my argument was that I was expendable, that there was a lot of help on the farm now and more on the way. Uncle Billy asked me what I wanted to do, and I said I wanted to be a writer and perhaps someday tell his story. He laughed; and as it always was with Uncle Billy, he surprised me again and did not try to persuade me to stay. Rather, he accepted my proposal and genuinely wished me good luck. As we turned back toward the farmhouse, he added that Beth had once told him I could do so much more, if only I left the farm.

My day of departure arrived. I got up early and finished packing my bags. I scratched a sleeping Cleary behind the ear and looked slowly around the room to capture the many memories. Then I whispered a benediction for the house and descended the narrow curving stairs a final time. As I reached the hallway, I sadly realized that for the first time ever, no one would be living upstairs with the ghosts. But then I remembered that Lil Joe would soon need a room of his own and he'd have two from which to choose, and my heart warmed some.

Grandma prepared me a very hearty breakfast and then wrapped up some of my favorite ham and biscuits for the train. I got the key down from the wall and slowly opened the door to the front room. Grandpa was sleeping with his chin down on his chest. I quietly approached his rocker and kissed him lightly on his forehead. He stirred, groaned, opened his eyes halfway, and then quickly fell back to sleep. I told him I loved him, and I thanked him for all he had done for me. As I backed out of the room into the sharp slant of a new summer day, Grandpa's old friend announced a quarter past nine.

Uncle Billy offered to drive me to the Warfield depot. He harnessed the mare and hitched the wagon under the buckeye tree. Grandma, Bella, Hudson, Rachel, and Lil Joe all came down the rise to Father's old wagon. Grandma went over the critical checklist of items I was required to take with me to the university: four single sheets, two blankets, a pillow and pillowcase, three towels, seven napkins with napkin ring, a clothes bag, and three pairs of strong shoes. I assured her I had everything.

I gave Rachel a big hug, placed my hand on the swell of her stomach, and said, "Take care of yourself and this little one here. You look a little peaked." I then gave all the others a long, last embrace, told them I loved them, and promised to return to see them as often as I could. I climbed up onto the wide pine bench next to Uncle Billy. He tugged at the reins, whistled, and steered the wagon out onto the entry road banked on both sides with yellow daisies, long purple, red pansies, and deep blue violets. As we turned onto the highway headed west toward Warfield, I waved my slouch hat vigorously to hide the fear, sadness, and guilt of leaving home for the first time.

Master Hudson had helped me choose a school that was strong in writing and the letters. He provided the headmaster with a certificate of good character and advocated on my behalf to secure work on the campus in exchange for my board, tuition, washing, and fuel. So I was now headed with Uncle Billy to catch the Nashville & Northwestern to the capital, where I'd board the Nashville & Chattanooga and then transfer to the Franklin Coal & Mining Railway, running daily to Cowan Station about ten miles from the university. Ever thoughtful, Master Hudson had also arranged for a driver to pick me up at the appointed time from my late-afternoon train.

I enjoyed my studies from the start and smiled inwardly every time my professor discussed one of the many topics near and dear to Master Hudson and me. During the fall term of my junior year at the university, we studied Dante's *Inferno* and his passionate sonnets for his Beatrice. Since I never seemed to get back to the farm, it was comforting to be reminded of my dear mentor and friend; yet as I read, my heartbreak over Beth was not far from my mind. My favorite of the love poems had two main sections: in the first, Dante lamented as Jeremiah the prophet had: "O all you who pass this way, listen and see, if there is any grief like mine"; and in the second part, he described what he'd lost:

> In her eyes my lady bears love,
> By which she makes noble what she gazes on.
> Where she passes, all men turn their look on her,
> And she makes the heart tremble in him she greets,
> So that, all pale, he lowers his eyes,
> And sighs, then, over all his failings.
> Help me, ladies, to do her honor.
> How she looks when she smiles a little,
> Cannot be spoken of, or held in mind.
> She is so rare a miracle and is gentle.

I usually continued my studies between the semesters, but I was now inspired to take the train up to Uncle Billy's farm before the spring term. As I walked up the entry road leading to Uncle Billy's farm, a gray-haired fellow sitting in one of the antique yellow rockers shouted something that sounded a little like my name, but he didn't get up to greet me.

When I got close to the front steps, I could see it was Uncle Billy and he wasn't the vibrant spirit I'd last seen some three years ago. Something had happened. His speech was slurred, his mouth drooped, and his right arm dangled at his side. He was wrapped in a black shawl and holding a cane across his lap.

Uncle Billy's wife, Mahaley, must have heard Uncle Billy shouting because she came quickly onto the front porch. I introduced myself and explained I'd not seen Uncle Billy for some three years. She could see from my face that I had not expected to find Uncle Billy in such a state. She took my hand, then described what had happened to her husband. Not long after I left, she told me, Uncle Billy went to Warfield to drop off eggs and butter and pick up the usual supplies. While he was at the general store he had an apoplectic attack and would have died if Dr. Simmons hadn't been close by. She said Uncle Billy recuperated at our farm until he was able to travel home. Without Uncle Billy, I knew Rachel and Hudson would have their hands full. I asked who was helping out at the farm and she said her eldest son and his wife had moved over to live on the property.

Mahaley invited me into the parlor. I helped Uncle Billy get to his feet and provided support until we got to his chair near the fire. I was dying to find out how Beth was doing, so I introduced the subject by telling Mahaley I felt I had already known her for a long time because of Beth's story about her mother. Mahaley smiled and replied she felt the same way about me. She said when Beth returned home from helping out on our farm, she couldn't stop singing my praises. I then asked directly how Beth was doing. Mahaley stopped smiling, paused, and then asked, "You didn't know Beth died?"

I couldn't accept what I was hearing; I didn't respond. Mahaley began describing Beth's last years: "Before Uncle Billy had his stroke, Beth married a banker and moved to Nashville. They hadn't been married very long when Beth contracted consumption. She gradually weakened, and when she became bedridden, she asked to come back to us on the farm here. She spent her last days staring out that window there at the cardinals building nests in the budding trees. After the wake, we buried her over there in the cemetery we share with the Episcopal Church."

I was stunned. I'd now lost Beth a second time. I'd always held out hope that we'd someday, somehow find each other, but that prospect was now extinguished. I didn't know what to say. I just sat there silently staring into the fire. The clock chimed three, and Mahaley tried changing the subject. "You must be starved. Please, let me get you something to eat." I thanked her for the offer but said I wasn't very hungry.

As dusk approached, I rose and politely insisted I had to be going. I hugged Uncle Billy tightly and thanked him again for everything. As I moved toward Mahaley to say good-bye, she raised her hand to stop me and said, "I almost forgot—please, wait just a moment." She left the room and returned several minutes later carrying a small cedar box. Mahaley smiled faintly and explained, "When Beth came back to the farm toward the end, she gave me this little box and asked me to pass it on, if I ever saw you." She handed the box to me. Holding it carefully in one hand, I removed the top, and a tear spontaneously rolled down my cheek. I gave Uncle Billy another big hug, embraced Mahaley, and slowly descended the front stairs.

I turned left and walked over to the walled cemetery between Uncle Billy's farm and the gothic revival church clad in scored stucco that resembled large stone blocks. I moved among the terraced headstones for several minutes before locating Beth's isolated plot in a treeless corner of the shared burial ground. I stood at her light-gray granite marker for several minutes with my head bowed, not really thinking, but feeling, sensing our past . . . repeating the chiseled inscription that captured her essence:

> Going up from us with the joy we had,
> Grew perfectly and spiritually fair,
> That she spreads even there a light of love,
> Which makes the angels glad.

I moved over to the left of Beth's headstone and used Father's pocketknife to hollow out a small pit in the moist spring earth. I removed a well-worn buckeye from my coat pocket and planted it, carefully mounding the black dirt above and around it. The dark brown seed was the timeless buckeye Beth had given me that painful morning just before she and Uncle Billy left for home.

I then moved over to the right side of the marker and burrowed out a second shallow hole. I removed the small cedar box from my inside coat pocket, opened it, and buried the pristine buckeye I'd lovingly given Beth the day before she left—a green act in a green shade. I stepped back in front of Beth's headstone and spoke softly and directly to her for a final time. "I hope these seeds I've planted will thrive, and you'll become the fulcrum, balancing my deepest love and respect for you, my Beatrice, my love."

So much has happened since I said my good-byes to Uncle Billy, Mahaley, and Beth.

On the home farm, the valiant warrior finally forgot how to breathe, and his beloved wife took his place in the rocking chair, chatting with his old friend, the inscrutable man in the moon.

In July '65 the Thirteenth US Colored was relieved from duty in the Middle Tennessee District and was ordered to report to Major General William Tecumseh Sherman in St. Louis. The storied regiment was finally mustered out of service in December '65, and Sergeant Basanater came home to make a life with Bella working on our farm.

About three and a half years later, Bella and the Sergeant informed Uncle Billy's eldest son they were heading on up to Franklin to start a new life on one of the few remaining plantations. Sergeant Basanater said he'd really tried making a life on our farm with Bella, but the folks around Warfield knew he'd fought for the Feds. There was still a lot of resentment, he explained, about the suffering the locals had endured. He said every time he ventured into Warfield for supplies, he'd sense the deep disdain the citizens had for a Negro who'd fought and killed their sons.

Mrs. Hudson, the reverend's supportive wife, succumbed to the dropsy, and from then on, the Reverend Hudson lost all enthusiasm to continue shepherding his parish flock. When the reverend told Master Hudson he planned to return to Europe, his son surprised and delighted the old cleric, expressing a strong desire to join him and raise his family in Stonehaven, his birthplace on the rugged northeast seacoast of Scotland.

When I learned Master Hudson would continue our quest in Europe, I understood how much Rachel's death during childbirth had played in his decision to leave the farm. But then I smiled. I could envision Lil Joe and his new brother, Benjamin, carrying on their great-grandpa's tradition. With the fierce North Sea winds blowing through their hair and the gulls calling and wheeling around the cliffs below, the young Hudsons would mount the ruined, precipitous parapets of Dunnottar Castle with Wallace and wave their imaginary swords in an enduring struggle for Scottish freedom.

As for me, after recurring bouts of winter fever over several years, I finally managed to earn my degree, board the train at Cowan Station, and begin my journey to Memphis to assume my first teaching position at the prestigious Westminster Academy. Their only English lecturer had died of cholera, and they hired me to replace him beginning with their spring semester.

Aboard the train, the Nashville & Northwestern conductor walked through the unheated railcar and announced the workers had almost finished replacing the rails, which had washed out during the floods of the night before. We'd been diverted to a siding just up the road from our farm. As I gazed out through the partially frosted windowpane, I could see most of our property stretching from the new Miss Owings School in the east to the massive rebuilt barn in the west.

When I looked to the south through the bare trees, I could see the farmhouse, the smokehouse, and our cemetery up on the back hill. It was so strange; it was as if nothing had ever happened. Everything was still there, standing frozen in a light gray layer of late-January frost. We were too far away to read the names on the bookmarks, discover the singe on the tall pines, or see the deep scar on our good luck tree. And no one here on board knew we were resting on the very cross-ties that had caused unspeakable suffering and massacred an innocent named Israel.

The metal groaned; the driving wheels sparked; and we began slowly moving past our entry gate. Thick gray smoke swept down around our car and disappeared to the east. I no longer had any desire to visit; everyone was gone now: Grandma, Grandpa, Mama, Father, Robert, Rachel, Bella, The Sergeant, Israel, Hudson, Lil Joe, Benjamin, and Beth. Repeating their names now was the forlorn sound of the successive nails piercing Father's coffin. As we approached the flickering, glistening platform at Warfield station, I looked out the window toward Grave's Bend on the Duck River and told my brother how much I loved him and missed him. And then I wished him well.